Pettikin

Abby Smith

Cover art and design by Sophie Mitchell
(www.sophiemitchellillustrations.com)

ISBN: 0-9983623-0-1
ISBN-13: 978-0-9983623-0-4
Library of Congress Control Number: 2016919673

Softlight Press LLC
Wilton, CT 06897

The moon bird's head is filled with nothing but
thoughts of the moon,
and when the next rain will come is all that the
rain bird thinks of.

Who is it we spend our entire life loving?

—Kabir

1

Aunt May's funeral was about as strange as Aunt May had been.

There were ten of us there, if you didn't count the alpacas. We had just arrived at the cemetery and were arranging ourselves on either side of the grave. Mom and I ended up on one side with five people from town I didn't know very well. I assumed they were there more from a sense of civic duty than any genuine affection for my eccentric great-aunt.

Aunt May's friends were on the other side of the grave.

They had arrived from out of town that morning, two men and a woman. The first man wasn't very tall but seemed big somehow—stout and with a broad chest like a lumberjack. He introduced himself to us as Theodore Theopolous the Professor, but failed to specify professor of what. The second man was tall but seemed small somehow—thin and gaunt, with mousy hair and a beard that looked like it had been eaten by moths over the winter. His name was Bob, and he insisted on bringing the alpacas. The woman, Mrs. Widgit, was short with a mop of gray curls and squinty eyes. She wore a long green dress with purple flowers and twirled next to the grave. They each held one of Aunt May's three alpacas and seemed oblivious that the people next to me were staring at them and whispering.

Well, it didn't take much to cause a stir in Wooster, Ohio. In my fourteen years I had already been a subject of gossip for the people in this small town more than once. I wondered if they included me in their whispers—if they thought I was standing on the wrong side of the grave.

The cemetery in Wooster covers most of the western side of the hill on Madison Avenue, out on the southern end of the town. It looks like a park but feels ominous, with gravestones tucked behind a black wrought iron fence, a row of towering spruce trees guarding the back perimeter like sentinels. On the slope next to the entrance, two rows of hedges are carved into a crooked welcome: WOOSTER CEMETERY.

A gated community for dead people.

Aunt May's grave was about a quarter-mile down a winding, blacktopped path from the main entrance, underneath a sprawling maple tree. There, we were tucked away from the road and, thankfully, the view of passing cars.

It was too warm for October, and I could feel prickles of heat forming underneath my wool dress. I knew that morning I would be too hot in it, but it was the only thing I owned that was black. In fact, it was my only dress.

Mom twisted her watch on her wrist with an almost imperceptible movement, her short, red curls gleaming in the sun.

"Your father's late," she murmured.

Dad was the minister of the local Presbyterian church and would perform the service. It wasn't like him not to be on time.

From across the grave, the alpacas shifted their feet and made soft, staccato honking noises. Aunt May had always said it was called *humming*, but to me it sounded like honking. Maybe they were too warm, as well. Bob had dressed them in colorful Guatemalan woven blankets and matching ski hats with long tassels that dangled down the sides of their faces. Because, I suppose, it wouldn't have been weird enough to just bring *plain* alpacas to a funeral.

I squinted through the sun at Professor Theopolous. If the alpacas and I were too warm, he must have been sweltering. The fabric of his faded pinstriped suit was as thick as cardboard, and he wore a cream-colored, wool fisherman's sweater underneath. He had just a monk's fringe of dark hair that morphed directly into a beard, a gold-framed monocle over his left eye, and a deathly solemn expression. I don't think he moved since we got there.

Mrs. Widgit, on the other hand, hadn't stopped moving. She was a little heavy, and it was obvious now as she leaned forward, balancing herself on one leg, that her giant chest was unrestricted by a bra. She pulled herself upright and bent her right knee, pressing the sole of a worn Birkenstock sandal into her left calf. She clasped her hands in front of her in prayer position, and then swung them out to her sides, like a giant bird about to take flight.

I stared at her. I was sure she was Aunt May's friend, and yet she bounced around as if the funeral were cause for celebration instead of mourning. Meanwhile, the people next to me wore black and feigned sympathy, but wouldn't give Aunt May a second thought once they left the cemetery, unless it was to gossip about the strange behavior of her friends.

Didn't anyone there feel the way you were supposed to feel when somebody died?

As soon as I thought it, Mrs. Widgit's head snapped toward me, dark eyes boring into mine. I dropped my gaze quickly, my cheeks flaming.

Because if anyone did feel that way, I knew it wasn't me.

A few tears came to my eyes, but I wasn't really sure why. I knew it wasn't because Aunt May died, and that made me feel worse. It seemed like if you were at someone's funeral, you should be sad about their death. But rather than sad, I was more uneasy, the way I get when the main character in a horror movie is about to go down into the basement alone.

It's not that I didn't love Aunt May. I spent most of my afternoons as a child with her while my parents were at work, and we always got along fine. I hadn't seen as much of her recently, though, not since I was old enough to be on my own after school. The news of her death surprised me, but only left me cold and numb.

Mom nudged me, interrupting my reverie. She had PhDs in both math and psychology and, with her own private therapy practice in town, was the main breadwinner in our family. I was sure she would have some psychological explanation for what I was or wasn't feeling, so I vowed not to tell her. I didn't want to know what kind of crazy I was.

She pointed up the hill. "Your dad's finally here."

Dad walked down the path from the entrance. Instead of his minister's robe, he wore a faded pair of jeans and a T-shirt with a large portrait of Aunt May on the front. Two young guys I didn't recognize followed him, carrying a large black trunk with brass handles between them.

"What's going on?" I whispered. Dad hadn't warned me about this.

"I have no idea." Mom wore that look I always thought of as her Psychologist Face—not showing any surprise or emotion no matter what bizarre human behavior she encountered.

Dad smiled briefly at us but didn't hesitate. He walked to the other side of the grave and gestured for the two young men to place the trunk at the base of the maple tree. They did so and left.

Well, of course Dad would be on Aunt May's side. Aunt May was my mother's aunt, but Dad was her closest friend and supporter all these years.

When Aunt May decided to buy the alpacas, Dad spent every weekend for the better part of a year fencing in a paddock behind the cottage that she rented from us, on the back of our forty-acre farm. When Aunt May painted the cottage fluorescent green and the shutters pink, Dad calmed Mom down and then, somehow, persuaded Aunt May to stick to a more reasonable palette when she repainted the cottage (which was often). Dad arranged for me to spend my afternoons after school with her, from the time I was five until I was eleven. I remember standing on a stool next to her kitchen counter, my long blond hair pulled back in a ponytail, baking cookies. I mixed the wet and dry ingredients in a large bowl while Aunt May told me stories about gnomes and dragons and far-off worlds. Original stories, though, not the stuff you heard in school.

When Aunt May sent me home with a bag of cookies, Dad ate them with me, destroying the evidence before Mom got home.

Dad turned away from us and huddled together with the strangers at the gravesite. The back of his T-shirt said "*Ask me about the bet I lost with Aunt May.*"

The people from town muttered to each other.

I leaned toward Mom. "What bet?"

"I have no idea," Mom said again. Her Psychologist Face morphed into her Slightly-Annoyed-Spouse face.

Dad opened the lid on the trunk under the maple tree. He distributed colorful Guatemalan ponchos and hats to the strangers, exactly like the ones the alpacas were wearing. They took turns holding the alpacas while putting the costumes over their clothes. Dad did the same with a fourth costume and then pulled a large manila envelope from the trunk.

Once they all looked equally ridiculous, Aunt

May's friends rearranged themselves with the alpacas, and my dad stepped in front of them, facing us. He was medium height and medium build, or dad-shaped as my friend Andie called it, with thinning brown hair and a neat beard. Our eyes met.

We are never going to hear the end of this, I thought at him.

He averted his gaze and adjusted his poncho. The murmuring died down, I assume because people were too stunned to talk.

"Friends, welcome," Dad said. "I guess it's fairly obvious that we'll be doing things a little...differently today."

A relieved chuckle swelled up from the crowd.

"You probably won't be surprised to learn that Aunt May prepared her own words for me to read to you today. She strictly forbade me, of course, to make any religious remarks on this occasion."

Soft laughter at that.

"However...." Dad became wistful. "Since this is the one time May will not be able to stop me, I wanted to say that she was a dear friend, and I loved her. She will be missed. And I know that in the eyes of our Creator, she was indeed a creation to behold. A real force of nature. And while I, personally, will miss her, I also believe that we pass her into good hands today."

A stillness seemed to wash over the group as Dad spoke. He had that effect on people, projecting strength and gentleness at the same time, even in such an outlandish getup. I suppose that's why he was a good minister. You felt somehow consoled when you listened to him, even if you weren't sure you understood or believed what he was saying.

"Now...." Dad held up the envelope. "We'll see what May has to say for herself." He slid a finger under the seal.

Mrs. Widgit bounced on her heels.

"I haven't actually read this," Dad said, a little nervously I thought, as he removed a sheet of paper. He scanned it quickly and read:

"Hello my dear friends and relatives, and the rest of you who have shown up for your own reasons." He threw a quick, apologetic glance at the townies. "If you are hearing this, then I am dead, and you are hearing it from my nephew-in-law Dan, who has lost his bet with me. Make sure to ask him about it on your way out." A grim look passed over my father's face, fading as he continued.

"We really make too much of death here on Earth. Trust me, it's not worth getting so upset about. It's all an illusion, you see. Nothing and no one we think we have is ever ours to begin with. Everything here is just on loan to us for a short time, and when we leave, we leave everything behind."

I suddenly felt much colder, as if the temperature had dropped ten degrees, even though the sun still shone as brightly as before. I folded my arms across my stomach.

"Today I must go, but there is one last thing I would like to leave behind. A poem--"

Dad broke off and looked up at me, surprised.

"A poem, which I dedicate to my great-niece, Allie."

Everyone turned toward me. Mrs. Widgit and Bob were smiling, but Professor Theopolous scowled, like I had done something wrong. I suddenly wished I could hop down into the grave next to Aunt May.

Dad read:

The Waking, by Theodore Roethke.
I wake to sleep, and take my waking slow.
I feel my fate in what I cannot fear.
I learn by going where I have to go.

We think by feeling. What is there to know?
I hear my being dance from ear to ear.

I wake to sleep, and take my waking slow.

Of those so close beside me, which are you?
God bless the Ground! I shall walk softly there,
And learn by going where I have to go.

Light takes the Tree; but who can tell us how?
The lowly worm climbs up a winding stair;
I wake to sleep, and take my waking slow.

Great Nature has another thing to do
To you and me, so take the lively air,
And, lovely, learn by going where to go.

This shaking keeps me steady. I should know.
What falls away is always. And is near.
I wake to sleep, and take my waking slow.
I learn by going where I have to go.

He turned the paper over, but there was nothing on the other side.

"That's it," he said, folding the paper in half. He grabbed a handful of the dirt piled next to the grave and threw it onto Aunt May's coffin.

"Earth to earth, ashes to ashes, dust to dust," he murmured, almost to himself. "Bye, May."

I tucked my icy hands under my arms. What did that poem mean? Why did Aunt May want me, of all people, to hear it?

The people next to me stirred, talking softly. They started walking toward Mom and me to pay their respects when a loud voice called out from across the grave, "OK, it's time! Let's begin!"

Everyone turned to watch.

Mrs. Widgit was in charge. "Bob, hold the alpacas! Theo, help me over here. Dan! We need you!"

Bob took the alpaca ropes as a bustling Mrs.

Widgit herded Professor Theopolous and Dad over to the trunk.

They pulled out three conical objects—wooden pipes, about four feet long, an inch and a half in diameter at one end, flaring to three inches at the bottom. They were painted blue and stenciled with white moons, yellow stars and red flowers. I assumed they were musical instruments, but there were no keys or reeds.

Dad and the strangers rearranged themselves in front of Aunt May's grave with Dad in the middle, the professor and Mrs. Widgit on either end, and Bob holding the increasingly distressed alpacas behind them.

They raised the pipes to their lips.

They can't be serious, I thought. Could Dad even play an instrument?

Mrs. Widgit inhaled dramatically, eyes wide, nodded her head once, and the three of them blew through the pipes, bugle-style.

It sounded like giant frogs dying. The noise coming from the pipes had no harmony or melody. They held the same notes for several seconds, inhaled, and played the same notes again, seeming unconcerned about whether they came in at the same time or not. Dad's face turned red with exertion.

I choked back a giggle and glanced at Mom. She had one arm folded across her stomach, the other hand covering her mouth. She refused to look at me.

Dad returned his pipe to the trunk and hurried over to Bob, who handed him one of the alpaca's leads. The professor and Mrs. Widgit kept playing. Dad and Bob began to weave around each other in a figure eight pattern, dragging the unwilling alpacas behind them. Dad's lips moved as if he were trying to keep time or count his steps. I wondered, horrified, if anyone was filming this.

After what seemed like forever, Mrs. Widgit caught the professor's eyes and, with a flourish of her pipe, ended the droning. Dad and Bob actually ran into each other at that point, mercifully concluding their dance, as well.

Everyone was silent. A car hissed by on the road.

Mrs. Widgit stretched her arms out wide, pipe dangling from her right hand, and beamed.

"This concludes our program today. Thank you all so very much for coming!"

After a pause, someone from town started clapping. A few others joined in, but seemed uncertain if they should be applauding at a funeral, so the resulting sound was almost as pathetic as the music had been, and died off quickly.

The murmuring and shuffling started again.

"This is going to be all over the Internet by tomorrow," I said to Mom.

Mom just raised her eyebrows and exhaled slowly. The townies converged on us.

"So sorry for your loss."

"But what an...*interesting* ceremony."

"And how wonderful that her friends could come, where are they from again?"

"Allie, this must be so hard on you."

"You were obviously very special to her."

I smiled politely and nodded but didn't speak. What was I going to say? That, no, I felt surprisingly un-sad? That I loved Aunt May but hadn't felt I was particularly special to her? I let Mom handle the niceties. She knew what to say to people, how to act normal. I gazed toward the main driveway, wondering how soon we could leave.

Dad joined us. He was folding his hat and poncho over his arm. I withdrew a few steps from him and Mom.

"Dan, Pat. Nice service." Mr. Cutter, a local land developer I'm sure Aunt May would never have been friends with, stepped forward to shake my dad's hand. He was tall with slicked-back hair the color of black shoe polish. His suit looked expensive, and his tanned skin seemed like it was stretched too tightly across his skull.

"Thank you, Jim." Dad grasped his hand.

"So what was the bet?"

"I don't want to talk about it."

My normally polite father was suddenly abrupt.

Something warm and soft touched my neck, causing me to make a ridiculous noise.

The little brown alpaca peered at me from under her hat. She had apparently gotten away from the others.

"Hey, Sunshine." I held out my hand.

She reached forward with her long neck and sniffed it, humming softly. I scratched behind her ears and ran my fingers through the soft, caramel fur on her neck.

Bob rushed over, her lead dangling from his hand.

"Hey, Allie, I'm sorry she got away." He looked into my eyes for just a fraction of a second.

"No problem. Sunshine is kind of my favorite. Aunt May got her when she was just a cria, and she used to let me feed her with a bottle."

Bob clipped the rope onto Sunshine's halter.

"Actually, I'm glad she came over to you." He dropped his voice. "I'm not sure all of these people are alpaca people, if you know what I mean."

I looked over at Mr. Cutter talking to my parents. "Yeah, well, I'm not sure all these people are even Aunt May people, if you know what I mean."

He followed my gaze, tracing a finger down the bridge of Sunshine's nose. "I know what you mean."

2

Mom and I drove home together so Dad could help Aunt May's friends load up the alpacas. I stared out the window as the town buildings changed into long, flat stretches of fields, old farm houses, dairy barns, and grain silos.

"How are you holding up, Al?" Mom's voice made me jump.

"Fine." I turned away from her and scowled out the window.

"You know, it's normal to feel upset when something like this happens." She reached over to touch my arm.

"I'm *fine.*" I shook off her hand. Even I was a little surprised at how mean my voice sounded, but now that I had said it, I wasn't sure how to un-say it.

"You shouldn't frown like that."

Mom let it drop, but I could almost hear the wheels turning in her brain, analyzing. I didn't like feeling that she was inside my head, trying to figure me out. I scowled harder. I didn't exactly know what I was feeling, except that suddenly everything about Aunt May's death and funeral was weirding me out, and not in a nice, normal, I-miss-my-dead-great-aunt way but in a freaky I-want-to-run-away-and-hide-from-everyone-and-not-think-about-this way.

We drove the rest of the way to the house in silence.

My parents held a reception for Aunt May in her cottage. The people from town arrived with cakes, pies, casseroles and other baked goods. I felt guilty about my behavior in the car, so I helped Mom arrange the food, a large urn of coffee, and pitchers of lemonade and iced tea on the shabby but sturdy oak table in Aunt May's kitchen. It was stuffy in the cottage after the heat of the day, so we opened the windows. There were no screens, but Mom said there probably wouldn't be too many bugs this late in the season. Once everything was set up and Dad arrived, my parents took pity on me and said I didn't have to stay if I didn't want to, so I slipped out the back door and trudged up the broad, grassy lane that led from the cottage to our house.

The lane ran down the middle of a large cornfield that we rented to our Amish neighbors. The corn had already been harvested for the year, the long, brown stalks dried and tied together into shocks that looked like giant teepees. When I was a kid, I used to play inside of them.

The tall grasses and timothy that bordered the lane gradually tapered into our back yard, near a grove of maple trees. Our tiny, antique farm house was over a hundred years old, storm-cloud gray with a rust-red metal roof and white trim. I steered past our garage, up a small hill to the back porch. The back door was unlocked, as usual. I pushed it open and a dark figure lunged toward me.

Two enormous paws landed on my shoulders, and my face was mopped by a pink tongue the size of a washcloth. I wrapped my arms around the neck of our oversized black German shepherd Socrates and stumbled backwards to push the screen door open again. He bounded outside, a whirlwind of frenetic dog energy. My only dress was covered with faint, dusty paw prints and fur.

I went upstairs to change. My bedroom used to be two rooms, but my parents had removed a wall when I turned ten so I could have more space. Half of the room was my sleeping quarters—an antique four poster bed with a colorful patch quilt, a dresser, and a closet. The other half was my workspace—a large desk with my computers, a wall of built-in bookshelves crammed with books, and an old yellow rocking chair with a pink cushion that had been there since I was a baby. A fluffy black and white cat, one of five who lived in the house, lay curled in the middle of my bed.

I pulled off my dress and wadded it in the corner of my closet. A voice in my head told me that probably wasn't the right thing to do with it, but I ignored it. I squeezed into my favorite pair of jeans, pulled a clean T-shirt over my head, and went downstairs.

I rummaged through the refrigerator but didn't see anything I wanted. I settled for a diet pop and sat down at the kitchen table. I felt better just being alone and in my normal clothes. A stack of mail and a fat, gray cat sat on the table.

"Hey, Blue." I scratched under her chin and began flipping idly through the mail while she purred.

A crunch of gravel made me look out the window. A pretty Chinese girl wearing a backpack way too big for her small frame steered her bike down our driveway.

Andie Wu. My best friend.

I stepped onto the porch.

"I'm going to kill him," she growled as she leaned her bike against our garage. "Oh, I'm sorry, are you OK? How was the funeral?" She adjusted her backpack and made her way up the red brick walkway to the porch.

"I'm fine. It was weird. Who are you going to kill?"

"Mark, of course. Down Socks!" Andie's words

were preemptive as she saw the familiar black dog loping toward her. He pressed himself against her legs, tongue lolling, while she rubbed his neck.

"What happened?"

"He frickin' asked Hope to go to Homecoming with him, that's what happened."

"*Hope*? Seriously? The freshman?"

"Seriously. After we stayed up until two last night texting." Socrates bounded off again and Andie came up to the porch.

I handed her my still unopened can of pop and went inside to get another one for myself. "That seriously sucks. What in the world was he thinking?" I called over my shoulder from the kitchen.

Andie was fifteen, but we were both sophomores because I had skipped a grade, thereby dooming myself to be too young to do anything for the rest of my life. If it wasn't for Andie, I probably would have been a complete social outcast.

"It's not the fact that she's cute that bothers me, but that she is *such* an airhead," Andie said when I returned. "How can I have any respect for him after this?"

"Did he get his Ritalin dosage wrong this morning or something? I was sure he was going to ask you."

Andie laughed, which made me happy, then hesitated. "You know Brett's taking Tracy, right?"

Why did my heart start pounding faster just hearing the name? It annoyed me.

"No, but I figured."

Brett Logan: seventeen, a senior, and the only guy I had ever kissed. We dated for three months over the summer, but he broke up with me when school started because suddenly I was too young for him. Tracy Sloane was also a senior and, he said, more mature.

Andie said mature was just a euphemism for something else.

She regarded me over her pop can as she took a

sip.

"So what was so weird about the funeral?"

I shook my head.

"Some of Aunt May's friends were there, and they brought the alpacas, wore weird costumes, played these weird instruments."

"You're kidding."

"I'm not kidding."

"This will be all over the Internet by tomorrow."

"That's exactly what I said. Please, can I have the brain back?"

Our inside joke that we shared a brain came from our propensity to finish each other's sentences, say exactly the same thing at exactly the same time and win at Pictionary no matter how bad our drawings, as long as we were a team.

I sat down on a small bench next to the side of the house.

"I can't wait until I graduate and can get the heck out of Ohio. Anyway, in addition to that weirdness, Aunt May dedicated a poem to me, of all things."

"What poem?"

"Something by Theodore Roethke. I need to go look it up. Dad has a book of his poems in his study I think."

"Oh, speaking of studies, I brought your assignments for you, and notes on the classes you missed, if you even need them. Mrs. Greene gave you a pass on the pre-calc problems, though. She said you would probably ace the test whether you did the exercises or not."

"Actually, I already did them yesterday in study hall. I was bored." I cringed a little admitting that.

Andie rolled her eyes at me.

"Of course you did. Anyway, I also brought all the notes that Mark and I passed in chemistry class after Mr. Steele confiscated our cell phones. I thought we could go down to Walden and burn them."

Walden was our name for a small pond hidden in the woods behind Aunt May's cottage. Andie and I had named it after we snuck a copy of Henry David Thoreau's book from my father's study when we were in the sixth grade. I'm not sure we completely understood the book, but it seemed like a good name for a pond, and Walden had served as our secret hiding place and strategy-planning headquarters ever since. My dad, who had been to the real Walden Pond, said ours was a pathetic excuse for the real thing. He called it Walden Puddle.

Even from this distance we could see that there were only a few cars left in the private lane behind Aunt May's cottage. Dad stood outside talking to someone. Was it Mr. Cutter again? What was up with him?

"It's too bad about your Aunt May. She was pretty cool. Like, the kind of old lady I would like to be someday if I have to get old."

I had thought the same thing more than once. Aunt May must have been in her late sixties or early seventies, but she was tall and thin and spritely somehow. Her hair was gray, but that sort of golden-gray color, so it made her look pretty instead of old. She was almost always cheerful, and was completely self-sufficient. My dad often said she had more energy than he did.

We watched as the last of the cars pulled away from the cottage, and my parents walked slowly, hand in hand, toward the house.

"Hey!" Andie turned to me. "Let's ask your parents if we can spend the night in the cottage!"

"Aunt May's cottage?"

"Yeah, I mean, it's Friday. Unless you have plans, or something I don't know about."

She knew I didn't. One of us almost always ended up at the other's house on the weekends.

"Yeah, but, I mean, she just died. Isn't that a little, I dunno, creepy?"

Andie snorted. "Oh, come on. It'll be so cool. We

can order a pizza and watch movies, assuming she has a DVD player down there. I brought all my overnight things anyway, just in case." She pointed to her bulging backpack.

I watched my parents trudge up the hill. "All right, I'm game. We can ask them."

"Hello, daughter. Hello, other daughter." Dad said as he and Mom approached the porch.

"Hi Mr. and Mrs. Thomas. How was the reception?" Andie asked.

Mom sat down next to me on the bench and snatched my pop can.

"Exhausting," she said, taking a sip and handing it back to me. "Oh, that tastes good. Allie, would you be a dear and go get one of those for me?"

"Me too!" Dad added as I stood up.

"Yes, master," I said in my best Igor voice as I set my can down and headed for the fridge.

"What was the bet?" I heard Andie asking from out on the porch.

"I don't want to talk about it."

I returned to the porch with the pop. Dad took my place on the bench next to Mom, and she was looking at him with an amused expression.

"I assume you are aware that your shirt says…" she said.

"I know what the shirt says. But I'm not going to talk about it."

"Well, geez, Dad, you might have thought of that before putting it on. Or you could have just kept that poncho on over it," I said.

I handed them their drinks and sat next to Andie on the porch.

"How bad could it be, anyway? It's not like I have some inheritance you could have lost or something."

"I don't want to talk about it, because I'm not convinced I lost the bet yet," Dad said. "But speaking of inheritances, Aunt May, it turns out, left everything she owns to you."

"To me?" I looked at Andie. "Seriously? Wait, what exactly does she own?"

"Pretty much nothing. I guess everything that's in the cottage, her books and what little furniture she has. The alpacas. The cottage, of course, your Mother and I still own, despite Mr. Cutter's best efforts."

"He's scary," Andie said. "My mom said he bought Mrs. Schmidt's property right out from under her after her husband died and she couldn't afford the mortgage payments anymore. She lived there for forty years and had to move into a nursing home. Mr. Cutter tore the house and barn down to build condominiums."

"'Heritage Estates,' I believe he named them," Mom said drily.

"He apparently just bought a bunch of land on the other side of our property as well, and for some reason he wants to add our cottage to his acreage," Dad said, looking serious. "He offered me more money than it's worth."

"I don't even get why he was at the funeral to begin with," I said.

"He and Aunt May go way back," Mom said.

"You're kidding me. They were friends?"

"Hardly friends," Mom said. "I don't know all the details, but I do know they grew up together. Mr. Cutter is just a few years younger than May. I get the feeling there was some type of rivalry between them, and that he was always trying to prove himself to her."

"Prove himself? What does he have to prove? Seems like he has everything, he's so rich and all."

"Teachable moment, daughter," Dad said, using his most pedantic voice. "Being rich and having a lot of material possessions won't necessarily make you happy."

"Is this my punishment for not going to church? You're going to preach to me anyway?"

We grinned at each other. Dad was always surprisingly cool about my not going to church, even though he was a pastor. It wasn't that I didn't believe in God, just that I wasn't sure I believed in God the way everyone else was saying I should believe in God.

"At any rate, I don't like the thought of him being our new neighbor," Mom said. "Who knows what he's planning to do with that land? He might put up oil wells."

"I should go put up some more "No Trespassing" signs in the woods tomorrow," Dad said.

"So I assume you're *not* going to sell the cottage to him, right?" Why did I feel nervous at the idea?

"Of course not," Dad assured me. "We would never do that."

Andie nudged my foot with her toe.

"Oh, yeah, so, um, speaking of the cottage, Andie and I were wondering if we could spend the night down there."

Mom and Dad looked at each other as if they were communicating telepathically.

"Isn't that a little creepy?" Dad asked.

"Yeah, well, ask her," I jabbed a thumb toward Andie.

"Oh, come on," Andie said. "It's not like we're going to see Aunt May's ghost or something. And even if we did, she'd probably be a pretty cool ghost."

"I guess that's true," Dad said.

"I suppose it would be all right," Mom said. "The phone still works down there, and you have your cells. I would feel better if you took Socrates with you, though."

At the sound of his name, Socrates' head popped up from a hole he was digging in the yard. He looked at us with his ears cocked and head tilted to one side, then bounded over to the porch. He plopped down on his haunches in front of Mom and gazed at her adoringly, nose caked with dirt, eyes expectant.

Mom laughed and stood up. "Well, now I've done it, I better get him a biscuit. Do you girls want to take the sleeping bags down there? I'm not sure what May has in terms of sheets. Oh, and if you could do me a favor and clean up the kitchen and put away the food. I put the perishable items in the fridge, but we were so tired, we left everything else out. I planned to go back down later, but you could save me a trip."

"Sure thing, Mrs. Thomas." Andie, as the guest, was more polite than I would have been.

I ran upstairs and threw my overnight things in my backpack. When I got back downstairs, Mom had taken the sleeping bags out of the closet for us, and Dad was testing the battery in a yellow flashlight the size of a large brick.

"Here, better take this with you, in case you need to come back up to the house for anything."

"And take a sweatshirt, Allie," Mom added. "There's supposed to be a cold front moving through tonight. We may actually see normal fall weather tomorrow."

I pulled a blue hoodie off the pegs next to the back door and tied it around my waist. I shouldered my backpack and picked up one of the sleeping bags.

Andie was already waiting for me. "Ready, Freddy?"

"Ready!" I replied. "C'mon Socks!"

The sun was just starting to set as we set off down the lane toward the cottage. Socrates trotted ahead of us carrying an enormous branch in his mouth, turning his head over his shoulder periodically to make sure we were still following. I wondered where he thought we were going. The breeze was cooler and dark gray clouds gathered on the horizon, moving in our direction.

We walked in silence until the lane forked, the right path leading into our woods and the left to Aunt May's property. We veered left, while Socrates took off into the woods on some unexplained dog mission.

Two ancient silver beech trees just past the woods towered over the eastern edge of Aunt May's property.

The cottage was about three hundred feet away, a tiny wood shingled house, painted a rather boring off-white at the moment, with a gray shingled roof, red brick chimney, and dark red shutters with pineapples cut out of the center hanging on either side of the windows.

The old red barn where the alpacas lived lay behind the cottage, next to the large paddock enclosed by the black post and beam fence my father built. The barn was dark and the paddock was empty. Apparently, the strangers hadn't returned with the alpacas yet. That was odd. What could they be doing with them?

We walked up a short path of uneven, mossy paving stones to the front door of the cottage. A welcome mat with a picture of a gnome in a blue hat standing under a mushroom greeted us with the phrase *Gnome Sweet Home.* OK, that was a little tacky. Like the barn, the cottage was dark, and eerily silent in the fading evening light. For the first time, it hit me that Aunt May wouldn't be coming back. I shivered.

My parents had left the front door unlocked, and I eased it open.

I stepped over the threshold, listening intently. An old cuckoo clock tick-tocked in the living room directly across from the entryway.

"Hello?" I called out, immediately feeling stupid. Who did I think would be here? Andie stepped up behind me and we both peered around in the dim light.

"Creepy!" I announced in a cheerful, singsong tone.

"Oh get over it," Andie put her hands on my shoulders and pushed me forward.

A small wooden staircase to the right of the entrance led upstairs to Aunt May's sleeping loft. I walked past it toward the kitchen, Andie following closely behind me. When I reached the kitchen door I stopped, and she bonked into me.

"Ow! Stop it!" We both started giggling. I fumbled

along the wall with my hand until I found the light switch.

The kitchen seemed smaller to me than it had when I was a kid. The wood-topped counter I stood at so many times roughly divided the room in half, with the cooking area in front of us and the kitchen table on the other side of it, in the corner of the room. The food was still spread out on the table where we placed it earlier, and the windows were still open, blue checkered curtains puffing in the breeze. Not much had been eaten. A few dishes and cups were stacked in the sink, a few left sitting out on the counters.

"We might as well leave the food out for now," Andie said. "Maybe we won't need to order pizza after all."

"Yeah. C'mon, let's go see what Aunt May left me."

The kitchen dining area opened into the living room. A large picture window faced the back yard with a view of the barn and paddock. Two bright blue squishy sofas sat on either side of a coffee table piled with books. Across the room, the cuckoo clock ticked on the mantle above a fireplace, and in the corner to the right, books splayed across Aunt May's writing desk. Books were stacked two rows deep on the bookshelves that lined the walls. If the shelves were full, books were stacked on top of the bookcases, or on the floor next to them. Andie dropped her sleeping bag and backpack to the floor and flicked on a lamp.

"So... your Aunt May liked to read?"

"Yeah, I mean, I remember lots of books in here, but I didn't remember it being this bad." I dumped my backpack and sleeping bag in the corner and rummaged through one of the piles on the coffee table.

"Hey, Andie, listen to this." I picked up the first book on the pile. "*The Book of Useful People.*" I continued flipping through them. "*The Importance of Color, Famous Gatekeepers, The Book of Useful Phrases....*"

"Hey, let me see that." Andie took the last book

from my hand and opened it.

"Chapter One: Please go away," she read.

We both laughed.

"What else is there?" I asked, grabbing a new book.

A loud crash from the kitchen interrupted us. We froze and stared at each other.

"Are those windows still open?" Andie asked.

"Oh, man. I wonder if a raccoon or squirrel smelled the food and crawled in." I rushed back to the kitchen, with Andie following.

I stopped abruptly at the entrance, causing Andie to run into me again.

And then I screamed.

At first I thought it was a squirrel or raccoon that had snuck in through the open windows, lured by the assortment of treats. But even before I finished screaming I realized that the little creature standing in the middle of Aunt May's kitchen table was definitely not a rodent or four-legged mammal of any sort.

He was about twelve inches tall, wearing a green tweed coat, brown trousers, and a pair of wooden clogs on his stocking-clad feet. A red Santa hat flopped down over his snowy-white hair and beard. He had frosting on his face, a fistful of cake in each hand, and enormous blue eyes, wide with terror. When I screamed, he opened his mouth and started shrieking, a high pitched wail that quickly rose to a hysterical, siren-like noise. Big globs of cake dropped out of his mouth, and crumbs sprayed around the table.

Andie started screaming too, making three of us. The tiny Santa creature turned red and looked increasingly hysterical, waving his cake-filled hands and running in circles around a pie on the table. He looked so ridiculous that my scream turned to a laugh.

"It's OK, it's OK! Shh! You win! Please stop!" I begged.

Andie put a hand to her chest and leaned into the wall.

I crept toward the kitchen table with my hands outstretched, hoping this was a universal symbol for *I'm not dangerous.*

"It's OK! I'm not going to hurt you."

He stopped screaming, panting a little from his effort.

"My name's Allie," I said, feeling ridiculous. "I'm Aunt May's—May, she's the woman who used to live here—I'm her great niece, which is, like, a type of relative, I mean she's my mom's aunt, but we all call her Aunt May."

I cringed. That probably would have left even a real person confused.

He breathed heavily, regarding me warily.

"Do you have a name? Did you know Aunt May?"

Could he even understand a word I was saying?

He pressed his lips together and swallowed hard. He wiped the remaining cake from his hands onto his stockings, grabbed his jacket lapels, and stood up very straight.

"My name is Pettikin—Pettikin Periwinkle, but you can call me Pettikin. I'm a gnome," he said in a small, clear voice.

I heard a thud behind me. Andie had fainted and was slumped on the kitchen floor.

3

"Andie, can you speak?"

I crouched over her, my mind racing through the CPR steps we had learned in Health class the previous spring.

"Is she dead?" Pettikin, on hands and knees, peered over the edge of the table.

My brain went into overload trying to process both CPR and a curious gnome at the same time.

"What? No, I don't think…"

Andie moaned, and I shook my head to clear my thoughts. Best friend. Fix best friend first.

"Andie, are you OK?"

She put one hand to her head.

"What happened?"

"You fainted, I think," I said, helping her sit up. She still seemed a little queasy. "Maybe you should put your head between your knees for a minute."

I had no idea if that would actually work, but it sounded good. She folded her arms across her knees and put her head, face-down, on top of them.

We were all quiet for a moment.

"Hey, Al?" Andie's voice was muffled under her

arms.

"Yeah?"

"There's a gnome on the kitchen table, isn't there?"

"Yes. Yes, there is."

"I'm glad you're not dead," Pettikin said, sounding quite sincere.

Andie raised her head and caught my eye. If my expression matched what I was feeling, she probably didn't find it reassuring.

"Uh, thanks. OK, I think I can get up now."

Pettikin retreated to the far edge of the kitchen table and glanced to either side as if searching for possible escape routes. I wished they taught how to deal with a stray gnome in Health class, instead of CPR.

"Um…is it OK if we sit down?" I slid a chair back from the table and sat down. Andie took the chair to my right.

Andie and Pettikin watched me as if waiting for me to say something. Why was I in charge?

Pettikin's earlier eating spree had left cake crumbs, half-eaten cookies, and brownie carcasses splayed across the table. Carrots, cauliflower, and celery, on the other hand, were strewn across the kitchen floor next to a silver platter, presumably accounting for the earlier crash. I wondered if it was OK that he bypassed anything with nutritional value.

"Did you get enough to eat? I mean, we kind of interrupted you—are you still hungry?"

He hesitated. Thinking maybe he was shy, I took three peanut butter cookies from a nearby plate, passed one to Andie and held another out to Pettikin.

For a moment he didn't move, as if making some internal decision. Finally he stepped forward and took the cookie from me. He plopped down on the table, his legs spread out in a V, holding the cookie in front of him like a shield.

In slow motion, we all took bites of our cookies and chewed.

I swallowed.

"So, Pettikin—I don't know where to start. I mean, we've never seen a gnome before, not a real one."

"That's because there aren't any gnomes on Earth. Not anymore."

On Earth? Was this a joke? Were we being filmed or something?

"What are *you* doing here, then? Did you live with Aunt May?"

"No, I don't live here. I should never have come here…." His voice trailed off.

I absentmindedly broke my cookie into ever smaller pieces as I watched him.

"I'm lost," he whispered, so quietly I could barely hear him. His eyes filled with tears. "I'm lost on a Forbidden World."

"What's a Forbidden World?" Andie asked.

"One of the worlds we're not supposed to travel to—at least not alone."

"Why not?" I asked.

Pettikin bowed his head so I had to lean forward to make sure I could hear his answer.

"Because on the Forbidden Worlds, the Gateways have been closed."

"What Gateways?" I asked.

"The Gateways to the other worlds, the other dimensions."

My cookie was a pulverized mound of dust in front of me.

"So you came here from another world?" I asked.

"Yes, Arcorn. I come from a dimension called Arcorn."

"So how did you get here?"

"Through the Gateways, of course." Pettikin looked at the confused expressions on our faces. "You really don't know anything about the Gateways?"

Andie and I both shook our heads.

"Then I guess it's true that, on the Forbidden Worlds, you're not even aware of them anymore."

"What are they?" I asked.

"They're the doorways that connect all of the worlds in all of the universes to one another. If you can see the Gateways it's very easy to travel through them, from one world to the next. On my world we can all see them and learn how to travel through them when we're very young."

"Are they like physical doorways?"

Pettikin glowed in the yellow kitchen light. "I don't think they're physical the way you mean. They aren't like the doors in this house, for example."

"What are they like?"

"They're made of light, of energy. They're part of the universe you *feel* around you but don't necessarily *see*."

I was trying to keep up with him. "So when you travel through them, is it like...are you traveling through outer space or something?"

Pettikin giggled. "That would be a really inefficient way to travel between the worlds. It would take forever!"

"Yeah, our astrophysicists *have* struggled with that," I said.

Pettikin nodded. "It's because they don't know about the Gateways. If they knew about the Gateways, they would know it's not necessary to travel through physical space to get from one world to the next. I guess you could say that instead of traveling through *outer* space, the Gateways allow you to travel through *inner* space to different worlds."

"*So* not following," Andie said. She reached for another cookie. "Hope you're getting this, Al."

I wasn't exactly getting it, but I could sort of follow Pettikin's explanation. Still, I didn't know why he was so upset.

"OK, so what happened? I mean, it sounds like traveling through these Gateways is natural for you, like you know what you're doing. So why did you come here, if you're not supposed to?"

Pettikin swallowed and blinked his eyes. "Your Aunt May was my friend. She always brought us cookies whenever she visited us—"

I cut him off. "She came to visit you?"

"Yes, Arcorn was one of the worlds she stopped at frequently during her travels. Most of the gnomes were too shy to talk to her, but I'm brave, for a gnome." He sounded very proud as he said this.

"You're saying Aunt May, *my* Aunt May, could travel through these Gateways you're talking about?"

"Your Aunt May was a Gatekeeper."

"What's a Gatekeeper?"

"Someone who guards the Gateways on the Forbidden Worlds. They know how to find and open them there, and how to travel through them."

A sudden breeze blew through the still open window, stirring the cotton puff tip of Pettikin's hat. I shivered and got up to close it.

"Your Aunt May came to visit us the other day, on an important mission for the Guardians. She seemed worried about something and left before I had a chance to talk to her. I wanted to make sure she was OK, and when I thought about being with her, I found myself here."

I sat back down, rubbing my arms for warmth. Pettikin's eyes brimmed with tears. "But I shouldn't have done it. I should never have come here."

"But Pettikin, I don't understand what's wrong." I hated seeing him so upset. "Why don't you just go back home? You don't have to stay here. I mean, if Aunt May could travel from here to Arcorn, obviously there's a way…."

"No, you don't understand." Pettikin's voice was strained. "*Only* a Gatekeeper can open the Gateways on a

30

Forbidden World. I'm not a Gatekeeper. I can't even see the Gateways here."

"Oh no. You came here by yourself, but you need Aunt May in order to get home."

Pettikin nodded.

"Pettikin, she... she's dead." My voice cracked.

Large tears spilled from his eyes and rolled down his cheeks. He wiped them away with a tweed sleeve.

"I know," he said.

I put my elbows on the table and pressed my fingers on either side of my forehead, as if that would help keep my head together. Andie leaned back in her chair, stunned.

Ideas? I asked her silently.

She shook her head.

From the living room, the cuckoo clock chirped once, marking a quarter hour and causing us all to jump. Pettikin inhaled deeply and, for a second, I feared he might start screaming again. But he just exhaled slowly. He finished eating his cookie, sniffling in between bites, tears sliding down his face.

"OK, don't worry," I said finally, trying to make my voice sound reassuring. "We'll think of something. I mean, if Aunt May really was able to travel to your world, then there just *has* to be a way. We'll find a way to get you home."

Pettikin stopped eating. "You'll help me?" He wiped his face with his sleeve again.

"Well of course we'll help you! You were Aunt May's friend! We're not just going to leave you here alone."

Pettikin got to his feet and ran over to me faster than I thought possible. He threw his arms around my arm and hugged it tightly. "Oh thank you, Allie, thank you!"

"Aw, it's OK, Pettikin. Don't worry." I patted the top of his head.

"Um, Al?" Andie said. "That's great and all, but

how are we going to do this?"

Pettikin let go of my arm and waited for my answer. His expression was so trusting that I felt a little guilty, since I had no idea what to do.

"Well, um. I'm not sure. Aunt May has a lot of books. Should we try browsing through some of those for ideas?"

"Yes! We must start searching for Gateways!" Pettikin ran to the corner of the table and slid down the leg like a fireman. As soon as he reached the floor he took off for the living room.

"Hang on, wait for us!" I said. How could he move so fast with such little legs?

Pettikin stood on the coffee table when we got there, pouring over book titles. He dragged the ones he didn't care about to the side by using all his weight and pulling with both hands.

"Here, let us help you," I said.

It was getting dark outside, so I found another lamp and flicked it on. Andie and I sat down on either side of the coffee table and rummaged through the books while Pettikin peered at the titles. *101 Cookie Recipes, The Guardians, Introductory Gatekeeping....*

"There, that one!" Pettikin pointed at *Introductory Gatekeeping*, and I picked it up.

It was a large book, with a creased and worn black leather cover. The title was engraved in fancy gold letters at the top, and beneath it was an intricate design of crisscrossing lines that alternated with every color in the rainbow, like long, thin prisms. I tilted the book back and forth in the light of the lamp, watching the colors change.

"Neat," I said.

I passed the book to Andie so she could see it. "It reminds me of an Escher drawing or something, the pattern of the lines," she said, mesmerized.

We put the book in the center of the coffee table so we could all see it, and I flipped it open.

Preface.

Pettikin got down on his hands and knees, peering intently at the page. I read out loud:

"*If you're reading this book, then you probably live on one of the Forbidden Worlds. Sorry about that. But just remember, it could be worse!*"

"What the..." I stopped reading. "Who wrote this?"

"A Guardian, probably," Pettikin said. "They're very funny."

Oookaaay, I thought, and continued.

"*The fact that you're reading this book also suggests that you have been chosen by a Guardian to be a Gatekeeper. This is a very good thing, indeed. As a Gatekeeper you will learn to open and travel through the Gateways on your world, helping the Guardians in their mission to protect the bright worlds and battle the forces which work against the light.*"

I stopped reading again.

"So that's what Aunt May was doing? She worked for these Guardians that you keep talking about?"

Pettikin nodded.

I wanted to ask what a Guardian is but decided to finish reading.

"*Your primary task as a Gatekeeper will be to help beings who work with the Guardians travel through the Gateways on your world, while making sure the dark forces on your world don't gain access to the other worlds through your Gateways. This book should serve as a useful first guide for understanding the Gateways on your world. Remember, only another Gatekeeper or Guardian can teach you how to travel through them safely. We wish you the best of luck on your journey!*"

"That's all it says in the preface," I said. "Does that mean anything to you?"

Pettikin sat back on the table.

"On worlds like mine, the Gateways are open. Anyone can use them. But on worlds where there are dark forces, the Guardians close the Gateways. They set up a maze of dimensions around those worlds, and only give Gatekeepers the keys to unlock them. So while you can travel to a Forbidden World easily, once you are there you can't get back out unless a Gatekeeper takes you through those dimensions."

"Oh man," Andie said.

"That's why we call them Forbidden Worlds. They're not exactly *forbidden*, you can go to them, but there's a chance you might never return."

"Was Aunt May the only Gatekeeper here? Isn't there another Gatekeeper who might be able to help you?" I asked.

"I don't know. If there are others, I never met them. Aunt May is the only Gatekeeper I ever knew from Earth. Actually, she is the only person I ever knew from Earth, until I met you."

"Hey, wait a minute, how can you speak English?" Andie asked.

That was a good point. It never occurred to me to question why a gnome from another world knew my native tongue.

"If you mean the language you're speaking, I can't speak it," Pettikin said.

"Um, clearly you can," Andie said.

"Yeah, I'm hearing English," I said.

"I'm speaking my native language, but you understand me and I can understand you because I'm communicating with you telepathically," Pettikin said, in a tone that sounded like one he might normally use with baby gnomes.

"You mean you're psychic?" Andie asked.

"Everyone's psychic. How else would all of us who travel in the dimensions communicate with one another?"

"But we don't travel in the dimensions," Andie said.

"But you're still part of the universe," Pettikin

said, as if this explained anything.

I flipped through the book. Its pages were filled with complex technical diagrams and explanations, as well as a few photographs. Some of them were of famous places I recognized, like the pyramids in Egypt and the Grand Canyon. Others were just random, unfamiliar places, most of them outdoors, near the water, woods, or other natural settings. They had all been superimposed with multicolored bright lines, which came together to create tightly woven webs of light.

My heart sank, thinking we wouldn't be able to figure this out easily.

"Are these crisscrossing lines supposed to be Gateways?" I showed Pettikin the pictures.

He nodded.

"It's a way of trying to show what the Gateways look like and where they are. If you can see the Gateways they do look something like that, although it doesn't translate exactly to the drawings, since the Gateways aren't really part of the physical world."

"So," I said slowly, "you said that you can't *see* the Gateways here. But what if we could find one in this book and take you to it? I mean, maybe if we got you to the physical location of the Gateway you could get through it the same way you usually do, even if you can't *see* it."

Pettikin thought this over.

"I suppose we could try that," he said, sounding doubtful. "Since I don't know another Gatekeeper here, that seems like my best hope at this point."

Andie picked the book up and flipped through some of the pictures.

"Great, we'll just hop on a plane to Egypt...."

"There's gotta be one closer than that, don't you think? I mean, I don't remember Aunt May flying off to Egypt or the Grand Canyon all the time, so there must be some Gateways nearby that she could travel through." It was amazing how quickly we had started discussing interdimensional travel as if it were something completely normal.

Andie set the book back on the coffee table and flipped through the pages, pausing on pictures with Gateways. Egypt. Flip. Ocean. Flip, flip. Pond. Flip. Woods. Flip, flip. Grand Canyon. Flip.

"Hey, wait, Andie, go back," I reached forward. Flip, flip, flip.

The photograph was grainy, like it was taken in the fifties or sixties. It was a picture of a field on the edge of a woods, apparently taken sometime in the fall, golden-brown grasses gleaming in the light of a setting sun. A row of large, silver beech trees bordered the edge of the field near the woods, and in between the two tallest trees was a web of multicolored lines.

"Isn't that here? I think this is here!"

I snatched the book off the table and scanned the photo.

"The cottage isn't there, maybe it wasn't built yet, and there were more beech trees then, but I really think this is here. I think these two trees"—I pointed to the beech trees with the Gateway superimposed between them—"are the ones at the edge of Aunt May's yard next to the woods!"

We all crowded around the picture.

"Oh wow, you might be right," Andie said.

"It would make sense that Aunt May would live close to her primary Gateway," Pettikin said cautiously.

I could hardly contain my excitement. "So it might be right here! We might be able to get you home easier than we thought!"

Pettikin's face was doubtful.

Andie, however, was catching my enthusiasm. "Let's go outside and look before it gets any darker."

Pettikin slid off the edge of the sofa onto my shoulder, clamping a hand against my head for balance. I set the book on the coffee table and stood up, using one hand to steady him.

"Hang on." I knelt carefully, bending my knees but keeping my back straight like I was in a ballet class, so I wouldn't dislodge Pettikin. I fished the lantern-style flashlight out of my backpack and eased myself up.

Andie was already waiting by the front door. She pulled it open, and we all stepped outside.

"Whoa," I said.

It must have been ten degrees colder than when we walked down to the cottage. A frigid wind blew across the yard, swirling the first fallen leaves from the ground up into the air. The sun had set and the last light of the day was fading. Dark clouds scuttled across the sky. I shivered.

"This is crazy," Andie said. "How can it already be this much colder?"

"Global climate change," I answered automatically, with a tiny doubt in the back of my mind. I wanted to put my sweatshirt on, but that would have been difficult with Pettikin sitting on my shoulder. I flicked the flashlight on and focused the beam on the front walkway.

Andie set off at a brisk clip down the path that lead to the woods. I tried to keep up with her without jostling Pettikin too much. He grabbed two handfuls of my hair like reins as I half-jogged, half-glided behind her, one hand reaching up occasionally to steady him.

Andie stopped abruptly near the entrance of the woods.

"Do you hear that?"

I stopped and listened.

"Hear what?"

She put a finger to her lips, her head cocked to one side.

"I think there might be something in there," she said in a low voice, pointing toward the woods.

I thought I could hear it too, a steady rustling in the underbrush.

"A deer? Maybe a skunk?"

Pettikin breathed heavily on my shoulders.

Andie's face was serious.

"Maybe you should hide Pettikin."

Before I had time to react, the rustling became louder and faster. A deafening noise almost ruptured my eardrums.

"Ow, Pettikin, don't scream!" I reached up and got a hand between his mouth and my ear just as a black figure came hurtling out of the woods.

I burst out laughing. It was Socrates lumbering toward us, his coat covered in leaves and burrs. He danced around me in a circle, jumping up to see if the object on my shoulders was some kind of new toy for him to play with.

"Down, Socks!"

I stepped back, worried that Pettikin would be terrified, but to my surprise the gnome slid down my arm and climbed on Socrates' back, his hands burrowed in the dog's neck. Socrates pranced in a wide circle, turning his head to see the creature on his back, before stopping in front of me and Andie with a wide dog-grin on his face.

"Do you have dogs on Arcorn, Pettikin?" I untied my hoodie from around my waist and slid my arms into the sleeves, rubbing them to try and create some warmth.

"No, dragons, but they are very similar," Pettikin said.

I was about to protest that dogs and dragons were nothing alike. But seeing Socks' gleaming white teeth, enormous paws and pointed ears, I wondered if he didn't seem like a dragon after all.

I can't believe I'm thinking this, I thought.

"OK, let's keep going," Andie said, walking along the edge of the woods toward the two beech trees.

I shined the beam of the flashlight along the ground near the first one as we approached it.

"I wonder if there's any evidence that there used to be more than just the two trees here—an old stump or something," I said.

Andie walked into the beam of the flashlight searching the ground, Socks sniffing next to her. "I don't see anything out of the ordinary."

"Maybe it's not the right place after all," I said.

"I wish we brought the book with us so we could study the picture more carefully," Andie said.

"Yeah, but it's so dark out now anyway." I moved the flashlight beam up and down the trunk of the first tree and around the surrounding area.

"Maybe on the other side? Next to the other tree?" Andie asked

We walked behind the second tree, searching along the ground for anything that might suggest there used to be more trees. It took a few seconds for my brain to register a new rhythmic sound: *crunch, crunch, crunch, crunch.*

Andie grabbed my arm, and we froze.

"Behind you," she said. I turned the flashlight beam toward the yard but didn't see anything.

Crunch, crunch, crunch, crunch. The noise grew louder.

"Are we just imagining things again?" I asked.

Socrates pinned his ears against his head and a low rumble emerged from deep within his chest. Pettikin's eyes widened with alarm. I squinted out into the darkness.

"Who's there?" I called, trying to make my voice sound deeper than it was.

The crunching stopped. The only sounds I could hear were the wind in the trees and my own loud breathing.

"You need to hide Pettikin," Andie hissed, taking the flashlight from me.

I hurried over to the gnome. He clamped both hands over his mouth to keep from screaming.

"It's OK, don't panic," I whispered. I picked him up and held him a few inches in front of me while I searched for some place to hide him.

"What am I supposed to do with him?" I hissed at Andie.

"Hide him under your sweatshirt," she hissed back.

"Here, Pettikin, just keep as still as you possibly can."

He trembled, but did what I said. I got him situated so he was inside the flaps of my sweatshirt but resting against the crook of my arm, with the jacket part zipped over him.

"This is ridiculous!" I whispered, "I look like I have a bun in the oven!"

Andie glanced over at us, and, totally inappropriately, we burst into hysterics. She covered her mouth with her hand, trying to muffle the chortles, while I doubled over in silent spasms of laughter, trying not to crush Pettikin and hoping I wouldn't pee my pants.

"Stop it, stop it!" I said in between gasps, "It's not funny!"

The crunching started again, and a dark figure emerged from the shadows. Andie recovered and whirled around. Socrates growled feverishly. I grabbed his collar just before he could lunge forward.

Andie swung the beam of the flashlight onto the dark figure.

It was Mr. Cutter.

"Hello, girls." He squinted into the beam of the flashlight. "It's just me. I'm sorry, did I scare you?"

"Mr. Cutter?" I was totally bewildered.

"Allie, is that you?" Mr. Cutter put one hand up to his eyes and tried to peer around the bright beam of light that Andie shone deliberately in his face.

Socrates snarled and pulled on his collar.

"What are you doing here?" I asked.

"Didn't your father tell you? We're neighbors now." His voice sounded too friendly, like a salesman's. He tried unsuccessfully to step out of the flashlight beam.

"Could you call your dog off?"

"I've got him," I said, although I wasn't at all sure about that. "I meant, what are you doing here, on our property?"

"I saw the lights on in the cottage and I just wanted to make sure everything was all right." He took a step toward us, and Socrates almost pulled my arm out of its socket. Pettikin slipped down on my hip, and I was afraid his feet would be hanging out from under my sweatshirt if we weren't careful.

"Easy, easy!" Mr. Cutter yelled, backing away. "Hey, could you put the dog inside?"

"I think you better just go, Mr. Cutter," I said. Seeing his expression in the flashlight beam, though, I wished I hadn't.

"Now listen," he said, taking a step forward.

Before I could do anything, Andie said in an unexpectedly loud voice, "Please go away!"

Mr. Cutter jerked his head toward her and vanished.

Socrates lunged. This time I lost my grip on his collar and fell backwards onto the ground. I heard a muffled squeak from Pettikin and felt him scrambling underneath my sweatshirt as he poked his head out to see what happened.

Andie dropped the flashlight.

"Oh my God, oh my God, oh my God." She stared at the place where Mr. Cutter had vanished while Socrates sniffed furiously around it.

"I can't...did you see...." I couldn't get out a coherent thought as I struggled to my feet, clutching Pettikin to my side. I stumbled over to where Andie and Socrates stood, but there was no trace of the man who had been there not thirty seconds earlier.

"Did that just happen?" My voice was high and loud. "Did Mr. Cutter just appear out of nowhere and vanish right in front of us?"

Pettikin shrieked, and almost reflexively, I clamped my hand over his mouth.

"Oh my God," Andie said one last time. She covered her mouth with one hand and stared at me.

To my horror, I heard more footsteps, this time accompanied by voices, heading directly for us.

"Pettikin," I said.

He nodded slowly, and I removed my hand from his mouth. He replaced it with both his own, I guess not trusting that he wouldn't scream. I tucked him against my side and zipped the sweatshirt over him again, feeling awful when I saw him squeeze his eyes shut. What in the world was he feeling right now? Andie grabbed the flashlight and shined it into the yard.

Socrates barked again, but this time it was his normal, friendly, welcoming bark.

"Who's there?" I called out.

"It's us, Allie!" a melodious voice replied. "We've come to return the alpacas."

Mrs. Widgit, Professor Theopolous, Bob, and the alpacas emerged from the darkness.

4

"Your parents told us you girls were spending the night down here." Mrs. Widgit stopped in front of us and put her hands on her hips. "I must admit, I'm impressed with your bravery."

Andie let out a kind of half laugh.

"Andie, this is Mrs. Widgit, Professor Theopolous and Bob," I said. "Friends of Aunt May's who were at her funeral this afternoon. This is my best friend, Andie Wu."

"How do you do?" Mrs. Widgit held out the edges of her dress and curtsied. Professor Theopolous nodded once without smiling. Bob ducked his head and scuffed the sole of one shoe against the ground.

Mrs. Widgit turned her head back and forth between Andie and me.

"Is everything OK, girls? We thought we heard screaming before."

Neither of us said anything.

"Did you see Aunt May's ghost or something?" She chuckled.

"That would have been preferable, actually," I muttered.

Andie frowned at me, as if to say, *what are you*

doing? I winced at my own stupidity.

Mrs. Widgit raised her eyebrows.

"Did something happen?"

We were both silent, and I shifted my weight uncomfortably. Mrs. Widgit peered at me through the flashlight beam with oddly crooked eyes.

"What's under your sweatshirt, Allie?"

I looked at Andie helplessly. Mrs. Widgit wouldn't believe me if I said "nothing," but I couldn't think of a single intelligent answer that wouldn't give Pettikin away.

Good guys? Andie asked me silently.

I shrugged and grimaced slightly.

I think so, you?

Andie nodded, almost imperceptibly. She turned toward Mrs. Widgit.

"Actually, we ran into Mr. Cutter just before you got here. He kind of startled us, which is why we were screaming."

"The rich man from the funeral?" I didn't think Mrs. Widgit really bought the explanation, but she seemed willing to let the topic of my sudden-onset teen pregnancy drop for the moment. "I believe he and May knew each other for quite some time."

"We weren't sure what he wanted, and Socrates kept barking and growling at him. Finally, he just, uh…disappeared."

Andie omitted the part about her possibly having "disappeared" him.

"When you say he disappeared…" Mrs. Widgit said slowly.

"She means one minute he was standing here and the next minute he was gone. Like he had just… evaporated or something," I said.

"Can you show us where this happened?" Professor Theopolous' voice was gruff.

"Yeah, I mean it was right here." Andie gestured toward the spot on the ground where Mr. Cutter had been.

Socrates had finished sniffing it and was sitting nearby on his haunches with a satisfied expression, as if he had taken care of everything.

The Professor and Mrs. Widgit huddled around the spot, conferring with each other. Professor Theopolous bent down and touched something on the ground. Bob watched them while rubbing an alpaca's nose.

Andie caught my eye.

"I'll be right back," I called out, then walked away as fast as I could, trying not to jostle Pettikin too much.

It was dark without the flashlight, so I went just as far as necessary to get out of their line of sight. I carefully unzipped my sweatshirt. Pettikin still had his hands over his mouth and his eyes squinched shut. I set him on the ground and crouched next to him, making sure that my body was between him and the strangers. His expression was forlorn.

"Pettikin, I don't know what to do," I whispered. "I think these people were Aunt May's friends, so they might be able to help us, but to find out, I'll have to tell them about you. Is that OK?"

Pettikin's eyes darted around, as if searching for escape. "I don't know, Allie. The man that was here—I didn't like him."

"Me neither," I said. "Heck, I didn't like him even before he got all weird and started trespassing and disappearing into thin air and stuff."

The wind picked up again and blew the puffed end of Pettikin's Santa hat over his face. He brushed it away and shivered.

"I can't be sure, but I don't think these people are like that," I said. "They seem strange on the outside, but they might be OK on the inside, if that makes sense. Dad knows them, and I think Aunt May trusted them. Socrates seems to like them too. They might know more about how to help you than I do."

Pettikin fidgeted with a button on the front of his

jacket. He was so small and alone, and I felt completely useless. Why hadn't he run into a human who could actually help him, instead of a doofus American teenager?

"OK," he said finally. "If you think it's a good idea, then let's tell them."

I sighed in relief.

"OK. Don't worry, I won't let them hurt you." I wondered how in the world I thought I could keep that promise. Pettikin grabbed the sleeve of my hoodie and pulled himself up my arm to my shoulder.

We didn't say anything else as we walked back to the group.

Everyone was still gathered around the place where Mr. Cutter had vanished, Andie explaining something while the others listened intently.

"Um, Mrs. Widgit?" I said.

They all stopped talking.

"This is what, or rather *who*, was under my sweatshirt." I stepped into the circle of light created by Andie's flashlight.

Mrs. Widgit gasped.

"My goodness -- it's a gnome!"

Bob's eyes almost doubled in diameter, and even Professor Theopolous seemed shocked, which was about the first discernible emotion I'd seen him express.

"Mrs. Widgit, Professor, Bob—this is Pettikin Periwinkle from Arcorn," I said, feeling ridiculous, like I was introducing him as *one of the Arcorn Periwinkles*. "Pettikin, these are Aunt May's friends I was telling you about. Ow! Hey, don't...."

Pettikin had grabbed two handfuls of my hair and was pulling on them with increasing tension as I spoke. He relaxed his grip ever so slightly as I reached a hand up to intervene.

"Sorry, Allie," he said so quietly that only I could hear him.

Mrs. Widgit gaped at us.

"He lets you touch him." She said, with evident amazement.

"Well, uh, yeah, sure, when he needs to. Why?"

She took a cautious step toward us, and almost instantly Pettikin started shrieking. He yanked on my hair so hard I thought he was going to pull it right out of my head.

"Pettikin, stop! Don't scream--ow…." I stumbled backwards, reaching up to try and calm him, and Mrs. Widgit immediately stepped back to her original position. The alpacas hopped up and down and honked while Bob tried to calm them.

Pettikin stopped screaming and let go of my hair. I felt the blood returning to my scalp.

"He is a little bit shy around people, I guess," I said, rubbing my head. I could hear Pettikin breathing heavily on my shoulder.

"I can see that," Mrs. Widgit said, "but that makes sense. Gnomes are notoriously shy. It's one of their defining characteristics. They normally wouldn't let themselves be seen by a human, let alone touched by one. So, from our point of view, the only extraordinary part of this situation, besides the fact that there is a gnome here on Earth, is that he seems to feel so comfortable with you."

"Well, I, uh…."

I felt weird talking about Pettikin in the third person, as if he weren't sitting right there on my shoulder.

"OK, wait a minute," Andie said. "You're talking about this stuff like it's totally normal, saying things like 'here on Earth', and you know what a gnome is and how a gnome is supposed to act. And we just told you some guy disappeared on the lawn, and you didn't even try to call our parents and tell them we were doing drugs down here or something. There is something way weird going on here, and it seems like you all know something about it, and since there's a gnome sitting on Allie's shoulders, and we need to find a way to get him home pronto, I'm thinking now might be a good time for you to start giving us some answers."

If they were worried about us doing drugs down here, this outburst probably hadn't done much to convince them that we weren't.

"Perhaps we should all go inside for a bit, Viola," Professor Theopolous said. "It might be easier to chat there."

I thought I could hear the faintest hint of amusement in his voice, but it might have just been an attempt on my part to humanize him.

"Of course you're right, Theo," Mrs. Widgit said. "Girls, could we join you in the cottage for a little while? I can make some hot cocoa for everyone, if you like. I'm fairly sure May will have the ingredients. And Theo can build a fire."

It was hard to believe we needed a fire after the heat of the day, but my nose and hands were starting to feel numb from the chill, and I could see my breath when I exhaled.

"A fire sounds nice," I said. "Actually, I think there's some firewood stacked behind the cottage. At least that's where Aunt May used to keep it. Andie and I will go get some."

I wondered if I was being too obvious, but I wanted a chance to talk to Andie alone, and also to take Pettikin to the beech trees one more time. If there was a Gateway and he could get through it, maybe we could just spare him the rest of this ordeal.

"That sounds fine, dear," Mrs. Widgit said, pulling a small flashlight from her pocket and flicking it on. "We'll wait for you. Come Socrates! You can help me make cocoa!"

Socrates pricked up his ears and trotted eagerly after them, in case "cocoa" meant the same thing as "cookie." When they neared the cottage Bob veered away, leading the alpacas toward the barn.

"Beech trees?" Andie and I asked at the same time, and laughed.

"We need to do it faster this time, and I'm going to need the brain to do homework at some point this weekend," Andie said.

We jogged to the beech trees, with me holding on to Pettikin's legs to keep him steady. As soon as we got there, Andie trained the flashlight beam in between them.

A break in the clouds allowed the nearly full moon to cast a pale glow on us. The trees were taller than any other ones in the woods -- their branches almost seemed to touch the moon. Their trunks were so thick in diameter that even if Andie, Pettikin, and I held hands we wouldn't be able to encircle them.

"OK, Pettikin." I lifted him off my shoulder, setting him down on the ground in front of the trees. "What do you think? Is it a Gateway? Can you get through?"

Pettikin approached the space between the two trees. Andie, coughed from the exertion of running in the cold, covering her mouth with the crook of her left arm, still keeping the flashlight focused on the trees.

Pettikin raised one hand and took a few tentative steps forward. Then he stopped. He dropped his hand to his side.

"I thought it might be a Gateway. It *feels* like a Gateway. But I can't open it, and I can't get through. I think it has been closed." He shivered as he said these last words.

I guess I should have known it wouldn't be so easy. I had a terrible feeling that things were about to get much more complicated.

"So what do you think?" Andie asked. "Do we trust Aunt May's friends?"

"I guess we have to," I said. "I mean, we can't tell my parents, that's for sure."

"And we're not going to be able to do much on our own unless we get some more information. We at least need to find out what they know," Andie said.

I knelt down by Pettikin, offering him my hand.

"Don't worry. This was just our first attempt. Maybe this wasn't even the Gateway we wanted -- that picture could have been from anywhere."

"Maybe Mrs. Widgit and Professor Theopolous know something about the Gateways, since they know about gnomes," Andie added. "They might even know where the right Gateway is, or how to get you home."

Pettikin took my hand and climbed up to my shoulder.

"OK, let's go get some firewood so they won't wonder what we were doing out here," I said, "and then let's go get some cocoa."

"What's cocoa?" Pettikin asked as we walked toward the stone patio behind the cottage where several cords of firewood were stacked underneath a green tarp.

I had already started thinking of Pettikin as a small person and forgot how alien all of this must seem to him.

"You've never had cocoa? It's warm and chocolaty and sweet. I think you'll like it."

I lifted the tarp off of the firewood while Andie stacked a couple pieces in her arms. In the distance I could see the lights on in the barn. Bob must have been down there with the alpacas, feeding them or changing their water.

We tromped into the living room. It seemed brighter and warmer than it had when we left. Someone had turned the steam radiators on, and dishes clattered in the kitchen. Mrs. Widgit alternately hummed and talked to Socrates. Professor Theopolous kneeled in front of the fireplace, futzing with the flue.

"I've got firewood for you, Professor T," Andie said.

I watched his face for any type of reaction to her

informality, but his voice was formal when he answered her.

"Thank you, Andie." He took the wood and arranged it on the metal grate. "Now let's see here..."

Mrs. Widgit came into the living room carrying a tray with five steaming mugs of cocoa and cookies from the funeral reception. Socrates trotted close to her legs, gazing up at the tray and making it difficult for her to walk.

"Welcome back, girls! The cocoa is ready. I hope you don't mind that I turned the heat on."

Pettikin grabbed a couple handfuls of my hair and tightened his grip as Mrs. Widgit approached. Fortunately, Socrates spotted Pettikin on my shoulders and sidled up next to me. Pettikin slid down my arm to the dog's back – maybe there he wouldn't get too stressed out by the humans in the room. Socrates wagged his tail so hard that his whole hind end wagged with it.

Andie I and hurried over to clear away some of the books on the coffee table so there would be room for Mrs. Widgit to set the tray down.

"I'm assuming Bob will stay out in the barn with the alpacas a bit longer. He's quite shy you know," she said. "If he decides to come in I can easily make another mug for him."

FWOOM!

A wall of flame exploded out of the fireplace. I yelled and Andie ducked down, holding a book up in front of her face like a shield. Pettikin screamed and Socrates started barking and running in circles. Professor Theopolous was still standing next to the fireplace, and, for a moment, it seemed like the flames might engulf him, but they died down to a comfortable, crackling fire in the fireplace.

"What the heck was *that?*" Andie lowered her book-slash-shield. Socrates was still barking, and Pettikin only stopped screaming because he burrowed his face in the thick fur on Socrates' neck.

Only Mrs. Widgit hadn't flinched as she carefully set the tray of cocoa down on the coffee table.

"Little out of practice there, Theo?" Her voice was mild, but her lips were twitching.

Professor Theopolous cleared his throat and straightened his suit jacket.

"Fire's all set."

Andie and I frowned at each other. Our collective brain expressed that it was reaching its limit for bizarre, fantastical occurrences for one evening.

Socrates trotted over to the fireplace, still carrying Pettikin on his back, and sniffed around it. He scratched the floor with his front paws, turned around three times, and plopped down. He put his head down on his front paws and sighed. Pettikin slid off of him onto the floor in front of the fire. He leaned against the dog and stared into the flames with a distant expression.

Mrs. Widgit handed me a steaming mug of cocoa on a red paper napkin, then reached into the pocket of her dress and pulled out a straw. She jutted her chin at the gnome and winked at me.

"Here, Pettikin, try some cocoa."

I stuck the straw in the cocoa and set the mug down next to him, pushing Socrates' inquisitive nose away. I took a small sip to show him how to use the straw. The cocoa was warm, but not too hot.

Pettikin took a tentative sip, and then started slurping eagerly. I rejoined the others—Mrs. Widgit and the Professor on the sofa closest to the kitchen and Andie and I on the one across from them. Pettikin finished his cocoa and snuggled into Socrates' fur, his eyelids drooping.

Mrs. Widgit tucked her legs up underneath her on the couch and blew across her mug.

"So, did you find what you were looking for outside?" she asked.

Andie and I glanced at each other.

"What, you mean the firewood?" Andie's

expression was innocent, but her voice sounded flat.

"Actually, I rather thought you might be searching for the Nexus Gateway. We thought perhaps you were going to take Pettikin home." She watched me carefully as she took another sip of cocoa.

It wasn't at all what I was expecting her to say, and something about her tone caught me off guard. Was this an ambush? Had it been a mistake to trust them? I felt something inside me hardening, putting up shields, the way I did when Mom was prying too much.

"We didn't know it had a name," I said finally, in a cold voice. Ugh. I was about to take a sip of cocoa, and then wondered if maybe I shouldn't.

"What *do* you know about it?" Mrs. Widgit's tone was sharper.

"Nothing. What do you think we know about it? I mean, shouldn't you be explaining this stuff to us, not the other way around?" I glanced over at Pettikin. He didn't seem to be suffering any ill effects from drinking his cocoa, so I took a tentative sip of mine. It tasted good, like Mrs. Widgit had made it by melting real chocolate in warm milk, not from one of those instant powders.

"If you don't know anything about it, then how did you know it was the right Gateway to get Pettikin home?"

"Dude, we didn't know, we were just guessing," Andie said. "Pettikin told us about the Gateways, we flipped though some of Aunt May's books, and we thought that might be the closest one to try."

"Pettikin told you about the Gateways? You had never heard of them before?" Professor Theopolous asked.

"No. Look, what is this?" I asked. "I thought we were supposed to be getting information from you about what's going on. All I know is my great aunt died and left me all of her things, and that poor little Pettikin is trapped here because apparently Aunt May was some kind of

Gatekeeper, and he needed her to take him home. That's it. That's all we know."

Mrs. Widgit and Professor Theopolous exchanged glances.

"You're saying that until this afternoon you had no idea that your Aunt May was a Gatekeeper?" the Professor asked.

"No idea. If Pettikin weren't here I probably wouldn't believe it."

"In all these years, May never talked to you about the Gateways? Are you sure?" Mrs. Widgit pressed.

"I'm sure. You think I wouldn't remember something like that?"

"But she spent a lot of time with you when you were younger, yes?" the Professor asked. Man, they wouldn't let this drop.

"Yeah, but we just made cookies, and she told me stories about dragons and gnomes and…"

"And?" Mrs. Widgit prompted.

"And…nothing. Only I just now realized that maybe the stories she was telling me weren't really stories. Maybe they were real."

"Do you remember anything about them?" Professor Theopolous prodded.

"No, honestly-they were just stories to me. I didn't know there was going to be a quiz."

"You're sure she didn't mention the Gateways in the stories…" Mrs. Widgit again.

"No!" I was exasperated now. "I would have remembered that because it would have been something I had never heard of. I would have asked her about it. I don't know anything about the Gateways. I didn't know Aunt May was a Gatekeeper. I just know we need to find a Gateway to get Pettikin home."

"Not just a Gateway, but a Gatekeeper," Professor Theopolous corrected.

"And not just Pettikin," Mrs. Widgit added.

"What's *that* supposed to mean?" Andie asked.

"Let's just say that Aunt May left more than one interdimensional traveler stranded this week." Mrs. Widgit said, a smile twitching on her lips.

Andie groaned. "Oh man."

"I don't believe this," I said, setting my unfinished mug of cocoa down on the coffee table. "This is a nightmare."

"Oh, it's not so bad for Theo, Bob and I," Mrs. Widgit said. "We do spend a lot of time here and are accustomed to Earth. We could stay if we had to, although we prefer not to. But the gnome does present a more pressing problem. I think I have a better sense of the situation now, Allie. We apologize. We were working under a slight... *misapprehension* here."

"What misapprehension is that?"

Mrs. Widgit rearranged herself on the couch. "Well, as you are now aware, your Aunt May was a Gatekeeper. Gatekeepers are special people who have been chosen by the Guardians to protect the Secret Gateways on the Forbidden Worlds, and to open them for other travelers who work with the Guardians of the Universe."

"Like you?" I asked.

"Yes, like us."

"But you're not a Gatekeeper?" Andie asked. "You can't open the Gateways here either?"

"No, I'm not a Gatekeeper, I'm a Facilitator," Mrs. Widgit said.

"What's a Facilitator?" I asked.

"A Facilitator is someone who brings exactly the right people together at precisely the right moment in time in order to accomplish a specific task, sometimes without even being aware of it." Mrs. Widgit said. "Facilitators help make things happen, get things done."

"So why don't you bring us a Gatekeeper?" I suggested sarcastically.

"It's not that simple, Allie," Professor

Theopolous' tone conveyed that he was Very Disappointed in my attitude, as only a teacher's could. My cheeks flushed and I scowled down at my hands.

"How is it not that simple?" Andie asked. "If we had another Gatekeeper here, then they could take Pettikin home through that Nexus Gateway thing. Problem solved."

Mrs. Widgit struggled to pull herself forward from the sofa she had nestled into. She set her mug down on the coffee table and perched on the edge of the couch.

"I notice that neither of you have asked yet, what exactly it is that *Professor* Theopolous teaches," she said, leaning toward us, smiling.

The Professor didn't say anything.

"Well, what do you teach?" I asked

Professor Theopolous' expression was stony behind his monocle.

"I teach Gatekeeping. I *am* a Gatekeeper."

5

Andie and I gaped at him, and Pettikin's head appeared from behind Socrates, his eyes no longer sleepy.

"Are you kidding?" Andie asked.

"Then what are we waiting for? Let's go back to the Gateway and—" I said.

"It's not that simple."

"Why not?" I sounded whiny.

"Because Gatekeepers do not have unlimited power to enter all of the Secret Gateways on all of the Forbidden Worlds. They are chosen by the Guardians to guard and protect the Secret Gateways only on their own world." I had a feeling we were hearing part of a *Gatekeeping 101* lecture.

"You might say the Guardians give the Gatekeepers the keys they need to unlock and enter the Secret Gateways on their world. Without those keys a Gatekeeper can't see or open the Secret Gateways on a Forbidden world any more than any other person can."

Those Guardians, again. I should have done more research up front.

Professor Theopolous pulled a handkerchief from his pocket, removed his monocle and rubbed the lens between his thumb and forefinger.

"So, even though I am a Gatekeeper, and even though I train other Gatekeepers, I don't have the right keys to open the Gateways here."

I let out a long, slow sigh and slumped into the couch.

"Also-" Professor Theopolous hesitated for a moment. "I'm rather a *retired* Gatekeeper. At the moment I only teach."

"Those who can, do. Those who can't..." Andie muttered.

"So, what are we going to do?" I asked. "I mean, do we have any other options? Is there something else we could try?"

I glanced over toward the fireplace. Pettikin leaned against Socrates, but his eyes were open now, and he appeared to be listening to the conversation.

"I imagine," Mrs. Widgit said cheerfully and, I thought, a little smugly, "that is what we are all here to find out."

Professor Theopolous rolled his eyes. "Facilitators can be so insufferable."

Andie pressed her lips together in a thin line. I was starting to wonder if we might have been better off without the grownups.

"Well, has something like this ever happened before?" I asked. "I mean, what usually happens when a Gatekeeper dies? Do the Guardians find another Gatekeeper, or are the Gateways just closed forever?"

"Ah, now, *that* is an excellent question," the Professor said. "Generally a Gatekeeper trains an apprentice, for exactly this reason. Take my case for example. I was the Gatekeeper on a world called Feron, but I trained an apprentice Gatekeeper for twenty years. When I left Feron to become a teacher, my Guardian empowered my apprentice to be able to see and access the Secret Gateways there. Because of his many years of training and dedication, he easily took over the job from me, and one day his apprentice will take over from him."

Professor Theopolous paused. "But your second statement is also correct. If a Gatekeeper were to die, and left no apprentice to take over, the Guardians could close the Gateways on that world for good."

"What does that mean?" Andie asked.

Mrs. Widgit sounded grim. "It means there's a danger the world could become a Shadow World-a world cut off completely from the higher worlds of light."

"So did Aunt May have an apprentice then?" I asked. "Someone she was training to be the next Gatekeeper?"

Mrs. Widgit and Professor Theopolous stared at me. Andie turned her head toward me. From the fireplace, Pettikin's face appeared above the bulk of Socrates' body.

"Why are you all looking at me?"

No one said anything.

"Oh come *on*. You can't be serious. No. There's no way."

"I mean, it kinda makes sense, Al," Andie said. "She left you all her stuff and you said that she dedicated that poem to you at the funeral-"

"Yeah, and with all that at no point did she say, 'Yo, Allie, if I die you're the next Gatekeeper.' I mean come *on*!"

"Well, it's definitely the impression we were left with dear," Mrs. Widgit said. "That's why we were so confused when it became clear that you knew nothing about the Gateways or Gatekeeping."

I wondered how they could continue to be unmoved by my incredulousness. "You're serious? You actually think I was supposed to be Aunt May's apprentice Gatekeeper?"

"The only thing we can't figure out," Mrs. Widgit said, "Is why she didn't complete your training after she started."

"OK," I said, trying to be reasonable, "I know why you might hope there was training, but there wasn't, I swear. I just found out about all this stuff, like, two hours ago! I don't even know what it means!"

"Then it's a good thing that we have not just an apprentice Gatekeeper here but also a Professor of Gatekeeping," Mrs. Widgit sounded triumphant.

Professor Theopolous scowled.

"I'm not an apprentice Gatekeeper!" I was totally exasperated. "I'm, like, marginally related to a Gatekeeper, I have no other skills!"

"Well, everyone has to start from somewhere," Mrs. Widgit said.

"Well, if we're just going to pick someone randomly, why not pick her," I pointed at Andie, "or better yet, him! The *actual Gatekeeper*," I waved my hand at Professor Theopolous.

Professor Theopolous thumped the palm of his hand on the arm of the sofa.

"Even if I wanted to consider this preposterous idea, it is highly doubtful that I could train Allie to be a Gatekeeper at this point."

"Why not?" Andie asked. "She's the smartest kid in our class. She can learn anything."

"Andie—what the—you're not helping," I said.

"Book smarts isn't all it takes to become a Gatekeeper," Professor Theopolous said.

"Theo, you know very well that she's got a lot more than just book smarts going for her," Mrs. Widgit chided.

"Yeah," Andie agreed, "so why can't you train her?"

Here it comes, I thought. He's going to say I'm too young.

"She's too old."

What?

Mrs. Widgit reached up with her index finger and

rubbed her forehead just above her eyebrows. "I hardly think we have time to find and train a Gatekeeper from a suitably young age, Theo."

"You know as well as I do that it takes years of discipline and practice to develop the skill and dedication required to be a Gatekeeper. Even if it were possible to train someone so quickly, it would be particularly difficult to do here on Earth."

"Here on Earth, nothing works the way it's supposed to any more. I think this is a situation screaming for us to act in accordance with the times and not get hung up on a set of moldy traditions."

"The traditions are there for a reason."

"The traditions are outdated and no longer practical."

I was starting to feel a little sick to my stomach.

"I know it may not have been what you consider formal training, Theo, but May did spend a fair amount of time with Allie when she was younger. Perhaps she was laying the groundwork for future training," Mrs. Widgit said.

"That may be, Viola, but a few afternoons spent together is not going to substitute for the years of training she should have had by now."

"I could help her." The voice was small and came from the fireplace.

We all turned toward Pettikin. He cringed and ducked behind Socrates.

"Thank you, Pettikin, but gnomes are not Gatekeepers. I'm not sure how you could help." Professor Theopolous' tone was at least softer.

"We're not Gatekeepers, but we know a lot about interdimensional travel. If the Guardian agrees to empower her, I can go with her on her initial tests and help her."

"Tests?" I asked.

Everyone ignored me. The Professor peered at

Pettikin with a thoughtful expression on his face.

"It's never been done before," he said finally. "It would be highly unconventional."

"Oh Theo!" Mrs. Widgit jumped up and waved her arms in exasperation. "You and your traditions! Blaze a trail for once for God's sake!"

The Professor shifted his weight uncomfortably on the couch. "It is an intriguing idea," he admitted begrudgingly. "Gnomes do have a natural understanding of interdimensional travel, and a certain magic of their own. It might be enough to help her through the initial trial."

"Trial?" my voice sounded weak.

"*If,*" Professor Theopolous ignored me and glared at Mrs. Widgit, "we can get the Guardian to consider it, and you know as well as I do that it is not likely."

"Perhaps we can convince him that May meant for Allie to be her replacement, and simply hadn't finished her training yet. We won't know unless we ask," Mrs. Widgit said.

"Without May here, we don't even know if he will give us an audience," Professor Theopolous said.

"Um, excuse me?" I said.

Mrs. Widgit appeared to have forgotten I was there. "Yes, dear?"

"Do I get any say in this at all?"

"Well of course you do dear. What did you want to say?"

"That I don't understand why we're talking about this like it's the only option. I mean, why not ask the Guardian to just give the keys to the Secret Gateways to Professor Theopolous? He's already a Gatekeeper. He can take Pettikin home."

"The Guardian won't give the keys to someone who can't stay here and guard the Gateways once they're open again," Professor Theopolous said, "and I still have obligations on Feron and elsewhere. I can't take on this responsibility."

"But why me?" I asked. "I mean, I don't understand any of this. I don't even know if I can do it."

"You're the closest thing we have to an apprentice here, Allie. You're our best hope," Mrs. Widgit answered. "Are you saying you're not willing to try?"

"I, no, but, I mean…"

Pettikin stood back up and leaned toward me, his hands pressing into Socrates' fur.

"Please, Allie," he said. "Please say you'll try. We can ask the Guardian together. I'll help you."

I froze. What was I going to do, say no to that?

"Oh, OK, fine. I'll try," I said. It felt like the most anti-climactic, unheroic statement ever in the history of time.

"Don't worry. It's highly unlikely the Guardian will even see us, let alone agree to this idea." Professor Theopolous said, nodding his head.

"Great." I said, with no emotion in my voice.

"So it's settled then! Good. Well, on that note," Mrs. Widgit stood up, "I think it is time for us to leave for the evening. I believe you girls were trying to have a slumber party when you were so rudely interrupted."

"Wait a minute, that's it? You're just leaving?" I struggled to my feet.

"Well there's not much more we can do tonight. And you'll need some sleep if we're going to take you to the Guardian tomorrow."

"What? What do you mean you're going to take me to the Guardian tomorrow? I'm not ready to meet any Guardian—I don't even know what a Guardian is," I said as I followed her toward the door.

"Oh, It's OK, dear. We'll explain it to you tomorrow before we go."

"Although you might want to browse through some of these books to see if any of them talk about Guardians and Gatekeeping," the Professor added.

Homework on a Friday night. He really was a professor.

"We'll be back first thing tomorrow morning," Mrs. Widgit paused with her hand on the door. "Oh, and it's probably best to keep the doors locked and not let anyone else in this evening. We don't want another Mr. Cutter stopping by."

"Now that the alpacas are here they should be OK," Professor Theopolous said incomprehensibly.

"But—" I said.

"Tomorrow, Allie. We will answer all your questions tomorrow!"

With that, Mrs. Widgit and Professor Theopolous stepped through the door and disappeared into the darkness.

6

I stood staring after them for a moment, then slowly shut the door and returned to the living room. Andie was lying across the sofa with her hands over her face. I slumped down onto the couch across from her. Pettikin emerged from behind Socrates and climbed up the sofa to perch on the armrest next to me.

"Andie, what have I done?"

Andie moaned, rubbed her face a few times and then sat up, her hair staticky.

"You think you've got it bad. I may have killed a man."

"Oh hey, yeah!" I said. "I almost forgot about that. Did they say anything to you about that? About Mr. Cutter disappearing?"

Andie shook her head. "No, but I told them that I used the phrase from that book. You came back with Pettikin before they had a chance to say anything."

"I'm sure you didn't kill him." I tried to sound reassuring. "I mean, if you'd killed him there would be a body or something, wouldn't there?"

"It looked like he went through a Gateway," Pettikin said.

We both turned to him.

"Seriously?" I asked. "But I thought the Gateways here are all closed. I mean, isn't that why we're in this mess?"

Pettikin slid off the armrest to sit beside me on the couch.

"The interdimensional Gateways-the secret ones-are closed. But there are other types of Gateways," he said.

"Like what?" Andie asked.

"Like, Gateways that connect two points on the same world-next to a river, or mountain for example. You can take the Gateway on one side of the river to get across to the other side, or use a Gateway to get to the top of a mountain or to the other side if you don't want to climb it."

"Are you serious? All this money to build roads and bridges and lifts and we could just be using Gateways?" I asked.

"Maybe you've gotten so used to not having Gateways that you've just forgotten about them. Or maybe you don't know how to *use* them anymore."

"What other kinds of Gateways are there?" Andie asked.

"Guardian Gateways," Pettikin said. "Those are the most special. They're different from the other Gateways, because instead of leading to another place they lead directly to a Guardian, in his or her realm. The Guardian Gateways are the hardest to find on any world, and they're almost always closed. You can only get in if the Guardian lets you in."

We were all quiet for a moment. The cuckoo clock chirped once. It was almost nine pm. Somehow it felt much later.

"I'm starving," I said finally. "All we've had to eat are cookies and hot chocolate."

"Yeah, let's see what's left in the kitchen," Andie said.

Mrs. Widgit had cleaned up the vegetables from the kitchen floor and tidied up the kitchen table for us. We rummaged through the refrigerator until we found a tuna casserole from the reception that didn't seem half bad. Andie and I nuked huge bowls of that in the microwave while Pettikin ate a piece of apple pie. I hoped that this was his normal diet and that we weren't killing him with sugar.

When we finished eating we returned to the living room and got the sleeping bags out. We zipped them together into a large square in front of the fireplace so there would be room for all of us, and I went upstairs to see if I could find some more sheets and bedding.

I flicked on the light in Aunt May's bedroom. Unlike the mess of books downstairs, it was very spare- a platform bed with a cream colored comforter, a night stand, and a fuzzy white rug on the hardwood floor next to the bed. A row of built in shelves on the far wall housed extra blankets and linens. I grabbed a couple blankets and two more pillows and was about to leave when I saw a small flash of light from the night stand. A necklace- a black leather strap with some kind of stone or charm on the end- lay next to an old, wind-up alarm clock and a box of tissues. I perched myself on the edge of her bed, tucking the pillows and blankets under my left arm and picked it up.

The stone was smooth and not particularly shiny, so I wasn't sure why I thought I had seen a flash of light. It was round, about the size of a quarter, maybe a quarter inch thick in the middle, tapering at the ends. It seemed to change color in the light, sometimes white like marble, sometimes gray like granite. I stuffed it into the pocket of my hoodie, hoisted the blankets and pillows and went back downstairs. Socrates took up the major portion of our bed, with Pettikin snuggled up against him. I dropped the blankets and pillows down next to them.

"Hey Andie, look at this." I fished the necklace

out of my pocket and handed it to her.

Andie held it up by the strap, then took the stone between her fingers and flipped it over in the light.

"That's pretty cool. What is it do you think?" she asked.

"I don't know. It changes color sometimes."

"It's attached to the strap with a clip," she unhooked the charm and held it out to me. "You could wear it on your charm bracelet-a memento from Aunt May."

My parents gave me the charm bracelet when I was twelve, and it was something I always wore. Most of the charms on it were gifts from Andie or my parents.

"Do you think it's OK?" I took the stone from her.

"Sure. I mean she left everything to you, it seems like she would want you to have it."

I clipped the charm onto my bracelet, then held my wrist up to the light for a moment to admire it.

"Cool. Thanks Aunt May," I said.

Andie and I arranged the rest of the blankets and pillows on the bed and then took turns in the bathroom changing into T-shirts and pajama bottoms. I rummaged through the books that had been relocated from the coffee table to the floor earlier in the evening.

"So, what should we read for homework tonight?"

"What are our options?" Andie was walking in from the kitchen carrying a half-eaten pan of brownies, her hair in two sleek ponytails on either side of her head.

"Uh, let's see. Here's *Introductory Gatekeeping* again. Guess I better grab that one." I put it into the 'maybe' pile. "Oh, and here's your *Book of Useful Phrases* Andie." I handed it to her as she walked by. "Try to use it only for good and not evil."

Andie rolled her eyes.

"Ohhh! Here's one we haven't seen yet. It's just called *The Guardians*."

"I love hearing about the Guardians," Pettikin said dreamily from in front of the fire.

"OK, let's try that one then," I said, picking it up and heading for the nest.

Andie and I each staked out a portion of the sleeping area.

"You read, I'll eat," Andie said, taking one of the remaining brownies and handing me one.

I propped my head up on a couple of pillows and bent my knees so I could balance the book on my stomach.

This book had a red leather cover with a faded picture on the front. I munched on my brownie for a second while I looked at it. A tall golden figure like a ghost, the kind you make from a sheet when you're a kid, stood on an enormous oval disc that glowed like the moon. Its round head tapered to a thin neck, and its body flowed down and outwards, eventually blending with the surface it was standing on. It didn't have legs, but it did have two small appendages like arms. Behind this figure were the now-familiar interwoven patterns of criss-crossing, multi-colored lines. Gold lettering at the top spelled out *The Guardians* in fancy script.

"So are Guardians like wizards or something, Pettikin?" I asked.

"More powerful than wizards," Pettikin said.

"*More* powerful?"

"Yes, they're the most powerful beings in the universe, but also the kindest."

"That's a relief," Andie said around a mouthful of brownie.

"I don't understand what they are, exactly," I said, a little frustrated as I opened the book. "I mean, are they people or something else?"

"They can look like people in some worlds, and in others they look like the beings in those worlds. But that's just an outer form they take. Even when they look like people, they aren't really people." Pettikin said, as I skimmed the first page.

"OK, let's see if this helps," I started to read:

"*If you could remember back as far as remembering goes, before this life, before all the other lives you've had, before you existed and even beyond the outer boundaries of time and space and existence itself, before all of this ever was, the Ancients existed. Tasked with the creation, preservation and destruction of all that would ever be, from the light of the universe, the Ancients created all these worlds and the doorways through space and time that connect them. From the Ancients, the Guardians emerged, powerful beings charged with the protection and preservation of this creation.*

"*The Guardians are not bound by time and space. They work with the ancient light of the universe to preserve and protect your world, all other worlds, and the secret Gateways that connect them.*"

"Yada, yada..." I skimmed forward a few sentences. "This isn't helping much, is it?"

"It's kind of general or something," Andie said. "I mean, I understand all the words but I'm not sure what they're trying to say. I still can't picture what a Guardian is in my mind."

I shut the book and tossed it to the side. "You know what, I give up. I can't take any more for one evening."

"Me either," Andie said. She stood up and put the pan of brownies on the coffee table. "Ready for me to turn out the lights?"

"Yeah."

She flicked off the lamps, then rejoined us by the fire. I fluffed my pillow and pulled a blanket up around my chin. Pettikin glowed white in the darkness, like a gnome nightlight.

"Good night Pettikin," I said.

"Good night, Allie. Good night, Andie."

I was pretty sure that both Pettikin and Andie fell asleep quickly, but I found myself wide awake. I stared at the low, orange flames in the fireplace as they licked at the remains of the firewood, the soft crackling occasionally punctuated by the muted crashes of the logs breaking down and readjusting on the metal grate. The events of the day played over in my mind. I felt like I was in a speeding car, and suddenly, more than anything, I wanted to jump out, or at least put the brakes on until I had a chance to think things through.

I tried to focus on the sound of the cuckoo clock, the fire, and Socrates' snoring, hoping it might have a soporific effect. Instead, I heard Professor Theopolous in my mind talking about the years of preparation required to meet a Guardian, about how I wasn't ready, even as Mrs. Widgit insisted I would meet one tomorrow-to do what? Ask to be a Gatekeeper? The idea was absurd, none of this was possible.

I could almost feel the thoughts and doubts swirling around in my head, as if they had physical mass. I pressed a pillow over the top of my head hoping maybe the pressure would make them stop.

The cuckoo clock chimed midnight before I finally fell asleep.

Once asleep I had the weirdest dream. I was walking down a crowded cobblestone street in a foreign city I didn't recognize. Pettikin was riding on my shoulder. The streets were lined with stalls where shopkeepers were selling fruits and vegetables, flowers, spices, and yards of silk and cloth.

Pettikin let out a small cry, slid down my arm to the ground, and took off running. I started running after him.

"Pettikin, not so fast! I can't keep up!"

Dozens of people were walking toward me, and I tried to dodge them, feeling like a salmon swimming upstream. Soon he disappeared, and I had no idea where he was. I stopped running, out of breath. I scanned the crowded streets, searching for any sign of him. Tears of anxiety formed in my eyes, and I blinked them back.

Aunt May appeared from out of nowhere beside me. She looked exactly as she had the last time I saw her—tall and thin, with her bright blue eyes and golden-gray hair cut in a sleek bob. She was wearing blue slacks and a crisp, white shirt. She motioned for me to walk with her. I walked behind her, trying to keep up with her brisk pace. She walked for several blocks, weaving through the crowd, occasionally glancing back to make sure I was still there. Finally, she stopped a few feet away from a vendor's stall and pointed inside.

It must have been a type of laundromat. People were steaming and pressing garments in the back, and customers were picking up bundles of clothes in front. I put my hand up to my eyes and squinted.

That's when I saw him. He was young, maybe seventeen, and really tall. He had platinum blond hair cut into shaggy layers that he sometimes shook or brushed away from his face as he worked. In between washing and pressing shirts, he delivered packages of freshly laundered clothes to the people stopping by the stall, greeting everyone with a huge smile.

He must have felt me staring at him, because he looked directly at me with eyes so green they could have been photoshopped. His face brightened, and with one graceful motion he leaped over the counter and jogged over to us. He stopped in front of me and grinned. I immediately grinned back, like a dork.

"You see, May?" He turned to my great aunt. "I told you I could make her smile."

Aunt May beamed at both of us, and that's the last thing I remembered until morning.

7

I awoke to the sound of a slow and steady rain washing over the cottage. The fire had burned out in the fireplace, and it was chilly in the room. I sat up and pulled my blanket around me. Andie was lying sprawled across the sleeping bags on her stomach, and Pettikin was still curled up against Socrates.

So Pettikin hadn't been a dream. I stared at him for a moment, then got up quietly, wearing my blanket like a cape. I padded to the nearest radiator and cranked the knob higher. It came to life with a soft hiss. I went over to the window and looked outside.

The sky was a solid swath of gray, and I wondered if it was supposed to rain all day. The paddock was turning into a sea of mud. One of the alpacas peered gloomily out from the barn.

Inside it looked like we'd had a wild party here last night. The coffee table was piled with mugs, some with cocoa still in them, half-eaten cookies, and the pan of brownies. Books were scattered across the floor, and our sleeping nest was a tangle of sheets and pillows. The fireplace and surrounding hearth were smudged with soot, a byproduct of the Professor's overly exuberant fire.

I wrapped my blanket tighter around me and wandered into the kitchen, wondering if there was anything to eat for breakfast. There were eggs and milk in the refrigerator, but not much else. Normally Andie and I would have walked back to my house to eat, but I wasn't sure what we should do about Pettikin.

The cuckoo clock chimed from the living room. It was only 8:00 am.

A sudden knock on the door made me freeze. Socrates jumped up and started barking, which caused Pettikin to wake up and start screaming.

"No, no, Pettikin, it's OK!" I rushed into the living room and scooped him up under my blanket. Andie sat up, her ponytails a disheveled mess, eyes heavy with sleep.

"Andie, can you go see who it is at the door?"

She scrambled to her feet as I pressed myself against the wall next to the fireplace so I was hidden from view. Pettikin stopped screaming, but I could feel his heart beating rapidly next to me.

I heard Andie trip over Socrates, and swear under her breath as she pulled the door open.

"Oh, hi Mr. Thomas."

It was just Dad. With all the strange events of the past evening, and people appearing and disappearing out of nowhere, I had pretty much forgotten about my parents.

Socrates was whining, and I heard him push his way outside.

Dad's voice was hushed. "Did I wake you up?"

"Oh, um, yeah—sorry. We went to sleep pretty late last night."

"Is Allie still asleep?"

"Yeah. Uh—did you want me to wake her?"

"No, no," Dad kept his voice quiet. "I don't want to disturb you. I came down to feed the alpacas, and Pat asked me to deliver some food for you girls." It sounded like he transferred a grocery bag to Andie. "This way you can sleep as late as you want and not worry about missing breakfast."

"Oh, that's super. Thanks!"

"You girls have any plans for the day?"

"Uh," I could almost hear gears whirling and clacking inside Andie's head. "We were thinking of going for a hike in the woods later. I mean, if it stops raining," she added as if she had just noticed the rain outside. "Or maybe we'll just stay here and watch movies."

I put one hand to my forehead.

Dad laughed. "OK, well, Allie's mom and I are going into town to take care of a few things from May's estate. We might be gone for most of the morning, but there's plenty of food up at the house whenever you girls feel like coming back to civilization. They're saying the rain should end later this morning, even though it doesn't seem like it right now."

"OK."

"Oh! And your parents called, and I let them know that it's fine with us if you wanted to stay for dinner or even spend the night again tonight."

"That sounds great. Thank you so much, Mr. Thomas."

"Sure thing. OK, bye now. You girls have fun."

"We will. Bye!"

Andie shut the door and brought the grocery bag into the living room. I let Pettikin out from under the blanket and onto the floor.

"So it sounds like we at least have a day to work on getting Pettikin back home," I said.

"Yeah. Let's go see what your mom packed us for breakfast."

We traipsed into the kitchen and rummaged through the bag which was stuffed with a loaf of bread, a jar of peanut butter, toaster waffles, butter, jam, syrup, a carton of orange juice, two grapefruits and a bunch of bananas.

"Jeez there's a ton of food here. What do you want Andie?"

"Waffles!" Andie answered immediately.

"Waffles OK with you Pettikin?" He seemed unsure so I added, "They're sweet."

"OK, waffles then," he said, as he shinnied up the leg of a stool and climbed onto the kitchen counter.

I toasted the waffles while Andie found some plates and silverware. Andie poured orange juice for us, and I cut a grapefruit in half and sweetened it with some sugar I found in Aunt May's pantry. Andie and I sat on stools at the counter to eat, and Pettikin sat on the counter itself with his legs stuck out in a V. Pettikin ate his waffle by holding it in his hands and dipping it in syrup before every bite.

"I wonder what we're supposed to do now," Andie said as we ate. "I mean, we didn't really make concrete plans with Mrs. Widgit and the Professor. Are they coming here today?"

"I'm not sure. I'm still having a hard time believing last night really happened."

After we ate, we did the dishes. I washed, Pettikin held the sprayer and rinsed the dishes off, and Andie dried them and put them away. Then Andie and I alternated turns in the shower and getting dressed.

I took a long hot shower to get some of the chill I was still feeling out of my bones. I pulled on my jeans and a clean T-shirt and sweatshirt, and wiped a circle in the steam on the bathroom mirror. My hair was wavy when it was wet, and it had gotten darker as I got older. If we were being charitable we might call it honey blonde, which is nicer than saying dishwater blonde or, "What color is your hair?" My eyes were gray-blue, and my skin was pale with a few freckles, like Mom's. I didn't think I was ugly, but I was the kind of pretty where grownups said how beautiful I was and kids my own age didn't seem to notice.

Sometimes I wished I could have Andie's flawless skin and shiny black hair. It would take me forever to dry my hair in this humidity. I sighed.

Back in the living room, Pettikin, with a dishcloth tied around his waist like a little apron, was using another dishcloth to dust Aunt May's books as he stacked them into neat piles on the coffee table. Andie was rolling up the sleeping bags.

"'Bout time you got here," she said. "We're finishing all the work."

"My plan worked out perfectly," I joked, as I started folding the blankets.

I was interrupted by another knock at the door. Pettikin froze in a pre-scream stance, dust cloth in the air.

"No, don't scream, don't scream," I said, tossing the blanket I was folding aside and heading for the door. I paused with my hand on the handle, feeling suddenly nervous. "Who's there?"

"It's us, Allie! Mrs. Widgit and Professor Theopolous!"

I relaxed slightly and pulled the door open.

Mrs. Widgit swirled into the room wearing a long, yellow rain poncho with a matching hat and boots. She had a large tote bag slung across her shoulder. She took the hat off with a flourish and gave it a shake, spraying droplets of water around the entrance hallway. Professor Theopolous was wearing the same outfit he had the night before, except he was also carrying a large, black umbrella, which he was using more as a walking stick than for protection from the rain.

"Good morning, girls," Mrs. Widgit said brightly. "Good morning Pettikin!"

"Good morning, Mrs. Widgit," Andie and I chorused like a couple of obedient schoolchildren. Pettikin retreated to the far end of the living room and hid behind the sofas.

"I hope you don't mind us stopping by so early,

but we have a lot to accomplish today, and there is no time to waste!" Mrs. Widgit stamped and wiped her feet on the entryway rug. "We've been up all night making preparations."

"All night? Didn't you sleep at all?" I asked.

"Oh, heavens no, Allie, there was so much to do, after everything you girls told us. What with this Mr. Cutter of yours appearing and disappearing, we became quite concerned that there may be sslorcs at work here, and heaven knows that's the last thing we need. But don't you worry, we had a long talk with the alpacas, and they agreed that it would be best to put some additional protective charms around you and the cottage until we can get this all sorted out. Bob's out there with them now."

Mrs. Widgit continued stomping and shaking water droplets from her hat until she saw Andie and I staring at her. She stopped. "What?"

"Oh, we just had a little chat with the alpacas," Andie said, clasping her hands under her chin, her voice a comically overdone Mrs. Widgit lilt. "They've agreed to protect you from the slorks."

"Not slorks, dear, sslorcs."

Andie looked at me and then at Mrs. Widget. "Slorks."

"No, no, dear the s is long and k is soft: *ssloooorrrcs.*"

"Slorks." Andie scowled and folded her arms across her chest.

"No, I'm afraid you're not quite getting it, it's…"

"Viola!" Professor Theopolous' arms puffed out from his sides as if from the force of his exasperation. "Do we really have time?"

"Yes, of course, quite right, Theo. Girls, are you ready to go?" Mrs. Widgit stared pointedly at our sock-clad feet.

"Go where? What in the world are you talking about?" I asked. "What do you mean you were talking to the alpacas? And what's a... s... sslorc," I tried to copy her phonics as best I could.

"Very *good* Allie! You are a quick learner!"

I rolled my eyes.

Professor Theopolous put a fist to his mouth and cleared his throat.

"Do we have time to explain just a few things to them, do you think?" Mrs. Widgit asked. As if on cue, her tote bag began humming and vibrating.

"Oh, dear." She sat her hat down on the small bench in the entryway, unslung her tote bag, and began rummaging through it. After a few seconds she pulled out a purple, clam-shaped item about the size of her palm. She flicked it open.

A glowing white sphere with several smaller spheres spinning around it, like electrons orbiting the nucleus of an atom, appeared above the shell. The orbs began spinning faster, shooting off rainbow colored sparks and small puffs of steam while the whole apparatus hummed and buzzed.

"Ah! I am afraid the Professor is right, we are out of time." She snapped the clam shell shut, and shoved it in the tote bag. "Hurry girls, there is no time to lose. Put your shoes on and get Pettikin. We'll explain on our way to the Gateway."

"The Nexus Gateway?" I asked as Andie and I searched for our shoes. Pettikin climbed silently onto my shoulder when I bent down to tie mine. It was starting to feel like second nature to have him sitting there.

"No, the Guardian Gateway. It's our only hope at this point, even if it's a remote hope."

I straightened up. "Pettikin told us about Guardian Gateways last night," I said. "Is there one around here?"

"There's one nearby, but it remains to be seen if we will be able to gain entrance. The particular Guardian we must deal with for this endeavor can be somewhat ...

problematic," Mrs. Widgit sounded distracted as she stuffed her rain hat into the pocket of her poncho.

Professor Theopolous waited for us by the already opened the door. Andie and I exchanged worried glances as we followed him and Mrs. Widgit outside.

The rain had stopped, but everything was still soaked. Water dripped down from the trees and the eaves of the cottage. The sky had lightened to a smoky white color, the sun a hazy, glowing orb low on the eastern horizon. It was chilly, but my sweatshirt provided adequate warmth, even without a proper jacket.

Mrs. Widgit and the Professor set off down the path toward the woods, Andie and I following behind. I eyed Mrs. Widgit's yellow, rubber rain boots enviously as my sneakers quickly soaked through.

"So, where exactly are we going?" I asked, shoving my hands into the pockets of my hoodie.

"The Gateway that leads to the Guardian that Aunt May worked with is a quarter mile or so behind the cottage in the woods. Viola and I know where it is, although neither of us has ever been granted access to it," Professor Theopolous said.

"And once we get to the Gateway, then what?" Andie asked.

"Our plan is for Theo and I to attempt to enter the Gateway. If we can persuade the Guardian to grant us access, we will visit him in his realm and explain the situation. If he agrees, we will bring him back to meet you, Allie."

"Why even bring us along then?" I asked. "Why not see if you can talk to him first, and then, if he agrees, bring him to the cottage?"

Mrs. Widgit drew her breath in. What emotion was that on her face? Horror?

"Allie," Professor Theopolous' voice sounded urgent. "I realize that this is all being done on incredibly short notice, and that you have not even been remotely properly trained, but let me try to impress upon you, as thoroughly as I possibly can, that the Guardians are not to be trifled with. Ever. In any way. No matter how small. They are the greatest, wisest and most powerful beings in the universe. You do not waste their time, or approach them lightly. This is doubly important in this case, because although Viola and I have been fortunate enough to encounter this Guardian before, he is not our usual Guardian, and he is a little... *different* from some of the others. Should he agree to even give us an audience in this matter, let alone come back to meet you, then it is imperative that you be waiting by his Gateway so as not to waste his time."

If his intention was to scare the crap out of me, he succeeded. "OK, consider the point impressed upon me," I said. Geez.

We turned down the main path into the woods. The leaves had just started to change to fall colors, but the rain made everything appear dull and brown.

"How is he different from the other Guardians?" Andie asked.

Professor Theopolous and Mrs. Widgit exchanged glances but didn't immediately answer.

"That is something you'll just have to see for yourselves. There's no way to explain." Mrs. Widgit answered finally.

We hiked in silence for about five minutes, and then the Professor veered off the main path to a smaller deer trail that had been worn through the ferns and underbrush. Andie and I stopped as the adults continued down the short, steep slope to the small pond that lay just a few feet below.

"Walden? The Guardian Gateway is at Walden?" I asked.

Professor Theopolous and Mrs. Widgit were waiting for us at the bottom of the hill. "You know this place?"

We half-jogged, half-skidded down the slope to meet them.

"Yeah, up until now we thought this was our oh-so-secret hiding place," I said.

Professor Theopolous peered at me from behind his monocle.

"Interesting," he said.

The pond lay in front of us, a long oval of smooth, gray water reflecting the sky above. It was about seventy feet long and maybe thirty feet across. A large, gray boulder lay on the right hand bank in front of us. On the far side of the bank was the small campsite Andie and I had created, useful for when we came down here to burn things.

Andie and I glanced at each other, and in unspoken agreement walked past the two adults. We each dipped the soles of our right feet and our right hands in the water, and then used the water to make one footprint and one handprint each on the boulder. The ritual was held over from our childhood, when we first started coming here, but we observed it religiously. It seemed wrong to ignore it now, even with everything that was going on. Professor and Mrs. Widgit watched us without saying anything. Pettikin, however, slid down my arm and dropped to the ground. He walked to the edge of the pond and stuck his right sole and right palm in the water and then placed a footprint and palm print on the boulder exactly as we had, albeit somewhat lower down on the rock.

"OK, Pettikin, you're in! Welcome to Walden," I said.

Pettikin surveyed the surroundings carefully. "This is a nice place. I like it here." He began wandering along the bank toward our campsite.

"So, what are we supposed to do now?" I asked as we all followed behind him.

"You girls can amuse yourselves while we make

preparations," Professor Theopolous answered. He and Mrs. Widgit stopped a few feet past the boulder, and then Mrs. Widgit set her tote bag down and began rummaging through it again. She pulled out a wrinkled and yellowed square of paper which had been folder over on itself several times, like a map. The professor held one corner while she unfolded it, revealing a diagram like a star chart, with more of those criss-crossing patterns of lines I was getting used to seeing. They got into a heated conversation, Professor Theopolous pointing at the map and Mrs. Widgit gesturing toward the pond.

Andie and I shrugged at each other, and followed after Pettikin.

When Pettikin reached our campsite, he gazed around for a few minutes, then walked over to a large oak tree set a few feet back from the water's edge. Humming softly, he began to clear away leaves from a small hollow in the old, gnarled root structure. Then he dragged an old pine bough out of the woods and used it to sweep away as much debris as possible.

Meanwhile, at the other end of the pond, Mrs. Widgit was standing on the boulder with her right foot pressed against her left calf and her hands clasped in front of her, just like she had at the funeral, only this time she didn't move for several minutes. Her eyes were squeezed shut and she frowned slightly, as if she were concentrating on something. I nudged Andie and gestured toward her.

"Well, this is obviously going to take a while," Andie said and walked over to the large wooden storage bin that my father had built for us to keep our camping supplies in. We pulled out two collapsible chairs and set them up at the edge of the pond to watch. Pettikin hummed and spread pine needles across the floor of his root hollow.

Eventually, Mrs. Widgit opened her eyes and hopped down from the boulder. Professor Theopolous took over. He stood next to the boulder, put his hands on his hips and did a series of deep knee bends. Then he took a deep breath and folded his hands in front of him so his left palm rested on top of his right and his thumbs were touching. He closed his eyes, inhaled, and then began chanting in a way that reminded me of the dying frog horns from the funeral.

Andie snorted and quickly slapped a hand over her mouth. I edged my chair away from her, knowing that if we got started laughing, we would never be able to stop.

When the chanting failed to produce any discernible result, Mrs. Widgit tried again, this time perching in a full lotus position on top of the boulder, her upturned hands on her knees, thumbs and forefingers touching. She too, began chanting. Andie rested one cheek on her knee, a pained expression on her face.

The two of them continued to go at it, taking turns like this, for the better part of an hour. Pettikin was settled into his root hollow home and was now digging a small fire pit with the sharp edge of a stone he had found. I picked up a handful of rocks and tried skipping them across the pond, but I'd never really learned how to do it, so I was basically just throwing rocks into the water. Andie folded her hands behind her head and leaned back in her chair.

"I should have brought my notes from class down," she said. "At least we could have been productive."

The Professor and Mrs. Widgit stopped, and Mrs. Widgit sighed. "I'm afraid it seem that we're not going to be successful, girls," she said.

"What was your first clue?" Andie asked softly without turning her head, so only I could hear her.

"So, what do we do now?" I asked.

"We'll need to come up with another plan," Professor Theopolous said, his voice serious.

From its resting place near the water's edge, Mrs. Widgit's tote bag began to vibrate and hum.

"Oh, dear," she rushed over and fished out her purple clamshell device. It almost leapt out of her hand, it was vibrating so hard, steam escaping from the seam where the two halves met. When she opened it, the orbs were turning and orbiting each other so fast they almost formed a solid cloud. "We really don't have time Theo. We need to think of something now, or we'll miss the opportunity altogether."

"If the Guardian doesn't let us enter his Gateway there is nothing we can do to make him," the Professor answered pragmatically.

"No, there isn't," Mrs. Widgit said slowly. She paused. "Allie, maybe you should try."

"Try what?"

"See if you can enter the Guardian Gateway."

"What do you mean? I already know I can't. I wouldn't even know what to do." I thought about all the posing and chanting I just witnessed.

"Well, the beauty of a Guardian Gateway is that there isn't much you have to do except convince the Guardian to let you through. He'll do all the work for you."

Pettikin was walking toward his root hollow home with an armful of twigs. He dumped them into his fire pit.

"I've been through Guardian Gateways before, the ones on Arcorn," he said, "I'll go with you Allie. We can ask the Guardian together."

"Well, uh," I found it almost impossible to say no to Pettikin, but I really had no idea what to do.

Pettikin turned and walked past me toward the boulder. Andie shrugged at me.

I followed after Pettikin, who, once again, despite his tiny size and what should have been correspondingly tiny stride, was making it difficult for me to keep up.

Pettikin examined the boulder for a minute, then scaled it like a miniature rock climber. I climbed up after him. The top of the boulder was flat, and it was easy enough for the two of us to sit side by side, me with my legs crossed Indian style, and Pettikin with his legs stuck out in front of him in what I was starting to think of as his signature tripod stance.

Mrs. Widgit bustled over. "Now Allie, if the Guardian lets you through, explain the situation as quickly and clearly as possible. You can tell him that Theo and I are waiting here and that we can explain everything to him."

"And for heaven's sake, remember to be polite," Professor Theopolous' voice sounded strained. "Don't waste his time and try to remember that he is one of the most ancient, powerful beings in the universe, and could turn you into a smoking pile of rubble if he should so choose."

"Theo…" Mrs. Widgit turned to him, hands on hips, annoyed.

My palms started to sweat and my throat felt dry. "You're sure you've done this before, Pettikin?"

"Oh sure, it's easy," he said cheerfully, his demeanor the exact opposite of the two fussing adults standing nearby.

"So, uh, what do we do?"

"Just close your eyes and try not to think too much, so the Guardian can take you through the Gateway."

"Don't think too much? How am I supposed to do that?" It reminded me of that stupid exercise my drama teacher had given us in school—whatever you do, don't think about a giant, killer rabbit with fangs—after which all you can think about is a giant, killer rabbit with fangs.

Pettikin didn't answer. He sat motionless on the rock with his eyes closed, his shoulders slumped slightly forward.

I closed my eyes, and tried to stop my thoughts. Instead, I replayed Mrs. Widgit's and the Professor's instructions in my mind, thought about how nervous I was, how ridiculous this all seemed, and the fact that I had no idea what I was doing. Then I started wondering inanely about school, homework, and even the stupid homecoming dance that I had not been invited to. Pettikin was going to be stuck here forever at this rate.

I could hear my own breathing, an occasional splash of water from the pond, and the sound of the breeze through the trees in the woods. I sat as still as I could and waited for something to happen. I felt a warmth against my forehead and could see a bright light from behind my eyelids. The sun must have finally broken out from behind the clouds, I thought.

I was going to say something to Pettikin, but I couldn't speak or move. That was strange. It didn't feel bad, it just seemed that there was some disconnect between my wanting to say something and my physical body. But I felt kind of peaceful and warm, so it didn't really matter.

The light and warmth gradually faded, and I felt like I was regaining my faculties. The sun must have moved back behind the clouds, I thought.

"I don't think it's working, Pettikin," I said. My eyelids felt heavy, like I had been asleep for hours. I pried them open, and things came into focus, like normal.

Except it wasn't normal. I was no longer sitting on top of the boulder on the edge of the pond in our woods, but instead on top of grass that was so lush and soft it almost felt like carpeting.

"What the..." I stood up but my legs felt weak and buckled out from under me. I landed hard on my tailbone. "Ow."

I was in a field of blue and green mountain grasses and wildflowers, somewhere in the foothills of a distant range of snow-capped mountains. Hazy white clouds hovered near their peaks and cast shadows that drifted across their gray stone peaks like a celestial shadow lamp. I could hear a gentle breeze rustling through the meadow, a few birds singing, and water running nearby, but none of the background noise I was used to—no planes in the sky or cars going by on a road.

"Pettikin, are you OK? What happened? Where are we?"

Pettikin was a few feet away exploring the new landscape but came rushing over to me when I called.

"I think we did it, Allie! I think we made it through the Gateway, but I don't know where we are. It doesn't feel like your Earth."

"Yeah, I'll say," a voice said from behind us.

I yelled and jumped up, turning toward the voice, but Pettikin started screaming and running in circles around my legs so I fell again. Once I was down, Pettikin dove behind me for cover.

"You have some serious balance issues," the voice sounded amused.

I squinted up at it.

I couldn't believe it. It was the kid from my dream—the cute guy with the light blond hair and impossibly bright green eyes. He was wearing skinny blue jeans, a green and purple button-down shirt, and shiny black boots. He towered over us, his arms folded across his chest, grinning broadly.

"Hi!" I blurted out without thinking and then cringed. He couldn't possibly have any idea who I was or why I thought I knew him.

"Hi!" he answered back, mimicking my enthusiastic tone and tilting his head slightly to one side.

Pettikin climbed up my back and peeked over my shoulder, then let out a small cry. He leaped over me, digging his clogs into my shoulder and pushing down on my head with his hand for support.

"Ow, Pettikin…"

When he reached the ground he straightened his jacket and walked toward the blond kid. He pressed his palms together and bowed formally from his waist. The boy watched him with a gentle, interested expression.

Pettikin rose up and said, "Oh great and wonderful Guardian, I am Pettikin Periwinkle from Arcorn. We have come to ask for your help."

Oh, crap. Guardian. This was the Guardian. I was already wrong.

The Guardian took a step forward, bent down and touched Pettikin gently in the center of his forehead. The light inside Pettikin got even brighter for a moment, like someone had turned the key on an oil lamp.

"Pettikin Periwinkle, I am Vala," he said.

He straightened up to his full height and turned his gaze toward me.

I scrambled to my feet, trying to collect my thoughts. I glanced down. My jeans and sweatshirt were covered with grass stains and dirt. I brushed frantically at them until I felt a gentle but firm force pulling my eyes upward.

His eyes locked on mine and I couldn't move or look away. It wasn't like looking at another person, but into some kind of void. No, void wasn't the right word because he wasn't exactly *empty*, but *vast*. He looked like a kid, but he felt ancient.

He squinted his eyes slightly, and I felt a strange sensation in my chest, as if there had been a knot around my heart that was loosened. He shifted his gaze, and I felt a tingling sensation in the top of my head. He looked at me for a few seconds more, then nodded his head once, as if he approved of something. He dropped his gaze to the ground, and a shy expression came over his face. He scuffed one toe in the dirt, like Bob sometimes did.

I stared at him, transfixed. This wasn't good. Professor Theopolous would probably kill me if he found out I'd fallen for the Guardian.

"So," he said finally, raising his head. "You wanted my help?"

A soft, golden-white light hovered around him,

and he had some kind of presence larger than his physical body that I could feel even from where I was standing a few feet away. I had no idea what to say to him, and I suddenly felt terrified.

"You were expecting an old guy with long white hair, flowing robes and a wizard's staff, weren't you?"

I relaxed a little. "Yeah, something like that."

He waited, as if expecting something.

"What's your name?" he asked finally.

"Oh!" I kept forgetting that the dream from the night before hadn't really happened and that we hadn't actually met. "I'm Allie. Allie Thomas." Feeling stupid, I tried to copy Pettikin since he seemed to know the protocol for this. I bent forward at the waist in an awkward bow.

Vala laughed, and Pettikin ran over to me, giggling. He climbed up my leg and arm to my shoulder, perhaps sensing I could use the moral support.

"You've got a major gnome situation going on there," Vala sounded impressed. "They don't usually like people."

"Uh, yeah, that's what everyone keeps telling me."

He folded his arms. "So, Allie Thomas, what is it that you want? Obviously I'm interested in helping you or you wouldn't be here, but I don't have all day. We Guardians are a tad bit busier than we might appear, you know."

"Right, sorry!" A looming image of Professor Theopolous' disapproving face appeared in my mind.

I took a deep breath and the words came tumbling out in a rush. "Well, my great aunt May died last week, but her funeral wasn't until yesterday, and afterwards my best friend Andie and I wanted to spend the night in her cottage…" I was completely rambling. I tried to remember what Mrs. Widgit and Professor Theopolous had told me to say, but my mind had gone blank.

"Oh, so *you're* May's niece!"

"Well...great niece, actually. She was my mom's aunt."

"She told me about you. She was my friend, you know."

"Uh..."

"That was rhetorical—you don't have to answer. Just continue."

I was seriously blowing it. "Well, uh, basically when Andie and I went down to the cottage last night, we found Pettikin there."

"Uh oh."

"I know I shouldn't have done it," Pettikin said. It sounded like he was struggling to hold back tears.

"It's not even that easy to do, Pettikin. I'm surprised you were able to," Vala sounded thoughtful.

"He didn't know Aunt May had died," I said, in Pettikin's defense. "When he got to Earth, he was trapped because she wasn't there to take him back through the...the secret Gateways, or whatever. And not just Pettikin, but some of Aunt May's other friends are stuck there too."

"Viola Widget and Theodore Theopolous?" Vala asked drily.

"Yeah."

"I felt them trying to get through my Gateway earlier."

"They seem to think that our only chance for getting Pettikin home is if you could reopen the secret Gateways on Earth. So they sent us here to ask you if you could do that."

Vala laughed. "Viola and Theo told you to ask me that?"

Not the reaction I was hoping for. "Um, something like that. I might be phrasing it wrong."

"They know I won't reopen the Gateways on Earth without a Gatekeeper to watch them."

"Yeah, they said that."

There was no way that I was going to mention that their plan was for me to be the Gatekeeper. Now that I had seen Vala I realized that the idea was patently ridiculous. Professor Theopolous was right.

Vala's countenance changed while I was thinking this, became more gentle.

"Tell me something, Allie," he said, moving closer and leaning down toward me. "Putting Mrs. Widgit and Professor Theopolous aside for a moment—why are *you* here? If they hadn't told you what to ask for, what would *you* want from me?"

A million desires ran through my mind, most of them highly inappropriate. Pettikin stirred on my shoulders bringing me back to earth. Or wherever we were.

"I just want to help Pettikin get home safely. He can't stay on Earth—he'd be miserable there. I'll do whatever you need me to do, but there's no one else to help him, and I don't think we can do it without your help..."

To my complete horror, my voice cracked and my eyes filled with tears. It was as if I had stored up all of my sadness over Aunt May's death and worry for Pettikin for this one moment, and now the emotions threatened to overtake me. I clamped my mouth shut and blinked my eyes furiously, determined not to cry.

Vala seemed to be considering my words very seriously. He turned away from us and paced slowly back and forth, looking down at the ground. His gait was uneven, weaving around instead of following a straight line, and sometimes he paused with a foot suspended in the air, as if he was deciding where to place it next.

Finally, he stopped pacing, and turned to face us.

"OK," he said.

"OK—you'll help us?"

"OK, I will help you to get Pettikin home, and then you in turn, Allie, will help me. Deal?"

It seemed almost too easy. "Oh, wow, yes, deal!

Pettikin, did you hear?"

Pettikin hugged my head. "Oh thank you, Guardian, thank you!"

Vala didn't seem to share our bubbly enthusiasm. "Tell me, Allie, are Professor Theopolous and Mrs. Widgit waiting on Earth?"

"Yes."

"You came from my pond? The one behind May's house?"

"Yes."

"All right, then let's go there. I need to figure out exactly what has happened."

He stepped forward and placed one palm against the center of my forehead, the other against Pettikin's, and then everything went white.

8

I felt like the atoms of my body were being reassembled—pulled together from the far reaches of the universe around a gravitational core of me-ness. It took a few seconds before I could feel my eyes, let alone pry them open. When I finally did, everything was too bright, like an overexposed photograph. I blinked a few times, and things slowly came into focus.

We were back at Walden, standing next to the boulder.

"Allie!" Andie ran toward us.

Vala stepped in front of her. She stopped and stared up at him.

"You must be Andie," he said. He gazed at her for a few seconds while she stood with her arms hanging limp at her sides.

"Don't worry, I'm a friend," he said finally, moving away with an amused smile. He walked over to the other side of the boulder where Mrs. Widgit and Professor Theopolous were standing.

Andie raised one hand weakly, index finger extended toward his back.

"Who…?"

"Viola Widgit and Theodore Theopolous! Once again you are causing me no end of trouble." Vala's voice was equal parts humor and irritation. He stopped in front of the grownups and folded his arms. Mrs. Widgit pressed her hands together in front of her, and Professor Theopolous bowed from his waist, like Pettikin had.

"Now, Vala, surely you're not still upset about that small matter last spring," Mrs. Widgit fretted. "It all ended for the best after all."

"Yes, because you had me to take care of everything." His voice was still severe, but he was smiling and gazed into each of their eyes for several seconds, just as he had with me and Andie.

Andie came up beside me, leaned her head close to mine and whispered, "That's the *Guardian*?"

"Yep."

"He's...hot."

"I know, right?"

Pettikin shifted himself on my shoulder, presumably so he could see better. It was bizarre watching the adults show such deference to someone who, from the outside, didn't look much older than Andie or me.

"You must forgive us, Vala," Professor Theopolous said. "It was our intention to approach you ourselves. We realize that the girl is quite young and untrained."

"And yet she and the gnome did what you weren't able to." Vala's voice was flat. "Do you know why?"

Mrs. Widgit and the Professor were silent.

"Well, come on, it's not that difficult. Or at least it shouldn't be for an old Gatekeeper such as yourself." Vala's eyes bored into the Professor, who still proffered no answer.

"Fine. Allie, do you know?" Vala's countenance changed, became more playful and less severe.

"Do I know what?"

"Why you were able to get through my Gateway

95

when Viola and Theo failed?"

I wanted to answer him, he looked so sincere and appealing, but I honestly had no idea. I shook my head, trying to convey apologies for my stupidity with my eyes.

"Then I'll tell you." Vala turned to the grownups. "When Viola and Theo tried to access my Gateway, they thought only of their own predicament, how they could help themselves. Allie, on the other hand," he turned back to me and, again, became softer and more gentle, "thought only of how she could help Pettikin."

He gazed at me for a long moment with an expression almost like adoration. I felt my cheeks flush with embarrassment. I certainly didn't feel I was being anywhere near as noble as he was allowing.

"And of course Pettikin," he turned his gaze to the gnome, "Pettikin thought only of his own Guardian. But gnomes are another story altogether. They're innocents."

I glanced up at Pettikin sitting on my shoulder. Even in the daylight he seemed to be glowing. He beamed at Vala.

Vala addressed the adults again.

"Remember why we do things," he said so quietly that I had to strain to hear him. "We help each other out." He dropped his gaze and played in the dirt with his toe for a moment. Mrs. Widgit and Professor Theopolous were silent.

When Vala finally raised his head, his expression was serious.

"And you're going to need my help. I feel sslorcs here, and normally, they wouldn't dare approach Aunt May's cottage or my pond. Do either of you know what happened?"

The Professor and Mrs. Widgit exchanged glances.

"Vala, we're worried someone may have made a contract with the sslorcs," Mrs. Widgit said.

A strange feeling spread through the air, like the

barometric pressure dropped a few points. Vala narrowed his eyes and set his jaw forward. He turned abruptly on one heel and began circumnavigating the pond with long, powerful strides. A strong wind kicked up behind him, stirring leaves up off the ground and causing his shirt to billow. The sky darkened, and I felt my hair prick up with static electricity, the way it did before a thunderstorm. Andie and I inched closer together. Pettikin clung to my neck so hard, he was almost choking me.

When he reached the far apex of the pond, Vala turned around. He no longer seemed aware of any of us. The wind grew stronger around him, and he reached both palms toward the sky and exhaled slowly. Bright light shot out of his hands, spiraled in the vortex of wind swirling around him, and then exploded into several beams which arced over the pond and into the woods. Andie and I ducked, and I clamped a hand against Pettikin to steady him on my shoulder. It sounded like he was muffling a scream in the crook of his arm. The light beams pulsed and ricocheted through the air for several seconds and then faded away. Vala lowered his arms and the wind around him died down. The charge in the atmosphere faded, and the sky brightened.

He walked toward us, his expression calmer, although I thought he looked tired. Pettikin was limp against my head, and Andie clutched the sleeve of my hoodie. He didn't look at us as he walked past, but I felt waves of soothing energy flowing our way.

He stopped in front of the Professor and Mrs. Widgit.

"There is a Contractor here. I stopped short of eliminating him, because something's not right. What was May keeping from me?"

"We don't know for sure, she didn't tell us anything, but..." Mrs. Widgit paused and glanced over at the Professor.

"She knew who it was? You know who it is?" Vala

asked.

Mrs. Widgit hesitated.

"We think it might be Jim Cutter," she said finally.

Vala's shoulders fell.

"Ah, that idiot." He brushed his hair from his face and paced slowly along the edge of the pond.

"OK, let's head over to the cottage. I need to talk to the alpacas."

"Right," Mrs. Widgit said, and she and the Professor turned and headed back the way we had come.

"You three stay close to me," Vala said to Andie, Pettikin and me.

We followed him up the hill to the main path, at which point Andie sped up so she was next to him.

"If I may ask a question," she said.

He gave her a brief, sidelong glance.

"Yes."

"Why do you all keep talking about the alpacas like they're the Godfather or something, instead of cute, but not necessarily useful, farm animals?"

Vala checked to make sure I was still following. I put a hand on Pettikin's legs and sped up so I was walking next to them.

"The alpacas work for me," he said. "They are magical beings that can protect Gatekeepers and travel in and through the secret dimensions with them."

I stopped walking.

Vala also stopped.

"What?" he asked.

"The alpacas are magical?"

"You have a gnome sitting on your shoulder and just traveled to another world not twenty minutes ago. Are you saying they're not? And you're not?"

"Well, I... OK touché." I wasn't entirely satisfied with that answer, but couldn't immediately think of a way to follow it up. We resumed walking.

"Anything else?" Vala asked Andie.

"Yeah, what's a s... sl..." she looked over at me.

"Sslorc?" I finished for her.

"Yeah."

"The sslorcs are shadow beings. In a way they're the opposite of the Guardians. If the Guardians represent light, happiness, peace, and protection, the sslorcs are anger, hatred, violence, and depression. They're strong on the shadow worlds and nonexistent in the higher worlds. On the forbidden worlds the two opposing forces struggle. Sometimes the good forces dominate, and sometimes the sslorcs do."

"And that's why you close the Gateways on the forbidden worlds?"

"Yes. The higher worlds vibrate at a much higher frequency than the other worlds and are filled with an inherent power—the light of the universe. The sslorcs know that their own power is weaker and constantly seek to steal the power of the higher worlds and corrupt it. Since there are no Gateways to the higher worlds on the shadow worlds, they try to get there through the Forbidden Worlds."

"But, I mean, what are they?" Andie asked. "What do they look like?"

"It depends on how much power they have. They can take some pretty ugly forms on some of the worlds—let's hope you never see them. Here on Earth they don't usually have enough power to take their own physical form. They are shadow beings, and would appear to you more as a darkness or a grim feeling. Here they gain power by either influencing people to do their work for them or, if someone is stupid enough, getting a person to enter a contract with them."

"What does that mean, to enter a contract?" I asked.

"The sslorcs have a type of dark power which they can temporarily transfer to a person. If someone is stupid enough to take it, this power can help them accomplish some goal their ego wants. But the transfer of power isn't free. Usually without the contractor knowing it, the sslorcs are actually feeding off that person's own, intrinsic power—power they had all along but were unaware of, or unsatisfied with. In the end, when the sslorcs have drained that person of their power, they will cut them loose. At that point, whatever temporary power that person gained from their association with the sslorcs will be gone, and they will be left desolate and confused, not understanding what happened. The sslorcs, meanwhile, increased their power and then look for another person to feed off of. In this way they spread like a virus through the worlds."

I shivered. "Then why would anyone do something like that?"

Vala sighed. "People can be so stupid. For many people, that type of dark power is enticing. Often they are tricked by the sslorcs into an alliance. They don't see or understand the consequences of what they are doing when they do it," Vala replied.

We reached the edge of the woods and could see the cottage. The sun wasn't even directly overhead yet. Instead of following the path, we cut through the yard on the eastern side of the cottage toward the barn. The alpacas were outside in their paddock, standing so close together that their bodies appeared to be a single mass of fur with three long necks sticking out akimbo, inquisitive faces perched on top.

All of Aunt May's alpacas were huacaya alpacas, with fluffy crimped hair that reminded me of giant poodles. Taos was the biggest, and the only male. He was white with golden brown shading on his withers and the tips of his ears, like a lightly toasted marshmallow. He stood protectively in front of the other two. Suzy, the oldest, was black with tan markings, warm chocolate eyes and long black lashes. Sunshine, the one who had come up to me at the funeral, was fawn colored, younger, and smaller than the others.

Vala walked up to the fence and leaned against it, one foot on the bottom-most board, arms folded across the top. The alpacas trotted over, honking and humming, then crowded around him, pressing their noses against his face and snuffling his ears.

Bob came out of the barn, wiping his hands on an old towel as he walked. When he saw Vala he froze, eyes wide. He threw the towel to one side, clasped his hands in front of him and bowed.

"Vala, when... when did you get here?" he stammered, as he straightened up.

Vala pushed himself up from the fence. He gazed into Bob's eyes like he had done with the rest of us.

"Just now," he said. "The alpacas were telling me what a fine job you have been doing taking care of them."

Bob's face turned scarlet underneath his patchy beard. He bent his head down and put one hand behind his neck, hiding his face with his arm.

Vala ran his hands through the fur on Suzy's neck, then began pacing back in forth in front of the paddock, his gait slow and meandering. Bob retrieved the rag he discarded earlier and climbed over the fence to join the rest of us.

Finally, Vala sighed, folded his arms and leaned against the fence, facing us.

"A lost gnome and a Contractor, huh," he murmured, then addressed Mrs. Widgit and the Professor directly. "This is a mess. Even with May here, you would have been in trouble, but I suspect you know that. We don't have a lot of time."

They didn't answer.

"So, Allie," Vala said. "Are you ready?"

"Ready for what?"

He looked at me, but not the way he usually did. His eyes were as hard as diamonds, and they flashed once, like kaleidoscopes turning into place. He pulled his mouth into a devilish grin, his gaze electric and intense.

"Are you ready to become my new Gatekeeper?"

"What? You mean right now? I didn't think…" I gestured toward Professor Theopolous, unable to finish the thought.

"You said you would help me. We made a deal."

"Well, yeah, but I mean, I didn't know exactly…"

Professor Theopolous exhaled slowly as though he had been holding his breath. "Ah, yes, Allie, perhaps I should have warned you about making deals with a Guardian."

"Warned me? About what?"

"Oh, about the eternally binding nature of such deals, things like that," Mrs. Widgit said airily, waving a hand in front of her face. "Yes, I suppose in retrospect, we probably *should* have mentioned something about that."

"In our defense we really didn't know that she would be in a position to be conversing with the Guardian, let alone making deals on her first meeting," Professor Theopolous was addressing Mrs. Widgit as if I wasn't even there.

I abandoned them as hopeless and turned to Vala, terrified.

His grin was gone. He was looking at me soberly with a gaze so penetrating, I felt he could probably see into the structures of my cells. For a long time, he just looked at me, his expression serious. My knees started to shake.

"You have a lot to learn," he said. Then, mercifully, his expression softened, and old Vala seemed to peek out from behind the new stone facade. "Quite a bit to unlearn as well," he said gently and finally turned away.

Andie stared at me with something of the same horror in her expression that I was feeling. I didn't know what to say. What had I done?

"Right, I better go get baking," Bob said briskly and hurried past all of us toward the cottage.

9

"I should probably go help him," Mrs. Widgit said cheerfully, as if nothing dire had just happened. "I know where May kept things. Theo, care to join me?" They set off for the cottage.

"Don't worry, Allie," Pettikin said, sliding down my arm and dropping to the ground. "I've spent a lot of time traveling through the Gateways. I'll help you. It will be OK."

Vala stood very still, staring off into the distance, but moved now, as if we had called him back from some faraway place.

"Yes, don't worry Allie. I'll help you too. And with a gnome and a Guardian behind you, how could you fail?" His smile was warm and friendly again.

"But Vala, there's still something I don't understand from before. Back at the pond it sounded like you know who Mr. Cutter is. Do you really think he made a contract with the sslorcs?"

"He may have," he said. "Before you were born, Allie, when your Aunt May was still young, there was another Gatekeeper here. That Gatekeeper was Harold Cutter, Jim Cutter's uncle."

"You're kidding," I said.

"No. Your Aunt May knew Harold because she worked for him after school. Both she and Jim trained as his apprentices."

"Mr. Cutter was an apprentice Gatekeeper?" If he had told me Mr. Cutter was a zombie, I would have been less amazed.

"That surprises you? You can't always tell the sum total of a person by the surface you currently see."

"So a Gatekeeper can have more than one apprentice?" Andie asked.

"It's unusual but not unheard of. Initially, both Harold and I thought Jim would succeed him. He was sincere and talented enough when he was young. But as time went on, he became obsessed with power. For someone whose business is exploiting the Earth's finite resources, you can imagine how tantalizing the prospect of gaining access to the resources on an infinite number of other worlds would be. He started to see the Gateways as something he could use to his own advantage to gain more wealth and influence here on Earth. May, on the other hand, impressed both Harold and me with her intelligence and work ethic, but even more so with her compassion. She was protective of everyone and everything around her. I watched them both for a long time, and, in the end, I was the one who chose to empower May instead of Jim to become the next Gatekeeper. Jim has resented it ever since."

"I can't believe this. I mean he's the last person I would have expected to be involved in something like this." I said.

"Yes, it's often like that. Life can be strange that way. At any rate, I can worry about Jim Cutter. Your only job, for now, is to become my Gatekeeper so you can take Pettikin home."

"Ah, yeah, about that, is it true what Mrs. Widgit and the Professor just said? About deals with a Guardian being eternally binding, or something?" I tried to sound really calm and disinterested.

Vala laughed. "Well the relationship you have with a Guardian is going to be very different from any relationship you have ever had with a human, but you don't need to take what they said so seriously. I would never force you to do something you didn't want to do. In fact, I couldn't. It's not in my nature. At any rate, there is still one more obstacle that we have to overcome before you can be my Gatekeeper."

"What obstacle?"

A car door slammed up at the main house. My folks had arrived home and were unloading groceries. Vala watched them.

"You may find out sooner than you think. Maybe you should go back to the cottage before your parents notice anything...unusual," he gestured toward Pettikin.

"Oh! Right. C'mon Pettikin, let's get you in the house."

Pettikin was already halfway up to my shoulders.

"Aren't you coming with us?" I asked.

"I'll join you in a bit. I have a few things to take care of out here."

"Aren't you worried my parents will see you?"

"No, I'm not worried. They won't see me unless I want them to."

Andie followed me to the cottage. A wash of warm, fragrant air greeted us when we opened the front door. Someone had turned on Aunt May's stereo and the Air from Bach's Orchestral Suite in D Major floated through the house.

"Something smells delicious," Andie said.

We kicked off our shoes and headed for the kitchen. Bob had tied one of Aunt May's old, checkered aprons around his waist and was whisking ingredients in a large red bowl tucked into the crook of his arm. He squinted down at a stained and crumpled handwritten recipe on the kitchen counter, a large smudge of flour streaked across his left cheek. When we entered, he glanced up at us with a distracted, almost frantic expression.

"Oh, hey, Allie."

"Hey Bob. What are you baking?"

"Snickerdoodles. They're easy and don't need a lot of fancy ingredients. We're kind of on a budget here on such short notice."

"I found some chocolate chips and walnuts!" Mrs. Widgit emerged from Aunt May's pantry brandishing two bags like trophies. "I'll get started on some basic chocolate chippies. It's not a lot, but it should be enough." She set the bags down on the counter and rummaged through one of the cupboards, humming along with the music.

Professor Theopolous was seated at the kitchen table with three open books and an array of graph paper in front of him. He alternated between squinting through his monocle at the pages of the books and quickly drawing patterns of interconnecting lines on the graph paper using a pencil and a ruler.

"If I may ask the obvious question," Andie said, "not that anyone will give me an answer that makes any sense, but what are the cookies for?"

Bob stopped stirring and looked at her like she was crazy. "For traveling through the dimensions!"

"Like I said," Andie replied.

Mrs. Widgit was creaming together butter, sugar, eggs, and vanilla in another large bowl with the same gusto as Socrates digging a hole in our back yard.

"You could think of the dimensions as each having their own vibrational frequency," she said, her curls bouncing up and down with each stroke as she stirred. "It can be very different from the vibrational frequency one is used to living in." She threw several handfuls of flour into her mix without even stopping to measure it properly. "It can be quite jarring to experience these shifts in energy, especially for someone who isn't used to it. The right cookies help one adjust to the energy shifts between the dimensions and maintain the proper stamina for interdimensional travel." She tossed aside her wooden spoon and began kneading the cookie dough with her hands like it was bread dough.

"Snickerdoodles and chocolate chip cookies," Andie said skeptically. "Breakfast of interdimensional champions."

Bob had already spooned the first batch of snickerdoodles onto a cookie sheet and was headed for the oven. "Well what do you expect on such short notice?" he said tersely. "They'll have to do."

Mrs. Widgit threw more flour into her dough. It seemed to me like more dough was stuck to her hands than was in the bowl at this point. "They'll do," she said mildly.

"What are you doing Professor T?" I asked.

The Professor didn't look up at me when he answered. "I'm drawing up some charts for you of some likely routes and markers you might encounter in the initial dimensions."

"Likely routes?" I walked over to the table and peered at the graphs he was drawing. I felt Pettikin lean forward from his perch on my shoulders. "What do you mean *might* encounter? Aren't there, like, fixed paths or routes or something we'll take?"

Pettikin giggled.

I twisted my head toward him. "And what's so funny about that question, Mr. Brave-for-a-Gnome?"

"The Professor can't draw out an exact path for you because the secret dimensions are different for everyone who experiences them."

"What?"

"The gnome is quite right. There is no way for me to know what your exact experience of the dimensions will be. But there are some general energetic markers that will be there. I should be able to help you orient to those," Professor Theopolous said.

"I don't get it."

"The dimensions are weird," Pettikin said without a trace of irony in his voice.

Professor Theopolous sat back in his chair and removed his monocle. "That's about as good an explanation as any."

"Oh come on, you've got to give me a little more than that," I said. "How is it possible, if you've been to these dimensions before, or at least if someone has, that you can't tell me how to get through them?"

"It's difficult to explain Allie, because you are used to thinking of the world around you as solid and real."

I was about to protest that it *was* solid and real, and had nothing to do with my thinking it, but he cut me off before I could say anything.

"You are familiar, I suppose, with Albert Einstein?"

"A little. Sort of. I read *The Universe and Dr. Einstein* last summer. E equals mc squared."

"Do you know what that means?" he asked dryly.

"No, not really. I know it means matter can be converted to energy and energy to matter, and I remember something about relativity—a twin who flies off into space at the speed of light and comes home to find his brother an old man while he's still young—" I broke off. That book also said things like color and form didn't really exist except in our minds, that everything was just different frequencies of energy that we perceived as being real— almost exactly what Pettikin and Professor Theopolous were hinting at now. When I read it, it just seemed like some abstract idea someone had, not something I could experience. If it were true…

I shivered.

"The world around you seems solid but is really made of energy," Professor Theopolous was in full

Professor mode. "It's how we perceive the energy in a dimension that creates the things we think of as solid and real. All of the dimensions are just different bands of perception, and how they will be perceived... well, that is greatly influenced by who is doing the perceiving."

"But, wait," I felt off balance, like when you climb up a tree too fast and your foot misses a branch. "If this world, Earth, is one of the dimensions, well, I mean, you could draw me a map of how to get around here."

"Yes, because here we are experiencing things together with the rest of the people, and we all hold very strong, common perceptual beliefs about how things operate. It's like that in some other dimensions as well, my dimension or Pettikin's for example. In those dimensions I might be able to draw you some more useful maps once you have been there. But in some others," he pulled one corner of his lip up, about as close to a smile as I had seen from him, "well, not so much."

I didn't totally understand, and I hated that feeling. "But aren't we going together, Pettikin? Will we be able to see each other, and will we see the same things?"

Pettikin hesitated. "I think so. I think for the dimensions we'll be going to that will be true. If we're together we'll perceive them the same way."

"For the dimensions we're going to? Are there some where that wouldn't be true?"

"There are a lot of dimensions out there," Pettikin said. "Just about anything is possible. There are some we wouldn't ever want to go to."

"You know, just when I start to feel OK about this stuff someone says something like that, and it doesn't exactly give me the warm fuzzies..."

A low, rumbling noise, like distant thunder, rolled toward the cottage. The whole room began to shake as if a train were roaring by. Professor Theopolous clamped his hands down on his books to keep them from sliding off the table.

I reached one hand up to hold Pettikin and put the other against the counter to steady myself. Andie was bracing herself in the doorframe between the kitchen and the front hallway. Mrs. Widgit was halfway to the oven, balancing a tray of chocolate chip cookies between her hands, her eyes wide with alarm.

A shimmering ripple appeared at the far end of the room and moved toward us like a wave. I felt a little dizzy as it washed over us. Once it passed the rumbling faded and the shaking stopped. For a moment no one said anything. Then Mrs. Widgit cried, "Vala! Oh no, I have to stop him!"

Bob maneuvered next to her and took the tray of cookies from her with oven-mittened hands before she could toss it to the floor. She sped toward the living room, muttering something about Vala and needing a book.

I followed behind her. She began clawing through the books stacked on top of the coffee table.

"What are you searching for?"

She slid books off the table one after the other until finally she grabbed one. "Here it is! I found it!" She flipped it open and fanned through the pages. A yellowed, folded piece of notebook paper fell onto the floor.

I held onto Pettikin's legs and bent down to pick it up for her. Mrs. Widgit snatched it out of my hand before I had fully straightened up. She unfolded it and scanned it quickly.

"This is what we need, come on!"

She snapped the book shut and tucked it under her left arm. I glanced at the title *The Importance of Color*. Clutching the piece of notebook paper in her right hand, she strode toward the front door.

Andie joined me in the front hallway and followed us outside.

Mrs. Widgit marched across the front yard toward the western side of the cottage. "Vala? Vala!" she hollered.

We jogged after her, but only went a couple of

steps before I gasped and stopped.

The cottage was a hideous shade of light brownish-purple. The shutters were pea green.

"Is 'vomit' a color?" Andie asked.

"Holy crap," I said.

"Vala!" Mrs. Widgit bellowed. His blond head appeared from around the side of the house.

"Something wrong?"

"You can't just change the color of the cottage willy-nilly like that!"

"I can't?" He walked over to us.

"No you can't! It makes Patricia suspicious, and that makes things difficult for Dan."

Difficult for Dan? Dad was in on all of this?

Mrs. Widgit whipped the book out from under her arm, smoothed the crumpled piece of paper in her hand on top of it.

"May spent months coming up with these conversion charts that use a reasonable spectrum of colors for the Earth people!"

Vala took the book from her and ran a hand through his hair, seeming contrite. I wanted to laugh at the complete reversal of their roles from their previous argument. He squinted down at the paper, pacing slowly as he read.

"This is fascinating," he said. "I'm impressed May was able to figure this out."

I edged closer toward him, dying to see what was on the paper. When I finally got close enough to peek at it I was disappointed. I was just a conversion table, with colors listed in one column equating to one or more colors in a second column, and some notes Aunt May had scrawled in the margins. I did notice that the colors in the left hand column tended to be gaudier and the ones in the right more neutral.

"Impressed or not, Vala, you've got to change it before someone sees!"

Vala ignored her. "It's quite interesting. As long as the trim is bright enough it pulls up the frequency of the rest of the surface, and if you include enough colors, according to May the sum of the frequencies matters more than—"

"Vala!"

Vala laughed, "OK, OK."

"I don't understand. Why do you need to change the color of the cottage at all? I thought Aunt May just liked to paint," I said.

"Well, an oversimplified answer is that activating the Gateways requires specific energies. Different energies are available on Earth at different times. For example, summer is very different from autumn. Sometimes, we have to make slight changes in order to have the right energy available to perform certain tasks. Right now, I need slightly different energy frequencies available to me so I can more easily reactivate the Nexus Gateway. Once it's reactivated, we can change the cottage back to the way it was before."

He handed the book and paper to Mrs. Widgit and turned toward the cottage. He closed his eyes rubbed his hands together.

Andie grabbed my sleeve and pulled me away from him.

He raised his arms above his head, palms open. I heard a kind of sucking noise and then everything became silent—so silent that I put one hand up to my ears, which felt like they were stuffed with cotton. White-violet light pulsed from Vala's hands and suddenly everything went into photo-negative—what was light before was dark and what was dark was light. I probably should have been terrified, but strangely, I had no reaction at all, as if suddenly being in a photonegative version of my world was completely normal.

The low rumbling sound started again, and a second pulse of light shot out from Vala's hands. A shimmering wave of energy rolled toward the cottage which began rattling and shaking. As the wave washed over the cottage, the color changed from vomit-and-green to light yellow with bright turquoise trim. As soon as the wave reached the far end of the cottage, the rumbling stopped, and the world returned to normal.

Mrs. Widgit's whole body relaxed into a slouch. "Much better!"

Vala seemed a little tired, but he was still smiling. "Well, we don't want to offend the neighbors."

"Forget the neighbors. We have a much bigger problem," I said.

"What's that?"

I pointed up to the main house. My father was running down the lane toward us, one hand holding his unbuttoned sweater closed, the other clamping an old wool cap to his head, Socrates bounding after him.

10

"Oh good, it's the obstacle!" Vala said cheerfully. "I thought that might get his attention."

"You *wanted* him to see? You wanted him to come down here?" I was aghast.

"I *needed* him to come down here. There's something we need to discuss."

Andie and I exchanged panic stricken glances. Was there even a standard grounding period for trying to leave one's home dimension with a gnome?

Pettikin rocked back and forth on my shoulders making a breathy, high-pitched squeal like a tea kettle. Vala walked over to him, arm outstretched.

"Here, Pettikin, try my shoulders for a bit. I'll keep you safe."

Pettikin scrambled from my shoulders up to Vala's. I briefly considered whether I felt jealous that he preferred the Guardian to me, but then Vala rested one hand lightly on my shoulder, and I decided that I really didn't care at all.

"What's he saying?" Andie asked. Dad was yelling something as he ran.

"'*Oh*'? Something with an '*oh*'? Sort of an '*ohhhh*'

sound?" Mrs. Widgit offered.

"What, you mean like, '*Noooo*'?" I asked as it became clear that was the word my father was howling over and over as he ran.

Socrates overtook Dad and arrived first. I watched with horror as he launched himself at Vala, who fortunately seemed to be a dog person. Guardian. Whatever. He intercepted Socrates in mid-flight and rumpled the fur on his head.

"Who's a good doggy? Are you a good doggy?"

Socrates mopped Vala's face with kisses, then plopped down on his haunches next to him, a love-struck expression on his face.

"Noooo!" Dad rounded the corner where the lane turned toward the cottage and hammered toward us, punctuating each stride with a syllable. "No, no, no, no, no!" He arrived in front of us, bent over, hands on his thighs, breathing heavily.

"Hello, Dan." Vala's voice was gentle, his hand on my shoulder again.

Dad's head snapped up.

"Vala? Oh no," he groaned.

"Wait, you *know* each other?" I asked, incredulous.

Vala laughed.

"Now Dan," Mrs. Widgit's voice was warm and maternal, "why don't we all just go into the cottage for a moment? I can make some tea, and there should be fresh cookies waiting by now…"

"Cookies? Oh no."

I had no idea what I should say. I was very aware of Vala's hand on my shoulder. It felt like a protective force field formed around me, as if he were pouring strength into me.

Dad seemed to notice this as well. "I'm too late, aren't I?"

"Pretty much," Vala said lightly.

Pettikin peeked out from behind Vala's head, his

curiosity getting the better of him.

My father gasped which caused Pettikin to yelp, and in one ill-thought-out moment, he leapt from Vala's shoulders high-dive style, toward mine.

"Pettikin, what are you…' It was clear he had overshot, but I somehow managed to lunge underneath him and catch him before he hit the ground. He scrambled up to my shoulder in a flurry of arms and clogs, clawing my face along the way and leaving my hair disheveled. He breathed heavily next to my ear.

I straightened up and tucked my hair behind my ears. "Uh, Dad, this is Pettikin. Pettikin Periwinkle. From Arcorn. He's a gnome. Pettikin, this is my father. He knew Aunt May."

"How do you do?" Pettikin squeaked.

Dad looked from me to Vala and then back again. "Explain."

"Why don't we all go inside like Viola suggested. It will be more comfortable to talk in there," Vala said.

Dad's face was ashen. He turned and walked toward the cottage, muttering to himself. I felt unsettled, like the ultimate authority figure in my life suddenly wasn't anymore.

Vala pressed his hand against my back to move me in the direction of the cottage.

Andie joined me. "We are so screwed," she fretted, glancing up toward the main house, as if she were expecting *her* parents to show up.

Mrs. Widgit was walking a few steps in front of us. "Maybe not," she said. "You may have secrets, but it would appear Allie's dad has a few, too. That should level the playing field a bit."

Andie snorted. "He's her *dad*. I don't think that playing field is going to be level anytime soon."

I didn't say anything, just followed them toward the cottage, staring straight ahead.

Socrates pushed through the door ahead of us and

ran into the kitchen. Bob had become an insanely efficient baking machine. Trays of freshly baked cookies cooled on the counter, and more trays were lined up next to the oven, ready to be baked. Bob stared into the oven, a new tray ready to go in his left hand. He glanced up at us as we walked in.

"Who is going to *eat* all of these?" I asked. No one answered me.

Professor Theopolous cleared away half of the kitchen table and sat with his arms folded across his chest. He was staring across the table at my father, who sat across from him with his head in his hands.

Mrs. Widgit picked up the tea kettle from the stovetop and filled it with water. Pettikin slid off my shoulders, darted across the kitchen floor and climbed onto Socrates' back. Socrates thumped his tail against the cupboards.

Vala walked to the kitchen table and stood next to Dad without saying anything.

My father didn't lift his head from his hands.

"You promised."

"I kept my promise. She came to me."

Dad dropped his hands to the table and raised his head. "How is that possible?"

"The gnome helped."

"What are you talking about? What promise?" I asked.

Dad had a strange expression on his face, something between anxiety and resignation.

"Did you really seek him out? Did you really somehow manage to approach him on your own?"

"Who, Vala?"

"Yes, Vala!"

"Well, yeah, I mean, we needed his help to get Pettikin home, so we had to go ask him, if that's what you mean. Pettikin showed me how to get through his Gateway I guess."

"Was this May's idea? Was the gnome May's idea?"

"Dad!"

Pettikin sat on Socrates' back, his head tilted to one side, observing my father.

"I know it must be tempting for you to think something like that, Dan, but you know better. May wouldn't use her friends that way." Vala's voice was calm.

"She might not use him, but he could be in on it." Dad glared at Pettikin, who cringed and ducked down behind Socrates' head.

"Dad, stop it! You're scaring him!"

"Well how else do you explain it?"

I had never seen my father like this before. He was usually so calm and reasonable.

"Explain what? Pettikin didn't want to come here. He came here accidentally because he was *worried* about Aunt May. The problem is, once he got here, Aunt May wasn't here to take him home."

I assumed at this point that Dad knew the whole *Aunt-May-is-a-Gatekeeper* backstory without my having to explain it.

"And I suppose you think you're going to do it?"

"Well, I, uh…" I glanced at Vala.

"Because if you are, someone here found a way around my agreement with May, and I want to know who it was."

Dad glared across the table at the Professor who regarded him from behind folded arms without changing his expression.

"What agreement?" I asked.

Mrs. Widgit set a steaming mug of tea down in front of my father.

"Don't look at us," she said lightly. "We assumed Allie was May's apprentice all along and were quite shocked to find out that wasn't the case."

"What agreement?" I was almost shouting now.

Dad seemed to suddenly remember that I was the daughter, and he was the father. He sighed, ran one hand across his thinning hair, and relaxed back in his chair.

"I'm sorry, Allie. I'm not doing this properly. I know this must all seem very strange to you and I should be explaining things, not demanding answers from you."

I was so not prepared to deal with consoling my dad on top of everything else. I shifted my weight uncomfortably.

"What agreement?" I asked again, in a calmer tone.

Dad leaned forward and wrapped his hands around the mug of tea in front of him, then let it go and sat back in his chair again without taking a sip.

"What have they told you so far?"

"That Aunt May was a Gatekeeper. That this is a forbidden world. That when she died, the Guardians closed all the Gateways here, including the one Pettikin needs to get home." I hesitated, and then added, "And that Aunt May apparently never trained a replacement Gatekeeper, which is a big part of the reason we're in this mess."

Dad pressed his lips together, and the corners of his mouth turned down slightly.

"So, as you've obviously figured out for yourself, your great aunt was a little different from most people."

"That's an understatement," Andie muttered.

"May was obviously quite fond of you, Allie, and she did have her eye on you to be her apprentice from when you were very young."

I couldn't believe it. Part of me had been expecting my father to contradict the absurdity of the past two days—to offer some rational explanation for what was going on, to make things go back to normal. Instead he was offering up the crazy right along with the rest of them.

"You knew about all of this? How could you not have said anything to me all this time?"

"As I'm sure you're starting to figure out, I couldn't really say anything about all of this. It's not something one talks about in casual conversation with everyday people."

"What about Mom, is she in on it, too?"

"No, your Mother doesn't know. She doesn't need to. She's a very practical and rational person. It would just upset her to know about ...this," he waved his hand in a vague gesture that encompassed the entire cookie-filled strangeness of the kitchen and its current inhabitants.

"If she doesn't need to know, why do you need to know?"

Dad smiled slightly.

"Because I was Aunt May's *ally*."

The timer bell dinged. Bob opened the oven, exchanged the baked and unbaked cookie trays, and closed the door again, all within a matter of seconds. He set the new cookies out to cool on the counter, hardly paying any attention to the conversation.

Mrs. Widgit handed me a mug of tea.

"Something we may not have told you yet Allie—every Gatekeeper has an ally."

My hands were cold again, so I wrapped them around the warm mug.

"What's an ally?"

"An ally is someone who assists a Gatekeeper in his or her home dimension. They are more of an integral part of society and help smooth things over for the Gatekeepers so they can work more easily in the world without attracting too much attention by their...well, their oddities," she replied as she continued distributing tea to everyone in the room. I noticed no one was drinking any.

I thought about how Dad had always been able to keep the townspeople from asking too many questions about Aunt May, the way he kept Mom from worrying too much about the color of the cottage. I wondered if he would have been able to do that if he didn't appear so normal on the outside. He was a well-respected minister at a local church—people expected normalcy from him, stability. If he tolerated Aunt May's behavior, it was understood others could, too, without worrying. It was the perfect cover.

"But why didn't you tell *me*?" I asked Dad. "If Aunt May wanted me to be her apprentice why didn't you say something to *me*?"

"Allie, you were only six years old. I realize you were and are precocious, but I really didn't think you were in a position to be making those kinds of decisions at the time. Decisions which would radically alter the type of life you were going to have."

He leaned forward again. "What I did do, when May approached me about training you as her apprentice, was come to an agreement with her. The agreement was that May could not tell you about what she did or approach you about any of this until you were eighteen, at which time you would legally be an adult and could make the decision for yourself."

"I can make decisions for myself now!"

Dad ignored my outburst. "Aunt May agreed to the terms of my contract, but with one caveat—that she could tell you the full truth at any time if *you* approached her...or, by extension, *him*." Dad gestured toward Vala. "Since, to my thinking, it didn't seem likely you would approach Aunt May, and it never occurred to me it would even be *possible* for you to contact Vala on your own, I agreed."

I felt an overwhelming combination of anger, frustration, and annoyance that I couldn't quite put into words, which annoyed me further because I really wanted to yell at somebody. Had anyone planned on asking me my opinion on any of this, ever?

"Well!" Mrs. Widgit said brightly, as she arranged cookies on a plate. "I think this has all worked out wonderfully then! Allie found her own way to Vala, Vala has agreed to initiate her as the next Gatekeeper, and, assuming she passes her trial, Allie can take Pettikin home and everything can continue as it was meant to be. I'm so glad we could all come together like this. Cookie anyone?" She placed a plate of cookies in the middle of the kitchen table.

Vala put a hand on Dad's shoulder.

"Dan, I know you meant well, and May was fond of you, so I never interfered with her agreement with you. But it was never your decision to make. Like it or not, she doesn't belong to you. Whether it's now or when she's eighteen, the decision is Allie's and Allie's alone. None of us can make it for her, not even me."

He spoke with a quiet intensity that had none of his youthful persona. He was very much a Guardian of the Universe at that moment.

My father nodded and gazed down at the table.

Vala dropped his hand, and his lips twisted into a playful smile.

"So what's it gonna be, Al?"

My heart started pounding and my throat felt dry. "I…" I started, but my voice sounded rough. I cleared my throat.

"I mean we're just asking you to make a major, life-altering decision, with ramifications for the rest of your existence in the universe, right here, right now, in this kitchen. Don't worry, take your time."

Vala's eyes were full of humor, like we were sharing some inside joke. Waves of happiness rolled off of him and washed over me. I felt the knot in my stomach relaxing and was tempted to smile back at him, but that reaction confused me so I looked away from him quickly. Could it be that easy?

Dad leaned toward me.

"But Allie, think seriously for a moment, now, while you still have a chance. I know that it all sounds tempting—easy, even—but what you're signing up for is anything but easy. It's a lifelong commitment. It means you will be doing the work of the Guardians for...well at least for the rest of your lifetime here. Once you agree to this, any plans you might have had for your life will be out the window. This will be the one thing you are most committed to. It might be hard for you to understand what that means now." His voice was earnest.

Vala folded his arms and closed his eyes. The air around him turned golden, and he seemed far away from any of us in the kitchen.

I thought about all the vague plans I had for my life, all of the things I had ever imagined myself doing in twenty years—wearing a business suit in an office, being a veterinarian, or a musician—no one vision had ever stood out to me as the right one. There was nothing I particularly wanted to do more than anything else in the world. I had plenty of ridiculous daydreams that mostly centered around me being married to Brett Logan and living in some farmhouse in Vermont—a replica of my parents' house and life. How much did I want all of that? I cast my mind forward to what it would be like if I became a Gatekeeper, trying to imagine where I would be, and what I would be doing. There was nothing, just a blankness, a feeling like a question mark. Dad was right. I couldn't even imagine it.

A soft voice spoke up from somewhere behind the pointed ears of our German Shepherd.

"Please, Allie. I'll help you."

Pettikin peeked out from behind Socrates, floppy Santa hat first, then big blue eyes.

I looked over at Andie. It was as if she were reading my thoughts.

"You were never gonna be normal anyway, Al."

We stared at each other for a second, like we were forging some kind of unspoken agreement.

"Dad," I started.

"Allie, I know you're kind, and that you want to

help the gnome, but there could be other ways, we haven't explored all options,"

I closed my eyes and shook my head as if to keep his thoughts from penetrating my brain and confusing me before I could speak.

"No, Dad, listen. I have to."

"That's what I'm trying to tell you, you don't *have* to do anything, there's still time..."

"No, that's not what I mean. I mean *I* have to." I opened my eyes. "Knowing that all of this exists, that there's a world outside anything I imagined, that I can be a part of it—I can't say no to that. I have to do it. I couldn't live with myself knowing there was an opportunity like this out there and I didn't take it. I would be wondering about it for the rest of my life. Yes, I want to help Pettikin, and Mrs. Widgit and the Professor, but also I'm saying that *I* want to do this. That's my decision."

Vala's eyes were still closed, the air around him still golden, but he was smiling. "That's my girl."

"So, if Allie's going to be the new Gatekeeper, who's going to be her ally?" Andie asked.

Vala opened his eyes and sort of came back into focus. "Duh."

It dispelled the tension in the room, if nothing else. Everyone laughed.

Dad sighed.

"OK, Allie," he said. "If this is really your decision, then I won't interfere anymore. Except, of course, in whatever way I can to help get Pettikin home while Andie's still learning the ropes of *her* job. Hope you know what you just signed up for, kiddo."

"No clue," Andie said. "Can I have a cookie? I'm starving."

Everyone laughed again, and we all crowded around the table to help ourselves to Bob's cookies, still warm from the oven.

11

Vala didn't eat.

At least not at first, although he was very concerned that Andie and I eat something more substantial than just cookies for lunch. We heated up the rest of the tuna casserole from the night before while Dad ran up to the house to make us a salad.

Vala stood a little removed from the rest of us while we ate and chatted. Mrs. Widgit passed the plate of cookies around again after lunch, but when she held the plate out to Vala, he held up one hand and shook his head. I noticed that Bob, who was still baking, seemed a little crestfallen. Vala must have noticed too because he then said, "I was hoping Bob would let me have one of the fresh ones from the oven."

Bob beamed and placed a freshly baked snickerdoodle on a napkin. He dusted it with nutmeg and carried it over to Vala, who smiled his thanks.

"Your cookies are delicious, Bob," Andie said from around a large mouthful. Bob shot her a shy smile.

"The chocolate chip ones, too," I added somewhat incredulously as I remembered Mrs. Widgit's baking technique.

Mrs. Widgit bustled around the kitchen clearing plates and napkins and checking tea mugs to see if any needed refilling (they didn't).

After a few more minutes of what almost passed for normalcy, Vala caught my eyes. His cookie was gone, although I hadn't seen him eat it.

"We should get started. There's a lot to do." His expression was solemn, but not unfriendly. I had the feeling that he was transmitting something to me telepathically, but I wasn't sure what. Maybe courage, because I didn't feel particularly worried or nervous. I pushed myself up from the table and glanced at the clock on the wall. It was a little after one o'clock.

Professor Theopolous pushed his chair back from the table.

"Yes. Well. There is the matter of the girl's training."

The girl—like I wasn't standing right there.

"She hasn't had much, really any, to speak of. I have agreed, however, to train her despite her advanced age. If we get started right away, I think that in a matter of weeks—"

Vala cut him off. "You agreed to train her, Theo? Well, you're fired."

Professor Theopolous blinked.

I scrunched my forehead. "So, who's going to…"

"I'll teach you myself," Vala said.

"Oh boy," Dad pressed a hand to his forehead.

"Allie, Pettikin, come." Vala's tone was commanding. He turned and strode toward the kitchen door.

Pettikin leapt down from Socrates, raced across the kitchen floor and up to my shoulders. I hurried after Vala.

"Where are we going?"

"You're going to take Pettikin home of course. Bob—we'll need the alpacas."

126

"Right!" Bob set down his spatula and hurriedly untied his apron. "Viola…"

Mrs. Widgit appeared by his side, took the wadded up apron he shoved at her with one hand and picked up the spatula with the other.

"I'll get the cookies together for them Bob, don't worry."

Bob rushed past us and out the front door. Dad, Andie, and Professor Theopolous followed behind me.

"Vala," Dad said, "While I know my *very-smart-but-in-these-matters-quite-clueless* daughter is no doubt honored that you have agreed to teach her personally…" he shot me a meaningful glance.

I was supposed to have felt honored by that? Crap. I was never going to get the hang of this Guardian etiquette thing.

Vala paused and waited for Dad to finish.

"As her father, knowing a little bit about you and, shall we say your *methods*, I can't help but wonder—what, exactly, do you have planned?"

"What methods?" I asked.

Professor Theopolous, perhaps feeling like he needed to have *some* input into my gatekeeping education, answered.

"Let's say, Allie, that you wanted to learn how to swim. And let's say, for argument's sake, that you didn't know how—had never even been near the water in fact." He looked pointedly at Vala who rolled his eyes dramatically, walked out the front door, and set off across the eastern lawn in the direction of the two old beech trees. The hazy clouds from the morning had burned away and been replaced by a bright blue sky with white meringue clouds. The air was cool, but the sun was warm, and everything had the feeling of being freshly scrubbed after the morning rain.

"There are some," Professor Theopolous continued, somehow keeping pace with me even though I practically had to jog to keep up with Vala, "who would feel that it's useful to take a gradual and measured approach to teaching you to swim. They might explain a few techniques to you, perhaps take you first into shallow water where you were able to stand on your own. They might give you an inflatable floating device to help keep you buoyant in deeper water while you were still learning."

We arrived at the beech trees, which seemed somehow more normal and less spectacular than they had in the moonlight the night before. Vala turned around, and appeared both exasperated and amused.

"That's great Theo, and after several months using your method, a person might be able to swim—*if* they had an inflatable floating device with them and if they weren't so terrified of the water after everything you'd told them that they were still willing to try!"

"Sooo...what's the other method?" I asked.

"We throw you into the deep end of the pool and see if you figure out that you already know how to swim."

I knew I should have been worried. "Does that work for gatekeeping?"

Vala was thoughtful. "I don't know. I've never tried it before."

"No one has ever tried it before!" Professor Theopolous flung his arms out to his sides, with an '*I can't believe no one is listening to me*' expression on his face.

Dad scratched his head nervously.

"Honestly, Vala, are you sure about this? I'm surprised the other Guardians would agree to it. Why the urgency in training her so quickly?"

Vala's face turned serious.

"There's a Contractor here."

Dad's hand was still on his head, but he stopped scratching.

"Who?"

"Jim Cutter."

Dad lowered his hand in slow motion. "Can you

break the contract?"

"Not on Earth, not without killing the Contractor."

"Then that's why May let them kill her," Dad's voice was grim.

"Wait a minute, what?" Andie and I said at the same time.

"Aunt May was killed? I thought she died of an aneurism," I said.

"The aneurism was likely caused by an attack from the sslorcs, Allie," Professor Theopolous said. "Normally, May was so powerful that she could easily defend herself against such an attack. But by making a contract with the sslorcs, Jim Cutter momentarily obtained far more power than he normally would have."

"He *killed* her?" I was incredulous.

"More likely the sslorcs did it without his knowledge, but the only defense against that attack would have been to kill the Contractor. It's the only way to break a contract on Earth." Vala said.

"Then why didn't she kill him? Better he die than her! And why don't you just kill him now?" My voice was a little too loud.

"Allie," Dad moved to put a hand on my arm but Vala stopped him. His eyes bored into mine, his expression serious.

"Is that what you want Allie? Is that what you want me to do? Or, if I handed you a gun, would you do the job for me?"

Dad sucked in his breath.

Vala's look was intense, and he was still holding my father's wrist. I felt a horrible sick feeling in my stomach.

"I...I..." I started.

"Because if that is what you want, tell me now."

I wished that an enormous hole would open in the ground and swallow me. I dropped my head, my face flaming.

"I'm sorry. I didn't really mean that. I don't even know why I said it."

"Vala," Dad started.

"Don't defend her Dan. Let her speak for herself."

I swallowed and forced myself to meet Vala's gaze.

"Even if you handed me a gun, I wouldn't be able to do it. I don't even want to. Maybe it's just because I'm a coward, not noble like Aunt May, but I know I couldn't do it, and I don't even know him like she did. I…I don't know why I said something like that. I didn't mean it. It was a really stupid thing to say. I'm sorry."

Vala's eyes narrowed, as if he were searching for something in my soul. "He was once my student. I don't abandon my students no matter how far they fall. I will save that man." His expression was almost pleading with me. "You understand me, right?"

I nodded. I felt a strange pressure around my heart, and my eyes welled with tears.

Vala released my father's arm.

"She's strong, Dan. I need her to be strong."

Dad gave my arm a sympathetic squeeze.

Vala addressed the adults again. "If I leave the Gateways closed now, with a contractor here and no Gatekeeper, what will keep Earth from becoming a shadow world? Do you have the power to stop the sslorcs on your own, without my help?"

"A shadow world? Is there really a danger of that?" Dad asked.

"The way things stood a few hours ago, yes. If I want to keep the Gateways open, I need to establish a new Gatekeeper quickly. Because Allie's younger and less experienced than May, they may try to take advantage of the situation. If we hurry, we have the advantage of surprise."

I felt really, really small and inadequate and stupid.

I just wanted to help Pettikin get home and now there were grand, cosmic issues at stake. What had I done?

Vala answered my thoughts as though he had heard them. "We're all just a small part of something that's much bigger than us. You're not required to know or understand the big picture—that's my job. All you have to do is perform the task that's currently in front of you as best you can."

But what if I can't? I thought.

If Vala heard that thought he ignored it. He gazed up at the old beech trees for a moment, then turned to me and Pettikin, scanning us up and down. He paced back and forth with his uneven, meandering gait for a while, staring at the ground. Finally he stopped in front of us.

"OK. This is what has to happen for this to work."

I felt Pettikin lean forward attentively.

"Normally, Allie, you would have already been training for several years before attempting something like this. The training you would have received is designed to help an apprentice Gatekeeper amass and store a certain amount of power—power that you need just to be able to *see* the Gateways and enter them. You don't have that much power yet, so I will have to give it to you.

"In addition, I will give you the keys to the secret dimensions around Earth. You will need them to open the Gateways between the dimensions and travel through them to the higher worlds on the other side."

Professor Theopolous made a noise that sounded almost like a whimper.

"Oh have a little faith, Theo," to my surprise it was Dad who answered, sounding a little irritated.

Vala started pacing again. "Now comes the hard part. In order for me to give the keys to you, or any apprentice Gatekeeper, you're supposed to first complete a trial—a series of tests to demonstrate that you have learned the disciplines of Gatekeeping and are worthy of owning the keys. Since you haven't had the benefit of years of training from your Aunt May, or even the torture of a week of training with Professor Theopolous—"

Andie snorted and then inched away from the Professor when he glared at her.

"—I've decided to keep it simple and, also, to accomplish two goals at once. Let's say that I will temporarily *loan* you the keys you need to get through the secret dimensions. Your trial will be to take Pettikin through them and stay with him on the other side, in the higher worlds, until he is safely home on Arcorn. Oh, and then find your way back here of course."

I pictured myself lost in some kind of void trying to find my way back to Earth. What would happen if I didn't make it?

"If you succeed, you keep the keys and become the new Gatekeeper. So do you think you can do that?"

I swallowed and tucked my hair behind my ears. "Well, I mean—"

"Don't be ridiculous," Vala answered for me. "Of course you can't. You have no idea what I'm talking about." His tone was teasing, not mean. I felt a wave of relief wash over me.

"Yeah, I guess I'm not sure I can do this. In fact, I may be pretty sure I *can't* do this," I replied with a nervous laugh. Professor Theopolous harumphed and folded his arms across his chest.

"That's why we're going to cheat," Vala said. "I can't release you from having to go through the trial, but I can give you helpers."

As if on cue, Bob appeared, leading the alpacas. The alpacas, with small day packs made from the same material as their funeral outfits draped across their backs, picked their way across the lawn delicately. I wasn't sure what the packs were for—presumably nothing too heavy since alpacas aren't normally pack animals.

Vala held out a hand, and Suzy approached it,

sniffed it delicately, then hummed softly. "Each alpaca knows the way through one of the secret dimensions. They can't get through the Gateways between them without you, but they should be able to lead you to them.

"Pettikin." Pettikin's weight shifted on my shoulders. "I also have a job for you. Once you are in the initial dimensions, I need you to translate what the alpacas are saying for Allie."

I looked up at Pettikin, surprised.

"You can understand what the alpacas are saying?" Pettikin sounded almost horrified.

"You can't?"

"She can't, so it would be very useful if you would help her to understand. I also need you to guide her once you're on the other side of the secret dimensions in the higher worlds, and to help her adjust to some of the complexities of interdimensional travel. Keep her grounded so we don't lose her. Can you do that?"

"Yes," Pettikin said immediately. "I will help her. I promise, Guardian. I won't fail you."

I made a mental note that this was probably the way I was supposed to be addressing Vala. No wonder Professor Theopolous and Mrs. Widgit were always so appalled by my behavior.

Vala took a few steps toward me and spoke so softly that I wondered if anyone else could hear. "And I will help you, Allie. Since you don't have enough power yet to open and enter the dimensions, I am going to have to hold them open for you while you're on this journey. It's hard to explain how it's done, but I won't be able to go with you physically and do that at the same time. But just know that, even if I'm not there physically, I am always with you, and if you need my help I will help you."

For a long time Vala looked into my eyes and then lowered his gaze. When he raised his head again, his eyes were faceted jewels that flashed in the sun.

"It's time for me to initiate you."

12

Everything was happening so fast, I didn't have enough time to think things through. Actually, I wouldn't even know *how* to think them through since I basically had no idea what was going on.

"Pettikin," Vala gestured toward the ground a few feet away from me. "Stand here just for a second, I'll do you next."

Pettikin zipped from my shoulders and stood in the spot Vala indicated.

Golden and white light radiated out from Vala, swirling down and around his body. I could feel him from where I was standing—a wall of warmth and light, a silent presence.

"Come," he said, smiling sweetly and holding out one hand.

I froze like a baby rabbit, heart pounding. Why was I so afraid?

"It's OK, it's OK!" He beckoned me forward with his outstretched fingers.

Somehow, I put one foot in front of the other until I was standing right in front him.

"Bye bye," he said, putting the palm of his hand

on my forehead and closing his eyes.

I closed my eyes and felt … nothing.

The best nothing I had ever felt. The fear I was feeling just seconds before was gone. Everything inside of me—thoughts, emotions, breathing, heartbeat suddenly became absolutely still. I waited for something to happen.

"Excellent," Vala said, lifting his hand and stepping back.

I opened my eyes. That was it?

And then I gasped.

White and blue light surrounded Andie, Dad and Professor Theopolous, like a soft haze. Bewildered, I spun around. Pettikin was a little orb of sunshine standing on the ground.

"What the…" I took a few steps back. The trees were glowing. Soft blobs of white light floated through the air between them, bouncing off one another like soap bubbles. In the sky, flashes of white light would appear out of nowhere and then disappear, like beams from unseen lighthouses. The ground was a maze of glowing interconnected lines stretching out to the horizon.

"Whoa." I eased myself down to the ground, worried that I might faint.

Andie rushed over. "What's wrong? Is she OK?"

"She's fine. I just opened her eyes a little bit more than she's used to." Vala watched me, smiling.

My mind seemed to be adjusting to its new state, so it didn't feel quite so overwhelming. As the initial effect faded, everything returned more or less to the way it was before, just a little brighter and more alive. If I focused my mind, I could still see the blobs of light in the sky and, also, the light around all of my friends, but if I relaxed my focus and just thought about everyday things, I didn't notice it so much.

Andie pulled me up to my feet.

"Things look a little different?" Vala asked.

I nodded, not sure what I should say.

"OK, the first part's done then."

"First part?" There was more?

"All I did so far was give you enough power to be able to see and enter other dimensions. I still have to give you the keys to the secret dimensions around Earth. Otherwise, you won't be able to find your way through them any more than anyone else here can."

"OK," I said again and waited for him to hand me the keys.

Vala gave me a funny look, and Dad chuckled softly behind me. Professor Theopolous covered his eyes with one hand.

"I should probably explain that I'm using the word keys metaphorically," Vala said. "They're not physical keys like keys to your house or something. They're internal."

"Oh," I wondered how much redder it was possible for my face to get.

Vala took a couple steps toward me. He held one hand up to the height of his shoulder, then looked at me apologetically.

"I have to touch you again, is that OK?"

"Uh, sure…" Since he had already touched me twice, I wasn't sure why he was asking this time.

He didn't look into my eyes as he bent his fingers and pressed the heel of his palm to my stomach, just a little below my navel.

Ah. Yeah. So that was weird. I tried not to flinch instinctively. He still didn't look in my eyes as he very quickly moved his palm to the center of my chest, being incredibly cautious about where he placed it. I tried to pretend I was completely at ease with this, and definitely not hyper aware of exactly where his hand was, or the fact that my dad was watching. Again it seemed he waited only as long as necessary before he quickly moved his palm to the center of my forehead. That at least was starting to seem normal. His hand felt warm. I closed my eyes and golden light stretched in front of me for as far as I could see.

Vala dropped his hand, and I opened my eyes. The whole process only took a few seconds.

I almost laughed at the expression on Andie's face, which said, *what the heck was that?*

"Three keys, three dimensions," he said. "That's how many you have to navigate through to get to the other side."

"But, I mean, I don't get it. What exactly are the keys, and how do I use them?"

"You have to figure that out yourself," Vala said, "It's part of becoming a Gatekeeper." Pettikin sat in the grass a few feet away petting a sparrow that had hopped up next to him. Vala knelt down next to him and touched his forehead without nearly the ceremony he had needed with me. Even without concentrating, I could see the light inside of Pettikin shine out more brightly.

Socrates came bounding up, startling both the sparrow, who flew away, and the alpacas, who bounced up and down like popcorn kernels, honking their annoyance. Bob tried to calm them as Mrs. Widgit hurried toward us carrying two large grocery bags, both stuffed to capacity, and three rolls of paper tucked under her arm.

"Sorry it took me so long," she called out, plopping the bags and paper rolls down near the alpacas, a little out of breath. She put both hands on her hips and cocked her head to the side. "You look good, Allie!"

"I do?" It hadn't occurred to me that I would look any different. I glanced over at Andie for confirmation.

"You look…brighter, or something," Andie said, "I don't really know how to describe it."

"Oh." I guess the Pettikin effect also happened to people.

"Well, let's pack up the alpacas then!" Mrs. Widgit said. I peeked inside the grocery bags. They were filled with dozens of smaller bags of cookies.

Bob undid the first pack on Suzy's back and held it open while Mrs. Widgit hummed and arranged several bags of cookies in it. "Next!" she called out, and they proceeded to the other side and then the next alpaca, until each one's carrying packs were filled with cookies.

"That's it?" I asked. "Just cookies? No water bottle or anything?"

Mrs. Widgit looked at me like I was deranged. "I hardly think you'll need one," she replied.

"But I need six day packs full of cookies?"

"Is six enough Theo?" Mrs. Widgit actually seemed to be considering this. "I thought it seemed like plenty but it has been awhile since I've done this."

"Six should suffice, as long as she follows Vala's instructions and doesn't do anything stupid or get completely lost, which of course we can't know for sure."

Andie grabbed two fistfuls of hair on either side of her head, "Oh my God, how is that even helpful?"

"I was merely answering a question and not, in this instance, trying to be particularly helpful."

"Seriously, Theo," Dad broke in. "Maybe not the best time."

"Where do you want me to put your maps?" Mrs. Widgit asked him, holding up the rolls of paper she had brought down.

The two of them argued about this and finally settled on unrolling the maps, folding them, and putting one map in each alpaca's day pack. Vala stood up and began pacing back and forth in front of the old beech trees again, striding purposefully this time, not meandering. A couple of times he paused and gazed into the woods or up at the sky, his eyes narrow, as if he were watching or listening to something. Finally, he stopped in front of the two trees.

"Are you ready?"

A rush of adrenaline made me light-headed, and my heart started pounding. My brain dredged up a memory of my biology teacher explaining that this was your body's way of preparing itself for death. Pettikin raced over to me and climbed up to my shoulder.

"OK, everyone who's going through the Gateway, stand over here." Vala pointed to a spot next to him. "That would be Allie, Pettikin and the alpacas," he clarified when I didn't move.

Pettikin pulled on a lock of my hair, and I moved forward to the spot Vala indicated. Bob led the alpacas over to me and handed me their leads. "Good luck Allie," he mumbled.

Taos hummed and pressed his nose against my cheek. I patted the poof of curls on his head. My hands were shaking.

"Andie."

Andie startled when Vala called her name.

"I understand you had a run-in with Mr. Cutter here the other night?"

"Oh, uh, yeah..." Andie said carefully, as if she were trying to determine how much she should admit to or whether she was in Big Trouble.

"I have to keep the Nexus Gateway open for Allie while she's in the other dimensions, since she's not strong enough yet. To do that I have to take a form in this dimension that limits what I can do here. If I get too distracted, Allie could get lost in the void."

"I could what, now?" I asked.

Vala ignored me. "The Gateway will also be vulnerable because I'm holding it open. We don't want anyone or anything else to get through it, so I need you to be on the lookout for Mr. Cutter, and if you see him, do whatever you need to do to keep him away from the Gateway." He gave her a significant look. "Do you think you can you do that?"

"Yes." Andie said, although she appeared to be wondering exactly how much Vala knew about her previous encounter with Mr. Cutter.

"Dan, Theo, Viola—"

"Of course Vala," Dad answered before Vala could finish. "We'll help Andie keep everyone and everything away from the Gateway until Allie returns."

"Well then," Vala said, "this should be interesting."

He faced the two beech trees, closed his eyes and rubbed his palms together. Then he held his arms up and out at angle, palms forward. White light shot out from his hands, and he started growing taller. His physical form dissolved into a solid mass of golden and white light. He kept growing until he became a luminous, ghost-like figure, like the one on the book we had read last night, almost as tall as the trees themselves.

I have got to start rethinking my relationship choices, I thought.

In his new form, Vala touched first one beech tree, then the other with a ghostly, arm-like appendage. Light shot down both tree trunks to the ground and then ricocheted back up, spreading out through every branch and twig until they were all glowing white. Then he waved an arm first to the left, then to the right. Two arcs of light formed in the sky and then dissolved, the particles descending slowly, and accreting like ice crystals on an unseen lattice, until a densely woven web of golden light appeared in between the trees. It was humming like a strong electric current or magnetic field.

Andie looked as terrified as I felt.

Ghost-Vala gazed down at me. I felt like he wanted to tell me something, but without a mouth, he couldn't speak. I wondered what I should do.

Pettikin yanked on my hair. "Go Allie, go! He wants you to go!"

"Oh, right!" Trembling and stalling for time, I looped the alpacas' ropes tighter around each hand. Mrs. Widgit, Professor Theopolous, and Bob stood close together, Mrs. Widgit with her hands clasped under her chin like she was sending her first child off to college. Dad was standing next to Andie twisting his cap in his hands.

Pettikin gripped tighter around my head. I took a deep breath, scrunched my eyes closed, and plunged forward through the Gateway.

13

Red.

That was my first thought when I opened my eyes. Not fire engine red, but red like the sandstone rocks of the Grand Canyon, or the deserts of the southwest.

We were standing on a bed of rust-colored sand that stretched on for miles. A range of purple and red mountains cut a jagged silhouette against the horizon, their peaks lit up every few seconds by silent flashes of heat lightning. The sky was dark lavender on the horizon and black overhead where dense clusters of stars formed unfamiliar constellations. I couldn't see a moon, but everything around us was illuminated somehow—bathed in a pale white glow from some unseen light source. Towering plants that reminded me of saguaro cacti, some more than ten feet high, were interspersed with lower, shrubbier sagebrush-like plants.

It was a twilight desert world.

I had a feeling of dissolving and re-materializing when I jumped through the Gateway, but I hadn't seen light or felt the peaceful emptiness that I had when I traveled to Vala's world. It felt more like being in a void— a darker kind of nothingness.

Pettikin slid down from my shoulders and dropped to the ground. He sank into the sand past his ankles. My feet had also sunk into the ground more than I would have expected. I lifted one foot and set it back down tentatively. Instead of coarse grains of sediment, this sand was made of small, round beads with a rubbery, gel-like consistency. The beads rolled to the side when I set my foot down, creating a deeper indentation than ordinary sand would.

"What is this place?"

Pettikin shook his head as he turned around, scanning the landscape.

"I don't know. I've never been to this world."

The air felt cool and somehow thick or electric—as if I could feel the individual molecules against my skin. It gave me goose bumps. A shooting star streaked across the sky and then disappeared into the darkness. I thought I saw a pair of glowing, white eyes peeking at us from behind a cactus, but they quickly disappeared.

Taos hummed and pulled on his rope.

"Easy, buddy," I said reaching up to pat him. "What's wrong?"

"He wants us to follow him." Pettikin climbed up to my shoulder. "This is his world—he knows where we need to go."

"Oh." I thought about this for a second, then reached up and unhooked the alpacas from their ropes. I assumed at this point they weren't planning to run away from us. At least I hoped not, because if they did, we were kind of screwed. I unzipped the day pack on Taos' back and saw the map Mrs. Widgit and the Professor had placed inside.

"Should we take a look at this?" I asked, pulling out the folded square of paper and tucking the alpacas' ropes into the pack.

I unfolded the map, and Pettikin reached forward to hold one corner while I held the other. The page was covered with dozens of long, straight lines, some intersecting in crosses or stars, and groups of concentric circles. We stared at it in silence for a few moments.

"Does this mean anything to you, Pettikin?" I turned it ninety degrees, then a full one hundred eighty. "Which way is north? Is there even a north here?"

I wadded up the map and stuffed it back in Taos' pack.

"Let's just follow Taos if he knows where to go."

Taos hummed and took off at a speed I'd never seen an alpaca run on earth. He glided over the sand, barely touching the ground with each leap, heading for the mountains in the distance. My heart sank when it seemed like he really might be planning to run away from us, but then he stopped and waited, humming impatiently. I didn't need Pettikin to translate that.

"Well—here we go I guess," I said and took a step forward.

Whoa. With just the single step I shot forward a good yard and a half. I flailed my arms to catch my balance, Pettikin clutching my head, while Suzy and Sunshine leap-glided their way to Taos like Super Alpacas.

I took another impossibly huge step forward, teetered for a second, then took another, and another, until I got the hang of it. Soon I was bounding forward effortlessly, yards at a time, barely touching the sand with each step. Instead of getting tired, I felt an energy building up in me as I ran.

After a few minutes I stopped. My tracks already trailed off in the distance behind us.

"Pettikin did you see that?" I felt dizzy, like I was buzzing with electricity.

"It seems like there's a lot of power in this world." Pettikin sounded thoughtful. "I imagine anything we do or think here will be amplified beyond what we're used to. Which could be good or bad depending on what we're doing or thinking."

The alpacas were waiting up ahead for us. I ran until we caught up with them and skidded to a stop, my body humming with energy. If we kept this up, I was going to be totally wired by the time we were done.

Taos hummed and ducked his head.

"He wants you to eat a cookie." Pettikin said.

"You're kidding."

"No, I'm not." Pettikin was oblivious to my sarcasm. "He says the energy here is too strong for us. He wants us both to eat a cookie."

I reached into Taos' day pack and pulled out a package of cookies. Snickerdoodles. I undid the tie, handed a cookie to Pettikin then took one for myself. It was soft and cinnamonny, and, as I chewed, the manic feeling that had been building up in me started to dissipate. I finished mine quickly and ate another while Pettikin finished his, dropping crumbs in my hair.

I tucked the rest of the cookies into Taos' pack feeling much better. He hummed and took off again with us following behind.

We ran for a long time. More than once, I thought I saw glowing, white eyes staring at us from behind the plants, or tall, shadowy figures looming out of the corner of my eye, but each time I turned toward them they disappeared.

The ground became rockier and large boulders were interspersed with the plants. The mountains loomed closer. Taos stopped abruptly, and we pulled up beside him. I had no idea how many miles we just ran. He turned his head, sniffing the air. Then he hummed and picked his way toward several large rocks, rectangular blocks of stone maybe four feet high, that were arranged in a semi-circle around a clearing, almost like a small fortress or campsite. The alpacas huddled together near one of the stones and closed their eyes, humming softly.

Pettikin eased himself down from my shoulders and plopped to the ground. "We're supposed to rest here for a while before we continue on."

I retrieved another package of snickerdoodles from Taos' pack. I felt dizzy, like I had been drinking coffee nonstop for the past ten hours or had taken too much Sudafed. I handed a cookie to Pettikin, then shoved one in my mouth, gulping it down in just a couple bites. I was beginning to see how we might go through a lot of cookies while we were on this journey.

Pettikin wandered over to one of the stones. He observed it for a moment, then quickly scaled it, using some unseen-to-my-eyes crevices for footholds. I gripped the bag of cookies in my teeth, placed my palms down on the top of the rock and hoisted myself up next to him. I opened the bag and held it out to him. He took a cookie. I took one for myself and sat the bag down between us. We munched in silence, observing the landscape in front of us. A long stone wall on the horizon just in front of the mountains stretched in both directions as far as I could see.

I saw another shadowy figure from the corner of my eye. I slowed my chewing.

"Do you seem them?" Pettikin's voice was barely a whisper.

Ever so slightly, I turned my head, and the shadow slipped away.

"They disappear whenever I try to look at them," I whispered back.

"Don't look at them directly. Use your other sight, the sight that Vala gave you."

Oh. Duh. I tried to remember how to do that. I stopped chewing. My mind was still amped up from running, so I tried to calm it. It was easier to do that here than it was at home. As soon as I turned my attention inward, my thoughts slowed down, and everything became more luminous. I focused on my breathing and waited. Another shooting star streaked across the sky and disappeared into the darkness.

The shadow being reappeared in the periphery of my vision. I resisted the urge to turn directly toward it, waiting until it moved forward into my field of view.

Its figure was like a giant man, as tall as Vala had been in his ghost form, taller than the old beech trees behind Aunt May's cottage. He had chiseled features that reminded me of the statues on Easter Island, long black hair pulled into a ponytail and a white headband with a blue crescent moon in the center knotted behind his head. He was wearing a long, flowing gray garment that was belted in the middle, and a sword with a black and silver woven hilt hung in a sheath at his side.

He folded his arms and gazed off into the distance, waiting for something. I held my breath. Another figure appeared on the horizon and glided over to him. They looked almost identical to me, except this one had a red moon on his headband. They weren't talking, but I had the sense they were somehow communicating with each other.

"What are they?" I breathed, barely moving my lips.

"Warriors. I've heard of them but never seen them. They are incredibly powerful. They work for the Guardians and protect the universes. They destroy dark beings." Pettikin shivered. He sounded almost reverent.

The first figure turned dark expressionless eyes in our direction. One corner of his mouth pulled up into what seemed like a smirk, and they both slipped away into the shadows.

I exhaled slowly and reached for another cookie. Pettikin leaned back on his hands and gazed up at the stars. His beard and the cottony tip of his hat glowed silver, his eyes wistful. I cast around for something to say.

"What's your world like, Pettikin? I mean—is it like this?"

He shook his head. "No. It's more like your Earth, but maybe how it was hundreds or thousands of years ago—when things were still clean and there weren't so many people."

"Yeah, we haven't taken very good care of the place." My cookie felt oddly heavy in my hand, and my appetite was suddenly gone. "Are there people on your world?"

"Some, but not very many. Most of them are Gatekeepers or Interdimensional Travelers, like your Aunt May. They come to see our Guardian, but they don't usually stay for very long before they leave again."

"What's your Guardian like?"

"She's the most beautiful being I have ever met," his voice was soft.

"She? Your Guardian is female?" I felt a like a traitor to my gender for finding that surprising.

"Yes. She's very mysterious and powerful. She lives on our world and takes care of everything that lives there, but I think she also does other work in other dimensions that we don't know about. Even the other Guardians come to see her and pay their respects to her from time to time."

"It's hard for me to imagine what she must be like."

"She's outwardly very different from your Vala, but inwardly very similar, if that makes any sense."

My Vala. I wondered what he was doing right now. "It kind of makes sense. I wonder if I'll ever get to meet her. Hey, do all gnomes know as much about things as you do?"

"We're all taught the same things, and some things we just *know*. But I've had more experiences in other worlds than most gnomes. Most gnomes are content to stay on Arcorn and tend to their dragons and gardens. I don't know why I've always wanted to travel and explore other worlds so much."

"Like me wanting to get out of Ohio. And *now* look at us."

Pettikin gazed out at the landscape. "The universe is strange sometimes. Maybe we were meant to meet each other."

We sat in silence for a while longer munching cookies and watching the stars. Even though I wasn't as wired as I had been when we stopped, I was way too wound up to sleep. I wondered if I would ever need to sleep at all if I stayed in this dimension.

It felt like several hours had passed before the alpacas finally stirred. Taos came over to our rock and honked up at us.

"Time to go?" Pettikin, who was lying on the rock with his hands behind his head, sat up and nodded. I jumped down off the rock, sinking into the soft sand, and Pettikin slid down onto my shoulders.

We set off at a slower pace, but it was still faster than I could ever run on Earth. Taos was choosing his path carefully, winding around the large rocks that were becoming more frequently interspersed with the terrain.

After several minutes I noticed that we were approaching the wall I had seen earlier. It was made out of large, stone blocks, similar to the ones we had been resting on, but taller. Something about it seemed odd to me, but I couldn't quite place what it was. Then I realized that even though we were getting closer, it still extended all the way to the horizon in either direction. There didn't seem to be a way through it or around it, and Taos didn't seem to be changing directions or slowing his pace.

"What's he doing?" I called up to Pettikin. "Doesn't he see the wall?"

Pettikin's voice was wobbly from bouncing on my shoulders. "I don't know. I don't like this," his pitch was higher than normal, as if he were building up to a scream.

Taos galloped at full speed directly toward the wall.

"No, no, no…" I cried out, my voice getting louder with each no.

Just before he careened into the wall he veered sharply to the right so he was running parallel to it and ducked into a gap between two of the stones. Pettikin started screaming, and I tripped and fell forward onto my hands and knees. Suzy and Sunshine disappeared into the wall behind Taos as I skidded across the sand, Pettikin clinging to my neck. I scrambled to my feet and stumbled forward terrified we would get left behind. I clamped Pettikin's legs to my shoulder to make sure I didn't drop him and charged through the gap in the stones.

We were in a narrow, dimly lit stone corridor. Pettikin's shrieks reverberated against the walls and died away, replaced by the echoey sound of him panting. The air felt cool and musty, like a basement, and it gave me the absolute creeps. I tried to adjust my speed to the smaller area, brushing frantically at real or imagined cobwebs that touched my face as we ran.

Suzy was waiting up ahead for us, and I raced toward her. As soon as we caught up with her she darted down a second corridor perpendicular to ours. I followed her down that corridor, and then a third and a fourth.

We were in a maze—a maze that I would have absolutely no idea how to navigate or get out of without the alpacas. A toxic mixture of panic and adrenaline coursed through my veins. I ducked blindly down each new corridor hoping to see an alpaca so I would know where to turn. Just when I thought I couldn't stand it anymore, we turned out of the maze and into the open.

Lightning flashed overhead, illuminating everything briefly. We were in a small clearing at the base of the mountain, its huge bulk looming in front of us.

"Gaaaah!" I bent over, resting my hands on my knees, panting. Pettikin dropped to the ground and lay spread eagle on his back. I was gasping for air, not because I was tired from running, but because of the wild panic I was still feeling.

Taos honked and hopped up and down urgently.

"He wants you to..." Pettikin intoned without moving.

"I'm already on it," I walked jerkily over to Sunshine and clawed through her pack like a junkie until I found a bag of snickerdoodles. I ripped it open and ate two before I remembered to offer one to Pettikin. I gulped down a third before I felt the panic subsiding.

"Holy crap," I said finally. "Can we never do that again?"

Taos hummed. There, on the face of the mountain almost directly across from us was a diamond shaped web of glowing red lines. Two of the shadow warriors we had seen before were standing on either side of it, arms resting on the hilts of their swords, faces impassive.

"Is that the Gateway?" I felt a rush of excitement. Except for that last part, it hadn't been that hard.

Taos snorted.

"It's a Gateway," Pettikin said slowly, "but not the Gateway we need. That is."

He pointed to the top of the mountain. A tiny, diamond shaped web of white light shone down at us from its highest peak.

"Aw, man."

Suzy walked toward the red Gateway. Several pairs of glowing white eyes appeared in the darkness on either side of her, tracking her progress. The Warriors didn't move. She ducked her head, stepped through the Gateway, and was gone.

"Why did she go through that one if it's the wrong one?"

"Because that Gateway leads to the top of the mountain and the Gateway we need to go through."

It was hard to see because it was dark and so far away, but I thought I could just make out Suzy's silhouette in front of the white diamond Gateway at the top of the mountain.

"Ah, that's great! Come on then. What are we

waiting for?"

I was about halfway to the Gateway when a Warrior suddenly appeared in front of me. I hadn't seen him move. One minute he was standing to one side of the Gateway and the next standing right in front of me, blocking my path with his enormous feet and legs.

"Hey," I said, but he ignored me. I tried to go around him to the right. He reappeared in front of me. I ducked to the left, and there he was again.

"Hey, c'mon," I whined. "We're with her!" I pointed up the mountain at Suzy. The Warrior didn't shift his gaze or acknowledge me in any way, except to continue to block me whenever I tried to get anywhere near the Gateway.

I finally backed away, and he returned to his original position. Pettikin also tried to approach the Gateway, but even his polite bow didn't sway the Warriors. They wouldn't let him pass.

I turned to the alpacas. "What about you guys?"

Taos nudged Sunshine forward. Sunshine approached the Gateway and carefully sniffed the ground in front of it. She honked once up at the Warriors, but they didn't move. She stepped through and was gone.

"So alpacas are allowed through the Gateway, but we're not?"

Taos hummed softly.

"He says that since they're part of this world, the Warriors don't see them as strangers and let them come and go as they please. He doesn't think they're going to let you or me through."

I tried one more time to approach the Gateway, but almost as soon as I thought about it, the Warrior was in front of me.

Frustrated, I glared up at him. "So what are we supposed to do?"

For the first time, the warrior locked his eyes on mine, and I immediately regretted it. They weren't normal eyes—no iris or pupil, just empty black hollows where eyes should be. His gaze was empty and vast like Vala's, but Vala was warm, and he was *cold*, like an icy wind howling through the blackness of space. My legs started trembling, and I wanted to back away from him, but I couldn't move. What was I even doing here? I was so out of my league it wasn't even funny. Professor Theopolous was right—I was going to end up dead.

The Warrior released my gaze and pointed to the left of the red Gateway. A narrow trail, maybe four feet wide, wound up the side of the mountain toward the top.

"So we hike up, is that it?" My voice was shaking and my breathing uneven.

Taos hummed softly.

"I don't like this, Allie," Pettikin's voice was strained. "Taos says the path isn't easy. It's designed to keep people away from the Gateway not lead them to it. I think maybe we should just go back."

I was terrified, and the energy of this world amplified the feeling. I wanted more than anything to turn back, to run away and pretend I had never agreed to this, never heard of gnomes or Guardians or Gatekeepers.

If we turned back now, though, Pettikin would be stuck on Earth forever. I was sure of that.

I had a strange feeling in my stomach, like a weight or force pushing downwards through my legs into the ground. The fear I was feeling didn't subside, but another part of me was detached from it.

"No, we're not turning back. We'll hike up." I said grimly. "Brute force over finesse—it's the American way."

Taos clucked and hummed.

"He says you should take his pack. He says we'll need the cookies." Pettikin was twisting the end of his beard in his hands.

"He doesn't want to go with us? That can't be good." I walked over to him, unclipped the straps from his neck and waist, and slid the pack off his back. The two halves folded together, and I was able to adjust the straps so I could swing it over my shoulders like a backpack.

Taos hummed, then walked to the red Gateway and disappeared through without so much as a glance from the Warriors.

I could just barely make out the figures of the three alpacas next to the tiny diamond that was now our destination. At least they were waiting for us.

"OK, Pettikin, let's go."

Pettikin hesitated. He wrung his hands and seemed like he was about to say something, but then just nodded. Perhaps because I was wearing the pack, he didn't climb up to my shoulder like he usually did, but followed behind me on foot.

The trail was rocky, but well-worn, as if someone or some*thing* used it frequently. It was bordered by scrubby desert plants and cacti, the face of the mountain on our left, the steep slope to the clearing below on our right. The Warriors watched us, and I shivered.

I glanced over my shoulder to make sure Pettikin was still following. He was, but he wasn't alone. Several pairs of glowing white eyes were following behind him.

"Uh oh." I relaxed my mind so I could use my 'other sight'. Slowly, their forms emerged from the darkness.

They looked like large cats, or maybe small mountain lions, about the size of Socrates. There were twelve of them, each with a faint, but distinct, pastel color—orange, lavender, yellow, light blue, turquoise—and different geometric patterns on their backs—blue spots, orange triangles, black stripes.

We were being stalked by a brigade of whimsical figurines from a Hallmark shop.

"Are those things friendly?"

Pettikin followed my glance, screamed and raced forward, climbing up my leg, scrambling over the pack on my back and up to my shoulders until he was almost sitting on my head.

"I take it that's a no?" I stopped walking and observed the creatures while Pettikin calmed down, gasping for air. They stopped when I stopped, eyeing me with empty glowing eyes.

"I… I don't know," Pettikin admitted, sheepishly. "I've never seen anything like them before."

"You're not usually afraid of animals though, only people," I noted uneasily, as I resumed hiking up the trail. Even with the additional gnome burden, I felt OK. The extra power on this world seemed to apply to strength, as well as speed. I glanced over my shoulder again. They were still following us, always matching our pace, always staying about ten feet behind us.

"They're hard for me to … to *read*." Pettikin said.

"You mean like the way you can *read* the alpacas?"

"Yes, and most animals."

I mulled that over. "Let's just keep going" I said. "They're not bothering us. If we can get to the Gateway and get through, it won't matter."

We hiked on for quite a while, making exceptionally good time, just as we had in the desert. I started to feel hopeful that it wouldn't take us too long to reach the top. The creatures had so far kept their disturbing, but as yet harmless, distance from us. I could, however, feel the excess energy of the world building up in me, buzzing like an electric current. We were going to need to stop soon and have some cookies.

Unfortunately, just as I realized this, I noticed new eyes peering at us from the shrubs on the sides of the road. Unlike the slanted cat-eyes that were following us, these were round and glowed red.

"Do you see those, Pettikin?" My head felt a little dizzy when I talked, and I wondered if I had already waited too long before stopping.

"Yes." An edge of hysteria crept into Pettikin's voice.

"We need cookies, or we're both going to start freaking out and do something stupid." I scanned the area for a shelter or clearing where we could stop and sit, but saw only the narrow path cutting through the mountain. I noticed, with some alarm, that the Hallmark brigade had closed their following distance to about half of what it had been.

"Eesh." I increased my pace up the path, and for the first time, had to exert myself to keep going. It wasn't anything I couldn't bear, but it was no longer effortless to be hiking up the mountain at a rapid pace. I willed myself on until whatever energy or chemical cocktail was swirling through my body bubbled over, and I got so dizzy I lost my balance.

"Whoa." I careened on one leg, and the shifting weight of the pack and Pettikin on my back nearly pulled me over. I stumbled into the shrubbery on the side of the path. Pettikin started shrieking. A violent hissing sound rose up from the bushes, and something pricked my leg.

"Ow!" I jumped back onto the path as dozens of tiny creatures poured out onto the road in front of us, blocking our way.

They looked like fluorescent hedgehogs, little roly-poly creatures about eight inches in diameter, with glowing purple quills tipped with silver.

I bent down to rub my leg. "Aww, they're kind of cute."

The creatures hissed in unison and puffed up their quills, turning into tiny, evil spheres. Pettikin let out a blood-curdling scream, as a stinging sensation spread through my arms and cheek.

"Ow, hey!" I jumped up and backed away. The creature closest to us shot quills at us, with surprising range and accuracy. Several were stuck in my arms and cheeks, and I brushed them off quickly. They were about three inches long, but very light, so they had only pricked my skin superficially. Besides some mild swelling and itchiness, I didn't appear to be mortally wounded.

"Take it easy, guys. We're not going to hurt you. We just want to… Ouch! Darn it!" I had taken a tentative step forward and was greeted with a hiss and another barrage of quills which landed on my leg. Only a couple pricked through the thick fabric of my jeans, and I hastily flicked them off, annoyed. Pettikin whimpered.

From behind me I heard a low, musical growl that sounded almost like purring. I turned around slowly to see twelve pairs of glowing white eyes half closed into slits, and twelve Hallmark ceramic figurines crouched low, ready to pounce.

The hedgehogs hissed.

Pettikin wailed.

My head was spinning, and I really wanted a cookie.

"OK, hold on, calm down everyone—"

No one listened to me. The Hallmark Cats were closing in on us. The hedgehogs puffed themselves up into prickly spheres. It seemed to be their single defensive move, and it had absolutely no deterring effect on the cats. Pettikin and I were about to become casualties of the Great Hallmark Cat-Purple Hedgehog massacre of our time.

I tried to press myself up against the mountain, away from the fray, but one of the cats turned and followed me. It pulled its lips into a snarl, revealing a set of gleaming, pointed teeth. Pettikin screamed.

That feeling in my stomach appeared again, the weight pushing downwards. The detached part of me took over, and I jumped into the middle of the path between the two warring factions. I turned toward the cats, my face a menacing scowl, and held up both of my hands.

"Stop it! That's *enough*!"

Some kind of force shot out of my hands, and knocked me back half a step. My voice reverberated off the walls of the mountain through the desert. The cats froze, and even Pettikin stopped screaming.

The echoes faded away, and I stood there for a few seconds while everyone stared at me. I couldn't believe it worked. I wasn't even sure what had just happened. I lowered my arms to my side, feeling self-conscious, but decided to press my advantage.

"Cats—sit!"

To my surprise, the cats sat.

"Um, right. Hedgehogs…"

I turned around, and a volley of quills from the nearest hedgehog landed on my shins. I gave him a stern look, and in unison, the hedgehogs pinned their ears to their heads and deflated, cowering away from me.

I almost started laughing at that, but managed to keep my voice firm. "Stop hissing and throwing quills at everyone. No one is going to hurt you. Pettikin…"

"Yes?" Pettikin's voice was hesitant, as if he were worried I was about to yell at him too.

"I need a cookie."

"Oh, right!" He rummaged around in the day pack, and soon a package of snickerdoodles appeared in front of me. I ripped the bag open, scarfing cookies as fast as I could. I could hear Pettikin gulping and felt crumbs dropping down my back, so I assumed he retrieved a separate package for himself.

Two by two, little hedgehog ears pricked up.

"What," I asked them with my mouth full. "You want some cookies?"

The hedgehog closest to me crept forward, sniffing my feet, his eyes huge, sorrowful, red saucers.

I took a cookie from the bag and broke it in half, then fourths. I bent down and handed him a piece. He grabbed it with tiny paws, stuffed it in his mouth, and scampered away.

Within seconds, I was surrounded by purple hedgehogs gazing up at me with forlorn eyes, mewling piteously. I broke up cookies and handed them out. One by one, they scampered into the bushes with their treats.

A plaintive yowl from behind me made me turn around. The cats were watching me, but instead of menacing, they looked hurt.

"Well, you can have some, too." Unfortunately, my bag was almost empty. I held out the last cookie to the cat that was closest to me. He took it and pranced away, looking smug.

"Uh, Pettikin," I was now surrounded by pastel cats, pressing up against me, and pawing my legs and arms. I was afraid they were going to knock me over.

"Here, Allie!" Pettikin dropped a fresh bag of cookies in front of my face. I quickly handed them out to the cats who trotted off with them one by one. We went through three full bags of cookies, but at least the hedgehogs and cats were no longer threatening to kill us.

I dropped the day pack to the ground and plopped down next to it, more emotionally than physically exhausted. Pettikin slid to the ground beside me. I snuck two more cookies from the bag without the animals seeing and handed one to him. We ate quickly without saying anything. The cats were splayed across the road, licking their translucent paws and rubbing their faces, a picture of contentment. From the bushes, the hedgehogs squeaked and made rustling noises, as if they were nesting. I hoped those were happy sounds. It certainly sounded friendlier than the hissing.

The web of light at the top of the mountain was closer than I expected. If we could keep the same pace we had when we started, we would get there soon.

We rested for maybe half an hour before I stood up and heaved the backpack over my shoulders. Pettikin seemed a little worse for wear. "Walk or ride?"

"I can walk for a while."

We set off at a quick pace, but once again, I noticed some resistance. It felt more like climbing at home, not the effortless running we did earlier. The bushes to our right rustled, and red eyes peered out at us from time to time. The Hallmark Cats were still following behind us.

We trudged on for what seemed like another half hour. The trail steepened gradually as we walked, and now we were hiking up a fairly sharp incline. The Gateway was hidden from our view by the mass of the mountain, so I could no longer judge our progress. I was getting short of breath, and each step seemed a little harder, as if something were pressing down on me. Pettikin was struggling to keep up, and his cheeks looked flushed.

"Is it just me or is it getting harder to walk here?"

"The mountain has power, and it doesn't want us to reach the Gateway. The closer we get, the harder it pushes against us."

"Oh. Great."

The trail steepened, and I had to grab on to the shrubs to pull myself up at times. At one point, it became a vertical stone wall, about six feet high, and Pettikin had to scale it first to show me where the best hand and foot holds were. I grabbed a twisted root at the top to pull myself the rest of the way up, breathing hard.

I wondered how the cats would handle the wall, but one by one they appeared over it, leaping up in one effortless step. They seemed to float whereas I had never felt heavier.

We were climbing another steep incline when my foot slipped. "Pettikin, hold up. What is this?"

An oily sheen spread across the ground. I bent down and picked up a handful of sand beads. Whatever substance was inside them that gave them their soft, rubbery consistency was leaking out. I quickly dropped them, my hand coated with slippery red, orange, and yellow oils. Gross. I wiped it on my pants.

We used the shrubs on the side of the path to pull ourselves up the slick incline, one of us slipping every third step or so, sometimes catching ourselves before we fell, sometimes landing on our hands and knees in the glop.

Pettikin, with his smaller surface area, was acquiring a faint, reddish orange patina.

A brilliant flash of lightning produced a crash of thunder so loud, I thought something exploded nearby. Pettikin screamed, and even I screamed and ducked, covering my head with my hands like they taught us in the tornado drills at school. The sky opened up, and we were pelted by hail the size of walnuts for about ten seconds before it changed into a torrential downpour of freezing rain.

Pettikin started to cry. "Let's go back Allie, I don't want to do this anymore."

"We *can't* go back Pettikin—we just have to stick it out a little further."

I tried to press forward, but the ground was a river of slime. It was like trying to climb up a waterslide at a water park. I slipped and fell face first into an oily red puddle.

Disgusted, I wiped my face, struggled to my feet, and started slogging forward again, like a hideous clown, arms flailing.

A second flash of lightning whizzed past so close, it made my hair stand on end. A second crash of thunder made me duck and cover again, tears of frustration and panic welling up in my eyes.

Pettikin cowered in a tiny ball, crying. I slopped my way over to him and scooped him up. I wondered if we should turn around after all. The cats were still there, completely unaffected by the weather and the slime, but offering no assistance. If we went downhill, at least gravity would help us.

I felt the pressure in my stomach, and a wave of energy pressing me down to the ground. *No.*

I could barely see the path up the hill through the wall of rain. The trail was an oil slick.

"Allie, let's go back," Pettikin wailed. "It's OK, we can try to get to Arcorn another day."

Human Allie agreed with Pettikin, but detached Allie took over again. "I don't think so, Pettikin. If we don't get through now, we'll never get through. We just have to keep going."

My mind was filled with grim determination—heavy emphasis on grim.

"Get on, and hang on tight!"

I held Pettikin up to my shoulders, and he scrambled around to my back, clinging to my backpack. I wiped the rain out of my eyes and slogged forward. It was slow and messy, and I kept slipping but I set my jaw and just kept climbing.

Eventually the rain stopped as suddenly as it started. The bulk of the water and slime rushed down the slope, leaving behind just a faint slickness. The air cleared, and I could see the path again. I picked up the pace, struggling against my own exhaustion, the buzzing feeling in my head, the weight of the pack and gnome on my back, and the weight of whatever force was pressing down on us harder than ever. I trudged around a small bend, and the path opened into a broad road, where several caves or indentations were carved into the face of the mountain. I let out a small cry. Up ahead was the diamond matrix of the Gateway, and Taos, Suzy and Sunshine waiting for us.

"Ah! Pettikin, look, do you see?"

His face appeared over my shoulder. He screamed.

"Ow!" I put my hand over my ear. "Wha…"

In front of me was a grotesque creature the size of a small elephant but with the appearance of a large ox with black leathery skin. It had yellow eyes and two twisted red horns on either side of its head, each about three feet long and each ending in a deadly point. It snorted, raining stinky, gray, ox-snot down on us and pawed the ground with a giant, cloven hoof.

I said a word that I'm not technically allowed to say.

Pettikin fainted and fell to the ground with a thud.

I scooped him up and searched frantically for some place to run. The ox bellowed.

The bushes next to us rustled, and a menacing growl rang out from behind us. The Hallmark cat brigade was crouched low and pressing forward, twelve pairs of luminous eyes locked on the ox.

I clutched Pettikin to my chest and backed off the trail toward the caves. As much as I was rooting for the cats, this appeared to me to be a battle between Satan incarnate and a bunch of Disney characters.

A swish, then a volley of purple quills shot out from the bushes on either side of the road, landing on the ox. Most of them bounced right off of his leathery hide, and he shook the remaining ones off easily. He bellowed, lowered his head, and charged forward, swinging his deadly horns from side to side.

Another roar, a lion's roar this time, echoed through mountains. All twelve cats charged forward, white hot light streaming from their eyes like laser beams. The Ox stopped and reared back, almost losing its balance. It closed its eyes and tossed its head, bellowing wildly in the searing light. The cats pressed forward, until it turned around and fled, disappearing into one of the caves.

Pettikin stirred in my arms. I was clutching him so tightly, I was surprised he could breathe.

"Is it over?"

"Yeah, I think it is over." My voice broke when I spoke. Arms shaking, I set Pettikin down on the ground and slid the backpack off my shoulders. My hands trembled so hard, I could barely open it. The outer cloth was still soaked from the rain, but fortunately, an inner lining kept the contents mostly dry. One package of snickerdoodles remained. I handed one to Pettikin and ate one myself. The cats crowded around and sat on their haunches, watching me expectantly.

"Oh yeah, you definitely get a reward," I broke the remaining cookies up so there would be enough to go around and quickly passed the pieces out to the cats. Then I walked over to the bushes and shook the remaining crumbs out for the Hedgehogs.

The alpacas hopped and hummed up ahead next to the Gateway.

The cats lay contentedly in the road grooming themselves.

"Thank you." I held out my hands, and a couple of them came forward to sniff them. I felt tears well up in my eyes like a dork. "Maybe we'll see each other again."

I re-shouldered the day pack, and Pettikin and I ran toward the alpacas, the closeness of our destination giving us a newfound energy. And then I stopped abruptly.

A warrior stood next to the Gateway, his arms folded. He was watching us.

"Oh no," Pettikin moaned.

I wanted to cry. It was so unfair.

The pressure in my stomach returned, and the wave of detachment ran through me. This time, the feeling was so intense that it pushed out into a sphere around my entire body. I was not letting this dude stop us again.

"Allie, what's wrong?" Pettikin asked.

"Nothing. Just—I think I know what the key Vala gave me is. Well, maybe. Hopefully."

With one part of me still terrified, I walked toward the Gateway.

The Warrior appeared in front of me, blocking my way.

I glared up at him. "We overcame all your obstacles fair and square. We got here on our own power." Well, ours and the laser attack cats. They had been a huge asset.

From a towering height, ancient, black eyes locked on mine, cold and intense.

Panic shot through me and I wanted to cower. Instead I clenched my fists, and stared back fiercely, legs shaking.

"Let. Us. Through."

A beat, then the faintest smile played across his lips, and he was gone.

The steely resolve left me like air gushing out of a punctured balloon. My legs gave out, and I fell to my knees.

"You did it Allie!" Pettikin came running up beside me.

I pushed myself up. Taos hummed and pressed his nose to my face.

"He can't go any further, since this is his world," Pettikin said. "Sunshine and Suzy will show us the rest of the way."

I put one arm around Taos' neck and rubbed his nose.

"Thanks for showing us the way," I said.

He hummed. Suzy and Sunshine stepped through the white diamond Gateway.

"Pettikin, let's get out of here."

14

Blue sky.

This was more like it.

I floated in a blue sky that stretched endlessly in every direction. Not just any blue, but the blue of the sunniest, happiest, warmest summer day that ever existed.

My body felt light and deliciously happy. I stretched out as long as I could, relaxed, and closed my eyes. I thought about taking a nap, although just floating here with my eyes closed was relaxing enough. As far as I was concerned, we could stay here forever.

I had no idea how long I floated there before I heard a faint honking noise.

At first, I didn't pay any attention to it because why bother? When it grew louder and more persistent, I thought I should at least open my eyes and see if it was something that warranted some kind of action. Perhaps I could ask whatever was honking to stop so I could go back to enjoying this world.

I opened my eyes.

Initially, I didn't see anything but blue sky, but then, an alpaca head appeared, fuzzy brown hair and round ears first, then nose and neck, like a swimmer surfacing from beneath the water.

"Hey Sunshine!" It was so great to see her.

Sunshine clucked at me, annoyed. Why was she annoyed when it was so beautiful here?

I felt something stir inside my chest, a gentle fluttering. Wait, was there something I was supposed to be doing here?

Pettikin appeared next to me, as if he too had just emerged from underneath the water.

"Pettikin! Hi!"

"Hi Allie!"

"Isn't this great?"

"It's so beautiful here! I love this world!" Pettikin clutched his hands under his chin dreamily.

"Me too! Can we stay here forever?"

HONK.

Sunshine was exasperated. I felt the flutter in my chest again.

"She keeps doing that, do you know what she's saying?"

"She says we need to come down there and follow her."

"Oh. Well, I guess we could do that."

The only problem was I wasn't exactly sure how to move. I had no real reference for up or down, except for the way I was oriented and the fact that there was an alpaca below me, so call that down. I also didn't seem to have any weight here, or maybe there was just no gravity to pull me in any direction. All I was able to do was rotate on my center axis.

"Uh—how do we do that?"

"I'm not sure," Pettikin stretched his arms and legs out to his sides and floated past me, spinning slowly, like a floating gnome version of da Vinci's *Vitruvian Man.*

I tried to move to my left, but all I did was rotate in a counterclockwise circle. Pettikin and I both giggled.

Sunshine honked, her front hooves appearing next

to her head as she pulled the rest of her body up from under the blue surface. She galloped toward us, the sky coalescing around her to form a soft surface that she could push against as she ran. Pettikin grabbed on to her neck as he floated past her and swung himself onto her back.

She hummed at me again, and I felt the stirring in my chest.

"She says Vala should have shown you how to move through this world. Also she wants you to eat a cookie."

My chest felt warm when Pettikin said Vala's name. There was something we were supposed to do here—what was it?

Pettikin reached into Sunshine's pack, and pulled out two chocolate chip cookies. He ate one and handed me the other as I drifted past them.

I took a bite. The cookie was still soft, and the chocolate chips were melty. The sweetness spread through my body, replacing the giddiness I was feeling with a calm warmth. I finished the cookie and held my arm out in front of me. If I focused, I could make the sky have a surface that I could feel. I focused harder and moved a foot forward, willing the sky to come up and meet it. My foot landed on something that felt soft and springy.

Cool. Sunshine snorted, and then turned and glided downwards, slaloming from side to side like she was skiing down a mountain. I followed after her. As long as I kept my mind focused, the sky came up to meet me wherever I wanted to go. I let my feet slip out from under me and slid the rest of the way on my backside. It was like sliding down a cushiony waterslide.

As we descended, the sky lightened and became translucent. I could see other figures moving below us, like we were looking through frosted glass. We passed through a boundary, and suddenly, we were falling through the sky in a new world.

We landed on a cloud, which, like the sky before,

coalesced to catch us. We bounced up once, over the edge, onto a rainbow and slid down onto the soft and springy ground, like an inflatable bouncy castle at a kid's birthday party.

Suzy was there waiting for us. She clucked and pinned her ears back.

Pettikin leapt off Sunshine's back, and he and I bounced on the ground. We were surrounded by trees made of pastel colored light, pink and purple trunks radiating out into thin branches decorated with white and gold blossoms. Their boughs waved in the air rhythmically. Beneath them were clumps of plants, some with colorful blossoms, some like giant reeds or cattails, hollow tubes of varying diameters and lengths, and others like fat gourds cut in half with long, thin tendrils stretching vertically down them. Everything was brightly lit, although I didn't see a sun. Light was emanating from all around—up from underneath the ground and down from the sky. Music floated through the air, a sweet melody with lots of flutes and a new-agey sound but no apparent source.

Suzy snorted and hummed impatiently.

"She wants you to eat a cookie." Pettikin stood on his hands, turning in a slow circle. I wondered how his hat never fell off. Maybe he secured it with pins or something. The thought gave me the giggles as I reached into Suzy's pack and pulled out a cookie. I continued to bounce and spin around, watching the trees and plants sway in time to the music.

I bit into my cookie and slowed my bouncing as I realized the plants weren't swaying in time to the music— they were producing the music. The gourds were like strings, the reeds like flutes, the flowers like horns and bells, the blossoms on the trees rustling like maracas. In a clearing just a few feet away from us, bright blue and green fuzzy turtles faced each other in a circle, bouncing yellow balls of light on their backs in time to the music—the percussion section.

"This is amazing!" I stopped bouncing and turned in a slow circle, taking everything in. The red world was a distant memory. From now on, I was all about the blue world.

Sunshine clucked and hopped, completely distressed. Pettikin had disappeared.

"Hey Allie, watch this!" The voice came from above me. Pettikin waved down at us from the highest branches of one of the trees.

"Hey be careful..." I started, but Pettikin had already leapt from the tree onto a rainbow. He slid down it like a slide, then bounced up from the trampoline ground onto a cloud. He bounced onto another rainbow, slid down and bounced up to another cloud, giggling like a maniac.

"Oh man, that looks awesome," I said.

Suzy honked at me and stamped her front feet, but I ignored her. I shoved the rest of my cookie in my mouth, bounced in place a couple times to pick up some momentum, then sprang up onto a cloud. Pettikin waved at me from one cloud over. Laughing, I waved back. Two rainbows appeared next to our clouds.

"OK, ready?" I said "On three! One, two... three!"

We both jumped and slid down our rainbows, bouncing on the soft trampoline ground and up to new clouds.

I had never seen Pettikin so happy. He was laughing, and his eyes were shining.

"Let's go again—race you!" I said.

I scrambled to the edge of my cloud searching for a rainbow. I heard both Suzy and Sunshine clucking at me as I slid down and sprang up to another cloud. It felt like my heart skipped a beat. Was there something I was supposed to do? Well, whatever it was it could wait.

Pettikin and I continued our game of cloud-slide until we got tired, then leapt up to a passing cloud and laid down on its surface. It was as soft as a feather bed. I sighed. Pettikin stretched luxuriously.

I propped myself up on my elbows. From here we could see the whole world. The musical plants beneath us gradually tapered off into a strip of pink and white beach that bordered a vast lake or sea. The water was a deep, dark blue, with delicate wavelets that rippled across its surface and sparkled in the light. Groves of pink and purple trees with large golden leaves adorned the water's edge.

I felt a strange feeling in my chest again, like something was wringing my heart between its hands. Was I missing something obvious? I gazed at the water, and my thoughts slowed down.

A diamond shaped web of white light glowed in the center of the sea, perpendicular to its surface.

My heart started pounding erratically. I felt a little dizzy.

Pettikin's eyes were closed, a huge smile on his face.

"Pettikin, can you understand what the alpacas are saying?"

"Who cares? They've been hyper ever since we got here."

I giggled, but felt a small, sharp pain in my chest. My grin faded a little as I saw the alpacas running in small circles below us and humming.

"No, but seriously, what are they saying?"

Pettikin sighed and sat up. "They want us to come follow them. They say we have to get to the next Gateway."

The next Gateway. My chest tightened. "Why would we want to do that?"

"I don't know," Pettikin yawned and stretched out again. "I think we should just stay here forever."

I loved seeing him this happy. In fact, I was pretty sure I loved this little gnome. I felt a warm glow in my heart, and then it was as if some bubble around it burst, and a huge wave of warmth and emotion engulfed me. I gasped.

"Pettikin, I remember now! We have to get to the Gateway because it's the only way to get you home—to Arcorn and your Guardian!"

As soon as I said the name of his world Pettikin gasped and sat up.

"How could I forget about my own world? What are we doing? What were we thinking?"

I was already to the edge of the cloud searching for a rainbow. "I think it's fairly safe to say that we *weren't* thinking. Man, the alpacas are going to kill us." A rainbow appeared, and I slid down it to the ground. Pettikin followed behind me and bounced from the ground up to my shoulder.

Suzy and Sunshine bounded over to us. As soon as they stopped, Suzy spat in my face and snorted.

"She says from now on you should listen to her when you're in the other worlds."

"Yeah, I got that," I said ruefully as I wiped my cheek.

I opened the pack on Sunshine's back and pulled out two cookies and Professor Theopolous' map for this world. I handed Pettikin's cookie to him and held mine in my mouth as I unfolded the map.

This one was even weirder than the one from the red world. It was just random arcs and wavy lines oriented every which way on the page.

"I give up," I said, finishing my cookie and refolding the map. "Is this your world Sunshine? Can you lead us to the Gateway?"

She hummed as I stuffed the map into her pack and, when she was sure we were following, began bouncing in time to the music down a path through the musical forest.

We bounced along after her, easily keeping pace,

just as we had in the red world. Here no buzzy energy built up inside me, only a gentle, peaceful feeling. The flowers in the woods all turned their faces to follow us as we walked, and the trees and reeds swayed in time to the music. Rainbow colored rabbits and squirrels darted around, humming the melody as they gathered nuts and berries from the ground. More than once, I found myself fighting against the urge to simply stop and stay there forever.

The music of the forest gradually softened, and we could see the lake up ahead, glittering on the horizon. Once we reached the beach, the music faded into the background and was replaced by the gentle lapping of water against the shore. I bent down to pick up a handful of the sparkling pink and white sand. Like on the red world, they were small, perfectly round beads. Unlike the red world, the beads were not rubbery, but hard like crystals and filled with light. Each one glowed like a tiny sun.

I dropped the sand and gazed out at the water. The light reflecting off the surface was so bright I had to shade my eyes with one hand. When we were in the clouds, the Gateway hadn't seemed that far from shore, but from here, it was just a tiny diamond on the horizon. I could swim, but I wasn't sure if I could swim that far, and I had no idea if Pettikin could swim. His roly-poly figure and stubby limbs didn't seem like they'd be suited for it.

Sunshine hummed.

"She said that this is as far as she can go, and that we should follow Suzy to the next world."

I reached up and patted Sunshine's head and smooched her cheek.

"Thank you Sunshine—sorry we were so stupid before." She hummed and pressed her nose against my face.

Suzy walked a few feet inland to a grove of trees. She sniffed the ground, grabbed something with her teeth, and pulled backwards. It was a large, golden leaf, almost as big as her. She dragged it to the water's edge and honked at me.

"She says we should go get a leaf."

"OK," I was confused but not in the mood to disobey her a second time. I walked over to the grove of trees. Underneath it was a large pile of jurassic-sized golden leaves which had apparently fallen from the trees.

"Man, these are huge. How big do I need?"

Suzy hummed.

"As big as we can find, she says it has to hold us."

"*Hold* us?" I turned around. Suzy stepped onto her leaf with her front hooves, pushed off with her back then hopped the rest of the way onto the leaf as it floated out into the water.

"Oh boy." My pulse quickened. I rummaged through the pile of leaves, until I saw one at the bottom that seemed like it would be big enough. I yanked it free. It was the shape of a large teardrop, maybe four feet across at its widest part and six feet long. It was about two inches thick and curled upwards at the edges. Whatever material it was made of was hard but not dense. It wasn't heavy, but its size made it awkward for me to carry, so I dragged it to the water's edge by its stem like Suzy had.

Suzy drifted out to sea, carried by some unseen current.

I pushed the leaf into the water. It floated, so that was good. I crouched next to it, holding on to the stem so it wouldn't float away. My sneakers got wet as water lapped over them.

"Want to get on Pettikin?"

He climbed back onto my shoulder, and then dropped down onto the leaf. It wobbled slightly but didn't tip over. He moved to the bow and sat down with his legs out in front of him in a V. The HMS Gnome.

I put my left foot gingerly on the leaf, pushed off from the shore with my right and pulled it up quickly. I flailed my arms and almost lost my balance as the leaf wobbled and floated out into the lake, so I quickly eased myself down and sat cross-legged. I wondered how Suzy could remain standing without losing her balance. She was already several yards in front of us, as if she had been surfing her whole life.

I dangled one hand over the side of our boat. The water felt warm. I wondered if I should paddle or try to steer, but after a few minutes I realized it wouldn't be necessary. Whatever current we were riding was carrying us directly toward the Gateway. A gentle breeze blew over the water and lifted my hair from my face. I closed my eyes, feeling warm and light and happy, and lost track of time. The overwhelming desire to stay here forever returned. As I was slipping into that mindset, I felt another stab in my chest and opened my eyes.

The Gateway loomed in front of us, as tall as a tree. I squinted up at the web of white light. For a minute, I thought we would just sail right through it to the next world, but, when we were about five feet away, the current shifted and began circling it instead. We joined Suzy in a slow orbit around the Gateway.

"So how do we get through?"

Suzy hummed.

"She says you're the Gatekeeper. You have to get us through."

"Oh man." I stood up, wobbling unsteadily. Could we just swim over to it?

Suzy hummed again.

"She suggests you use your other sight."

"Oh. Right." Would I ever get the hang of this stuff?

I took a deep breath and relaxed my mind. Everything became luminous. Something shimmered around the Gateway – something that had shifted the current. I concentrated as hard as I could, and slowly, it came into focus.

The Gateway was inside a spherical structure made

of smaller interconnecting geometric shapes, like a giant golf ball, but translucent instead of white. I reached over the side of the boat and paddled, trying to get us closer without crashing into it. Pettikin went to the stern to help steer, like a little rudder. We drifted up beside the sphere, and I reached out for it.

Its interconnecting blocks were as cold and hard as stone and at least a foot thick. I rapped it once with my knuckles then had to shake my hand to take the sting out of my fingers. It didn't feel fragile, like glass, but solid, like rock.

I put both hands on it searching for any type of entrance, but the lattice was solid. I got down on my hands and knees and peered into the water. The sphere extended below the surface, so no underwater entrance. We circled the entire structure once before I gave up that approach.

I put my hands on my hips. Had we come this far only for me to blow it? Getting around the warriors seemed easy compared to this. How was I supposed to move a wall of stone? Suzy chewed her cud with her eyes closed. At least she didn't seem worried—only like she planned to be here for a while.

Pettikin stood up and wobbled over to me. He put a hand on my leg, and I felt a flutter in my chest.

The sphere rippled.

Huh? Had I imagined that? I reached out and put my hand on it again, but it was still solid.

Pettikin didn't say anything, but the smile he'd had up in the clouds was gone. He seemed lost and lonely, and if I didn't think of something soon, he would stay that way. The feeling in my chest was almost wrenching. The sphere rippled again. I was sure of it this time. I felt, as well as saw, a tiny wave across its surface. A small beam of pink light inside the structure near my hand bounced back and forth between the outer walls of the crystalline block.

I shifted my weight on our leaf to steady myself, put my hands against the sphere, and closed my eyes. I thought about Pettikin and how much I loved him. I thought about everyone I loved back home—my parents and Andie and Socrates. The fluttering in my chest almost made me dizzy.

I thought about Aunt May. Was she watching over us now, from some other place? Could she help me get Pettikin home? I thought about her friends, Mrs. Widgit, Bob, and even grumpy Professor Theopolous, who already seemed like family, even though I barely knew them.

I could feel the stone rippling under my hands.

I focused harder. I thought about the alpacas, holding Sunshine in my arms and feeding her from a bottle when she was a baby. I thought about Vala, how I had felt when I first saw him, how it felt when he smiled at me. I thought about the moment when he had touched my chest. The feeling in my heart welled up and crashed over me like a wave of soft, white light.

"Allie. Allie!" Pettikin was tugging on my leg

I opened my eyes. Hundreds of beams of pink, blue and golden light ricocheted through the crystalline structure, softening it. I took my hands off and stepped back. When the streams of light crossed, they magnified each other, moving faster and filling the structure with vibrating light. The surface of the sphere undulated and exploded in a beam of light so bright, I had to cover my eyes with my arm. When I lowered my arm, the crystal had evaporated. A shower of pink, blue and gold sparks hung in the air where it had been, then slowly drifted down to the water and dissolved like snowflakes. The Gateway was free.

The breeze felt cool against my face, and I realized there were tears running down my cheeks. I wiped them away hastily, embarrassed.

"Well, I totally don't believe that worked," I said.

Suzy hummed, possibly in agreement.

Pettikin hugged my leg. "You did it! You found the key!"

"I think *you* were the key this time," I said. The current shifted and was pulling us around to the front of the Gateway. I sat back down cross-legged at the back of our leaf. Pettikin ran excitedly to the front.

Suzy's leaf got there first. She ducked her head and disappeared through the Gateway.

The web of light towered over us.

"Well, here we go again."

I closed my eyes, and my mind dissolved.

15

Light. Blinding white light, like it reflected off of snow. I cringed and lifted a hand to shield my eyes. My arm was translucent—a faint, pinkish-white glow. Pettikin and Suzy were flickering apparitions standing next to me. I opened my mouth to say something, but no sound came out.

We can't talk here... it's too noisy for this world. The thought was faint in my mind, but I knew it came from Pettikin. The silence here was so deep it was like anti-sound—like we had moved through a sound continuum and come out the other side of it.

Slowly my eyes adjusted to the light, and the physical forms of the world came into focus. The entire world was golden, and even the ground was glowing, light radiating out from underneath it, as if we were standing on the surface of a sun. A massive mesa, a huge imposing slab with steep sides that shimmered like rosy quartz, rose in the distance. A shining city of pyramids and domes perched on top of it. I wanted to get out Professor Theopolous' map but wasn't sure I would be able to. It would probably be a useless blank page anyway.

I felt really out of place—afraid that if I moved I

might break something fragile or disturb the profound silence. Suzy's apparition flickered and started floating down a long, golden path that lead toward the mesa. Pettikin shut his eyes. His image wavered, almost disappeared completely, and then began floating after Suzy, slowly at first but with gaining speed.

I tried to take a step forward, but my legs, despite being mere phantom legs, felt like they were bolted to the ground. Frustrated, I watched Pettikin and Suzy getting further and further away. I closed my eyes and willed myself to move forward but felt like I was pushing against a brick wall. I took a deep breath and tried to calm my mind. Finally, as if my emergency brake had suddenly been released, I jerked and began gliding forward. I felt off kilter, and my progress down the path was wobbly and uncoordinated compared to Suzy and Pettikin, but at least I was moving.

I fought to keep my mind calm and to use the 'other sight' that Vala had given me. It seemed to be the only way I could see anything in this world. Pastel yellow and pink trees lined the path we were floating down, and ghostlike figures with round, featureless heads, flowing cape-like bodies, and tiny arms drifted through the air next to us. They looked like Vala did in his ghost form, but they were different colors, less bright, and more ethereal. Some were carrying large gourd-shaped objects that reminded me of water jugs. They stopped and turned toward me as I passed, holding the objects they were carrying up and away from me, as if they thought I might be dangerous. They were so delicate I felt like a grotesque, snot-oozing goblin traipsing along next to them. I wanted to apologize for intruding in their world, but didn't know how.

Most of the beings we passed seemed to be heading toward the mesa and the diamond shaped web of white light at its base. Was this the Gateway to the next world? It seemed too easy.

Suzy and Pettikin arrived before I did and waited

for me. I wobbled to a stop next to them and glanced around nervously, but, although some of the beings seemed to be watching us, they didn't try to stop us. Suzy turned and dissolved through the web of light, and Pettikin glided through after her.

A pink ghost hovered next to me, its featureless head tilted to one side, observing me. I took a breath, closed my eyes, and willed myself forward through the Gateway.

It was like stepping into a vacuum tube. My stomach immediately dropped, and I was sucked rapidly upwards. A cold wind whipped silently past my head and down my body. I clinched my eyes shut and gritted my teeth. Just when I thought I couldn't take it anymore, I felt a jolt and was pushed forwards. I opened my eyes and wobbled precariously until I got my bearings.

We were in the city on top of the mesa. The pyramids and domes which had seemed so small from a distance towered above my head. Some of them were silver or gold, but most were clear or opaque and hard, like they were made of frosted glass or crystal. They were arranged in long, diagonal rows radiating out from a central dome, with wide streets of pinkish-white paving stones between them. Beautiful glowing trees and small gardens of flowers woven from strands of pastel light decorated the paths and areas between the buildings. Just a few yards from us was a silver fountain gilded with a delicate gold leaf pattern. White and rose colored light bubbled up from some unseen well and flowed silently down the sides of its broad basin.

Ghosts were everywhere now, dissolving in and out of the building walls and floating down the streets. Some were gathered in the open areas along the street, a group of them surrounding a central figure, like a teacher and students. Others were off by themselves filling their luminous jugs from the fountain of light, or picking soft orbs of fruit from the branches of the trees. One being was sitting on a bench under a tree by himself. He dipped an arm into a large basin filled with molten light, and pulled out a long, taffy-like strand. With his other arm he cut the rope off and deftly rolled the light into a ball. He stretched and massaged the light between the ends of his arms until he had molded it into a figure that resembled a tiny dog. He placed the figure down on the ground, and it came to life, scampering off down the street. I gaped at him, but he seemed unaware of me, already pulling another rope of light out from the basin. Down the street, the little dog of light jumped up and down next to a ghost being until it bent down and patted its head.

I felt Pettikin in my mind, *"Suzy says we need to go."*

I pulled my attention away, and we drifted down the street toward the giant central dome. A now-familiar network of interwoven lines of light at its base formed the shape of two ornately decorated doors. Two tall, white ghosts stood on either side of the doors like palace guards. They inclined their heads toward us as we approached but didn't stop us from going in. When I passed them, they looked up at each other, and I wondered if they were laughing at me.

I felt just the tiniest ripple as I stepped through the Gateway doors, like stepping through a curtain. We were in a large hall that reached the entire height of the dome, which must have been at least thirty feet at its apex. The ceiling was pitch black. Stars, planets, and galaxies turned slowly in it as if it were a window out into the universe. As I watched, the picture gradually zoomed in on a particular galaxy then readjusted itself for a few seconds. Then it zoomed in on a particular solar system and readjusted itself again. After zooming in on each planet in the solar system, the entire display went dark and a new universe appeared, starting the same process over again.

The walls were stone blocks lit by bright, white, egg-shaped crystals that rested on narrow pedestals of different heights spaced evenly around the room. Down the center of the hall, two rows of tall, golden thrones faced each other, six on each side and about twelve feet apart. A golden or white being, brighter and more intense than the beings that floated outside, sat on each throne. They sat upright, their phantom arms resting on the armrests of their thrones, and gazed up at the galaxies that turned in the ceiling above us. That is, until I drifted backwards into a torch, which appeared to be the one solid thing in this ephemeral world. The torch wobbled precariously, causing weird shadows to leap around the room. Twelve heads turned toward me. Oops. I willed my arms up and tried to steady the torch until it finally settled in its place.

Suzy gazed at Pettikin for a few moments from under long, dark lashes. Then I felt Pettikin speaking in my mind.

"This is the Council of Guardians." Even in my mind Pettikin sounded awed.

"What does that mean?" I glanced nervously around at the figures, then up at the ceiling where another universe faded and a new one appeared.

"Some Guardians roam through the universes and take different forms, performing different tasks on different worlds, like my Guardian or your Vala. The Council of Guardians is a group of Guardians that remains here to watch over the universes and direct things from a higher level. Sometimes they trade places, and a Guardian who was on the Council will return to the worlds, or one who was in the worlds may come back to serve on the Council for a while. We learn about the Council when we are small, but no one I know has ever seen them."

The Guardian closest to us turned to Pettikin.

"He says they know who you are and why you're here, but they can't show us the final Gateway or open it for you."

"Then what are we supposed to do?"

Pettikin seemed to be speaking telepathically with the Guardian.

"The world we're in now exists in between all the other

worlds—all of the Gateways are here. We have to find the final Gateway, the one that will take us out of the realm of the forbidden worlds and into the realm of the higher worlds, and get through it ourselves."

Except for the torches, the hall was empty. The vast universe spun slowly above us, and twelve golden heads turned toward us with silent curiosity and possible bemusement.

"But I don't see a Gateway here—I don't know what to do."

The Guardian that addressed Pettikin turned his head toward me. I felt a warmth spreading through my forehead, behind and above my eyes, and I suddenly felt very happy, like I did when Vala was around. I felt something friendly, a gentle humor coming from the Guardian.

I gazed up the ceiling again, and watched as one universe faded away and another appeared.

"Pettikin," I thought slowly, *"could it be some type of Gateway?"*

"I think," he hesitated, *"that all of the Gateways in all of the universes must be there somewhere."*

"So from all of the Gateways in all of the universes we just have to find the correct one? How is that even possible?"

As we were speaking, or, rather, thinking, the universe we were currently viewing zoomed in on Galaxy, then a solar system, then a planet. From there, one by one a series of Gateways flashed past—webs of different colored light woven into diamonds, squares, hexagons. They flashed by so quickly it created a strobe effect in the room—red, blue, white, gold—and then they were gone. A new universe appeared, zoomed in on a new planet, and the process repeated.

I felt a pressure in my head, like I was trying to understand a subject that was too advanced for me, and the repeated strobe effect was making me dizzy.

Suzy floated forward and nudged my cheek, a

faint, feather-like touch.

"*Suzy says that it's your mind that's making the display do that.*"

"My *mind?*" I was incredulous. "*You're telling me* I'm *controlling what's being displayed?*"

As my mind raced, the picture zoomed out again and spun toward another solar system, another planet.

"*Yes, and she says it's not the right way. You're trying to think about which Gateway you need, and the only way your thinking mind can do it is to randomly run through every Gateway in the universe.*"

I had to admit that was my thought process, and it did seem to be what the display was doing. "*OK, well, then we just need some more information. We need to go about this more systematically, find a way to narrow down the choices. I mean maybe the Gateway is on your planet, Pettikin, on Arcorn—that would make sense right?*"

"*I don't know Allie—I don't know if it works that way…*"

But the projection had already shifted, was honing in on a golden white sun, and a blue green planet similar to Earth. A brilliant series of Gateways flashed past and then were gone, replaced by a second of complete blackness.

I felt frustrated. "*Even if one of those was the Gateway I wouldn't know which one it was.*"

I felt a brief, sharp pressure in my mind, which I was pretty sure was an alpaca snort.

"*Suzy says as long as you are thinking with your logical mind, you will never be able to find the right Gateway, except as a freak accident. You need to use the higher part of your mind, something above thought.*"

"*But I don't even know what that* means!"

"*Suzy says you do know and to stop being so impatient and try to calm your mind.*"

Scolded by an alpaca. Again. A couple of the Guardians seemed to be conversing telepathically. Were they amused or questioning Vala's choice for a

Gatekeeper?

I turned toward the display above us, sighed, and closed my eyes. My mind was still trying to come up with some algorithm for finding the right Gateway. I felt like I had to physically wrench it away. What else could I think about? For some reason Vala appeared in my mind. I wondered what he was doing right now—was he still on Earth somehow keeping the Gateways open for us? Did he know where we were now and what we were doing? He told me if I needed his help he would help me. He must know which was the right Gateway.

"*Allie, look.*"

I opened my eyes. The display had returned. A new universe was overhead but turning much more slowly. Afraid that I would start thinking again, I closed my eyes.

"*OK, Vala, you're a Guardian, and it's obvious to me now that I have no idea who you are or what you're capable of. But I know you must know where the Gateway is, so please, if you can, show it to me. Otherwise poor Pettikin will be stuck on Earth forever.*"

Thinking about Vala, I felt my mind grow lighter. Somehow everything that seemed so impossible just a few seconds before seemed silly. The frustration disappeared from my mind and was replaced with a flood of golden light that washed down the length of my body. I felt warm and happy, almost giddy.

"*Allie*, look!"

I opened my eyes, startled, feeling dazed.

"*Look* up!" Pettikin sounded excited now.

I raised my eyes to the ceiling. Above me was a shining diamond made of interwoven strands of light. The display was completely still, frozen on this one Gateway.

"*Well, huh. You think that's it?*"

"*Do we have something else to try?*" I wasn't sure if Pettikin's question was innocent or if hanging around with a cynical earthling was starting to rub off on him.

Now the only problem was our candidate

186

Gateway, assuming it was a real Gateway and not just a projection, was a good thirty feet above our heads.

"So how do we get through it?"

Pettikin hesitated. *"I—"* he started, but then closed his eyes, and pressed his palms together, almost as if he were praying. After a few moments, to my surprise, he began to rise slowly through the air, floating up toward the Gateway.

"How are you doing that?"

Pettikin didn't answer. He seemed to be concentrating as hard as he could. To my alarm I also noticed that his ghost form was becoming fainter the higher he went. If he went much further, he would disappear completely.

I felt a little panicky. Was I supposed to do that too? What would happen when we reached the top? Would we disappear completely before we made it through the Gateway? Twelve golden faces and one ghost-like alpaca watched me. For some reason, I felt almost more resistance to this than I had to standing up to the warriors, but what other choice did I have?

I closed my eyes and tried to concentrate. I guessed that moving upwards might not be all that different from moving forwards, but I guessed wrong. No matter how hard, I strained I couldn't will myself to move upwards instead of forwards. I opened my eyes. Pettikin had reached the ceiling and was barely visible, his body surrounded by an orb of soft white light. When I heard his thought in my mind it was very faint.

"I can't go any further without you Allie. You have to open the Gateway."

I swallowed and closed my eyes and tried to concentrate again, but nothing was happening. If anything, I now felt so agitated that I wasn't sure I could even move forward anymore. Frustrated, I opened my eyes.

The Guardian nearest me beckoned to me with one arm. I somehow managed to float over to her. She leaned forward and gently touched the center of my forehead.

A wave of light washed down me so powerfully that I felt scared. Unlike the warm, happy light I felt when I was thinking about Vala, this light felt like a power jet that was washing out everything heavy in my being and pushing me upwards. Wave after wave of light rushed down me, making me feel lighter and lighter, pushing down into the ground. I began to sail upwards.

With each passing wave I felt simultaneously lighter and more terrified. It was happening too fast. I knew that soon there would be nothing left to wash away, nothing left of me, only this light.

"Stop, wait, I can't do this…"

A strange voice in my mind, not Pettikin's. The Guardian's? It wasn't talking in words, but I felt it sending me waves of reassurance and peace, saying that everything would be OK.

I was almost to Pettikin. The Gateway loomed above me and, as I drew near it, suddenly came alive, as if someone flipped a switch and all its filaments glowed. My body was almost gone, only a faint white light, like a mist, remained.

The Guardian's voice telling me to let go.

"No wait…"

After a blinding flash of light and a sudden rush of energy, I felt myself pulled up through the Gateway, and I dissolved.

I saw nothing, only darkness extending in every direction. Where was I? I felt some type of consciousness returning, some semblance of a body around me. I opened my eyes. I was drifting through darkness. I couldn't see anything.

"Pettikin?"

"I'm here Allie." His voice sounded distant and hollow.

"Where are you? I can't see you. I can't see anything—where are we?"

"I think…" Pettikin's voice trailed off. I had the uncomfortable feeling there was something he didn't want to say.

In the distance, a small circle of light appeared.

"Pettikin do you see that light?"

"I see it Allie!" Pettikin sounded relieved. "We need to go there."

The light grew larger, whether because we were moving toward it or because it was moving toward us I wasn't sure. I could see Pettikin's form next to me now. It was faint but growing stronger the closer we came to the light. I could see my body returning as well.

Relief washed over me, and I focused as hard as I could on the light. I felt a sense of urgency, like we needed to get there quickly.

"Hurry, Allie," Pettikin clearly felt the same, which worried me.

From my left a dark shadow, darker than even the blackness of the void around us, flew past my face. I recoiled and put my hands up to my head.

"What was that?"

"Allie…" Pettikin sounded scared, and now I was, too.

From my right, another shadow and a cold and clammy wind whipped past my face. Something brushed my cheek. A bat?

I flailed my arms and screamed.

"What are they? Get away!"

Another one from the right, another from the left. Like rips in the ether, I heard a noise like distant thunder, growing louder and louder until it became an ominous roar. Thousands of black bats came spiraling down toward me in a great cyclone of icy black wind that engulfed me. I could feel the bats tearing at my face and arms as I tried desperately to beat them away.

Pettikin shrieked.

"Pettikin!" I stretched my hand out toward him, tiny scratches appearing on my arms as the bats whipped past. He reached for me, but before I could grasp his hand, I felt an icy stab through my neck. I screamed.

It felt like something reached through my skin and was wrapping itself around my throat—an icy blackness with an iron grip unlike anything I had ever felt.

"No, no! Get it off me!" I shrieked.

"Allie!" Pettikin's voice sounded desperate. I caught a glimpse of him through the whirlwind of void bats. He had his palms pressed together again, and his eyes were closed as if in deep concentration. A soft orb of light blue energy surrounded his body. The bats beat down on it, but the sphere deflected them, shooting off tiny sparks of electricity each time one touched it.

The thing in my neck pulled tighter. I reached up my hands to pull it off, but there was nothing to grab onto. Was it completely inside me? This was so gross. More bats dove toward me, tearing the skin on my cheeks and arms. I tried desperately to fight them off, but each time I moved, the thing in my neck pulled tighter, shooting icy hot flames through my body. I wasn't going to make it.

"Vala!" I screamed desperately. The being tightened its grip on my throat so I could barely speak. "Vala, help!" It pulled so tightly that I could no longer speak or breathe. I felt my consciousness starting to fade.

And then light.

Brilliant white light pierced through the darkness, lighting up every corner of the void. The bats emitted a hideous, high pitched shriek as they withered and dissolved in the light. The thing in my neck loosened its grip, and I could breathe. The light swirled around me, and I felt whatever was in my neck withdraw. My eyes grew heavy with exhaustion. I thought I saw Vala in his human form, felt human arms around me. In the distance I saw Pettikin. He was OK. I heard him calling for me, but I couldn't answer.

I closed my eyes, and everything went dark.

16

I was lying against something hard, voices talking softly around me. My head pounded and my body felt stiff and sore. With enormous effort, I pried my eyes open. Everything looked as if it were under water. I blinked until my vision cleared. I was lying on the ground. Familiar Ohio grass and mud. I pushed myself up to a sitting position like an ancient, arthritic dog. From the corner of my eyes I saw a dim flashing.

"Allie!" Andie came running over. "Are you OK?"

"What happened?" I rubbed my forehead with the heel of my hand. "Where's Pettikin?"

"I'm here, Allie." Pettikin appeared from behind me, wringing his hands. Andie, Mrs. Widgit, and the Professor were standing in front of me. I tried to orient myself. We were in the yard next to the cottage, just in front of the Gateway. The faint flashing continued.

Pettikin put his arms around my neck and hugged me. "Oh, Allie, are you OK?"

I closed my eyes, pulled him tightly against my neck, then set him down on the ground. "Yeah, I'm OK. Are you OK?"

His eyes welled with tears. "Oh Allie, I used a

protective charm, and I was able to hold them off, but I couldn't keep them from grabbing you."

"It's OK, Pettikin. I'm supposed to be helping you not the other way around," I said ruefully. "Although maybe you should teach me that protective charm," I added, rubbing my neck, which still felt cold. "Where's Vala?" I peered around anxiously.

"He's right over there." Andie pointed toward the Gateway, but Vala wasn't there. "Hey, where did he go?"

I felt a horrible stab of guilt. I had totally failed. He probably didn't even want to talk to me. The Nexus Gateway was dark and silent again — two old beech trees in Ohio, nothing more.

"He'll be back soon," Mrs. Widgit said quietly.

I felt miserable. Pettikin edged closer to me.

"We failed, Allie," he whispered. "We failed the Guardian."

I hung my head and stared at the ground. The strange flashing from the corner of my eyes continued— blue, red, blue. I turned my head toward the main house.

"Is that a police car?"

Andie's voice was grim. "You think you failed. We *totally* blew it."

I had been so caught up in my own drama that I hadn't even registered what was going on around me. Now I saw that Andie's hair was a wreck, and a small scratch trailed down her left cheek. Mrs. Widget's hair was also disheveled, and Professor Theopolous' monocle was missing. Socks was lying under one of the Gateway beech trees panting, as if he had been running. A police car with its flashers on was parked in the driveway up at the main house, and my father was leaning through the driver's side window talking to the officer inside.

"What's going on? What happened here?"

Andie took a deep breath. "OK, here goes. Everything was going just fine for a good five minutes after you left. We were all just standing around, bored, waiting for you. Then, suddenly, that cop car pulls into your driveway with its lights flashing. Your dad swore, some minister by the way, and started running up toward the house. While he was running, he yelled something up at Vala, and Vala did something that I think kept the people at the house from being able to see what was going on down here." Andie glanced at Mrs. Widgit for confirmation.

"That's right dear—he put up a shield around us. You can still see it if you look closely."

I squinted my eyes. I could see just the faintest ripple in the air extending in a dome-like shape around us, the Gateway, and the cottage.

Andie continued. "So, even we don't know what's going on up there at the moment because, almost as soon as your dad left, Mr. Cutter appeared. Only, he wasn't like normal creepy Mr. Cutter, he was like some über-creepy Mr. Cutter, with this black haze around him and kind of a... a...possessed aura I guess."

I stared at her.

"I know. It gets weirder. This haze or fog around him, it started to...to *materialize* or something, like these creatures started growing out of it. They were sort of like, miniature dinosaurs or something, that's all I can think of to describe them. Like turkey-sized black velociraptors with red eyes and claws, which doesn't sound that bad until you've suddenly got four or five of them attacking you."

Pettikin was squeezing my arm so tightly it was cutting off the circulation.

"So I'm trying to get to Mr. Cutter so I can get rid of him, but instead, I'm covered in miniature dinosaurs..."

"Sslorcs, dear," Mrs. Widgit interjected.

"OK, fine, I'm covered in sslorcs, so I start yelling *'Please go away'* at them, and it worked, but I could only dissolve one at a time that way, and Mrs. Widgit and the Professor were being attacked, as well. Fortunately, Vala was able to dissolve any that got too close to the Gateway just by directing his attention toward them, which I think is something you might want to keep in mind for the future, by the way. But I got the feeling that it was hard for him to do that while trying to keep the Gateway open for you, and that it would have been better if we could have handled the situation. Unfortunately, it seemed like Mr. Cutter could regenerate the sslorcs almost as fast as I could dissolve them, and one of them started running directly toward the Gateway. Socks started chasing it, and I yelled up at Vala for help. Vala dissolved the sslorc, but poor Socks had too much momentum and went right through the Gateway."

At the sound of his name Socrates' ears pricked up. His eyes were half closed as he panted.

"At that point Vala changed into his normal—well his *human*—form and jumped through the Gateway to go get Socks, but that left the Gateway unguarded except for us. So now, all of the sslorcs that were left made a beeline for it. It was a madhouse. I sounded like a complete moron shouting '*Please go away, please go away*' over and over, Professor T was beating sslorcs with his umbrella, and I swear I saw Mrs. Widgit put one in her purse at one point."

"Oh, thanks for reminding me!" Mrs. Widgit unslung her tote bag, grabbed it by the handles and slammed it back and forth repeatedly into the ground. Then she jumped up and down on top of it until the bag gave off a tiny burp, and a puff of black smoke wafted up from it.

"Hmph!" Mrs. Widgit nodded with satisfaction and re-slung the bag across her shoulder.

Andie shook her head. "So despite being the not-ready-for-primetime crew, we actually stopped most of the sslorcs, but unfortunately, one of them got through the Gateway just as Vala returned carrying Socks. He obliterated the sslorcs that were left, at which point I managed to get rid of Mr. Cutter before he could create any more. But at that point, the damage was done, and the Gateway seemed to be losing power or flickering or something. Vala said, 'I have to go help Allie,' and jumped through just before it went completely dark. He returned with the alpacas, you, and Pettikin just a couple minutes ago. Bob's down at the barn with the alpacas now."

I put one hand up to my head, which was throbbing. My neck felt stiff and sore.

"But all that sounds like it only took a few minutes. Why are you all still here? Why is the police car still here? What day is it?"

Andie glanced at Mrs. Widgit and the Professor. "It's still Saturday, Allie. You were only gone for a few minutes—less than an hour."

Less than an hour? How could that be? It seemed like we had spent days in the other dimensions.

Andie was watching my face. "What happened to you in there, Al?"

I opened my mouth and then shut it again. My throat felt dry. "It's a long story," I said finally. "But obviously the fact that Pettikin is still here means I totally failed, and I'm not going to be a Gatekeeper anytime soon. We never should have gone."

Andie shifted her feet nervously. I lay down on the ground and stared up at the sky. Normal blue sky, normal clouds. No rainbow slides or trampolines. Pettikin sat down in his tri-pod stance next to my head.

Professor Theopolous eased himself down with some effort on my other side. Was he going to gloat? Tell me how he knew from the start this would never work? He crossed his legs and folded his hands in his lap, resting his forearms on his knees. For a long time he didn't say anything.

"Do you want to know who you really are, Allie?" he asked finally in a low voice. His eyes were fierce and dark and made me want to look away.

"Whenever you have failed, when you are lying on your back in the mud, completely and utterly defeated—"

I sucked in my breath.

"—you are the person who gets back up."

He stared into my eyes for a moment without smiling. Then he pushed himself up stiffly and started walking to the cottage. I exhaled slowly and watched his retreating figure.

Mrs. Widgit smiled at me sympathetically, then followed him.

"Well come on, Allie!" Andie came over and held out her hand to me, sounding a little desperate.

Pettikin rested one hand lightly on my forehead without saying anything.

"OK," I said finally. "Let's go back."

I grabbed Andie's hand and let her pull me up. Pettikin climbed up to my shoulder, and we walked back to the cottage together.

17

I excused myself to the bathroom because it was the one place I was sure I could be alone for a few minutes. I closed the door behind me, sank back against it and closed my eyes. I could hear the clatter of dishes and everyone talking in the kitchen. I took a few deep breaths and walked to the sink. My hair was a disaster. I had small scratches on my face and a kind of crazy expression in my eyes that didn't seem like me somehow. I pushed my sleeves up, turned on the cold water faucet, and splashed handfuls of water on my face and throat, rubbing it around to the back of my neck. I straightened up and let the water run over my hands and wrists for a few seconds, then rubbed it up to my elbows. Worried this was going to turn into a full on sponge bath, I turned off the faucet and groped around for something to dry myself off with. I rubbed my face and arms with a rough hand towel that was hanging next to the sink, then ran my fingers through my hair a few times. I put my palms on the counter and leaned toward the mirror to check my reflection again. I hadn't washed off the crazy expression, and now, my cheeks and skin were bright red as well. I sighed.

I left the safety of the bathroom for the kitchen. Mrs. Widgit was brewing coffee in an old French Press she found in Aunt May's pantry. Cookies were set out on a plate on the kitchen table, but I found I no longer had any appetite for them. Professor Theopolous sat at the table perusing a book he had taken from the living room. Andie sat next to him, her hands wrapped around a mug. Socrates was lying in the corner of the kitchen, and the tip of Pettikin's hat was visible from behind the bulk of his body. Bob was nowhere to be found, and I wondered if he was out at the barn with the alpacas.

The front door banged open, and Dad came rushing into the kitchen.

"Allie, are you back? Are you OK? What happened?" He walked toward me like he wanted to hug me, but then stopped short, unsure.

"I'm OK, Dad. We're both back," I pointed toward Pettikin, assuming that information was enough to let him know that I had failed.

"Ah. Well, with everything that went on here, I didn't figure it was going to be smooth sailing for you either," he rubbed his neck, glancing at me curiously, but didn't say anything more.

I was grateful that he spared me a load of Parental Concern. I didn't think I could handle it on top of everything else.

"What was going on up at the house, Dan?" Mrs. Widgit turned briefly from rinsing dishes in the sink. Professor Theopolous closed his book and set it to the side.

Dad groaned. "Oh it was just Mr. Cutter. Apparently, he went to the police to press assault charges against you two." He pointed a finger at me and then Andie, peering down his nose at us with mock severity.

Andie and I protested at exactly the same time.

"Assault charges?!"

"What the—"

"Fortunately Chief Miller is an old friend of mine and recognized how ridiculous it sounded, considering you girls have never been in trouble. He decided to come talk to me first. I convinced him there was nothing to the story, especially considering that Mr. Cutter was the one trespassing. The whole thing was bizarre, and about halfway through the conversation, it dawned on me that it might just be an elaborate diversion."

"Diverting attention from the sslorcs trying to get through the Gateway down here," Andie said.

Dad listened carefully as Andie retold the story of what had gone down dirt-side while Pettikin and I were in the dimensions.

Mrs. Widgit handed me a warm mug and steered me toward the table.

"Sit!" She pulled back a chair for me.

I sat, and sipped. She had mixed a little coffee into some cocoa to make a sort of mocha for me. The sharp, bitter taste of the coffee cut through the numbness I felt since we returned and made me feel a little better.

Dad took a cup of coffee from Mrs. Widgit and slid into the chair across from me. "So, what happened on the other side, Al?" he asked, his tone artificially casual.

Everyone pretended to be very engrossed in their drinks and tasks, and barely interested in what I had to say.

I took a deep breath and started talking. Andie gave up her pretense of not listening, watching me intently and becoming more and more incredulous as I described the maze and the warriors in the red dimension. When I got to the part about the pastel mountain cats, Professor Theopolous gasped so comically that we all turned toward him.

"You had a run in with the knarren?" He pronounced the k and rolled the r's dramatically.

Dad sprayed the mouthful of coffee he had just sipped across the table onto me. Pettikin appeared from behind Socrates, his face ghost white, and screamed until he fell over backwards in a faint.

"Sorry, Al," Dad handed me his napkin.

"What are the knarren?" I asked, mopping myself off. Socrates licked Pettikin's face.

"One of the deadliest creatures in the universe. They can obliterate anything they want with the white light from their eyes." Professor Theopolous' voice was strained.

"Oh. Well these ones were friendly."

"Friendly?" Pettikin gurgled from behind Socrates, apparently revived by the face licking.

"Well, once I got them calmed down and gave them cookies."

Professor Theopolous was incredulous as I explained the rest of the story with the purple hedgehogs (truffalos, he called them) and how the knarren defended us. When I finished, he pressed his palms into the edge of the table and leaned back in his chair, seeming, I thought, a little impressed. "Getting the knarren to work for you—I never would have thought of it."

Dad shook his head. "I guess you've got more of Aunt May in you than even I realized, Al." He blew on his coffee and took another sip.

I continued the story, glossing over the part about the bat creatures a bit because Dad had a sort of strained expression on his face listening to it. I glanced at Andie instead. Her face was grim but her countenance was one of solidarity, which was easier to take.

"So that's it," I said finally. "We tried, but we didn't make it." I set my mug down on the table and leaned back in my chair, hoping to convey a sense of finality about the whole matter.

An uneasy silence filled the room.

The phone rang. Mrs. Widgit grabbed it.

"Hello? Oh hello, Pat. It's Viola Widgit. Yes, Theo and I are down here with the two delinquents—Dan was just telling us the whole story."

I pushed away from the table and went into the living room with Andie following me. Mrs. Widgit's voice faded, "Oh yes, I'll be sure to tell them. I know they will be delighted."

I slumped down on one of the blue sofas, and Andie squashed down onto the one across from me. If Mom were here, I imagined she would tell me my current posture was bad for my back.

Socrates followed us into the room, Pettikin riding on his back. He lay down by the fireplace and gazed at me with adoring dog eyes. Pettikin slid down to the floor and leaned against the dog's fur. Our eyes met briefly, but neither of us said anything.

Andie picked up a book from the coffee table and began flipping through the pages.

"I still have ten pre-calc problems I have to do before Monday," she said.

"I did them before the funeral. You can copy mine this once if you want."

"I'll have to make sure to get one of them wrong, or Mrs. Greene will know I copied."

I folded my arms across my chest and stared out the window. The numbness I had been feeling was starting to wear off, and, in its place, waves of pain washed over me. It wasn't physical pain but a kind of icky, emotional pain, like something deep inside me had been wounded. I tensed my jaw. More than anything, I wished I could be alone.

In answer to that wish, Mrs. Widgit, Professor Theopolous, and Dad came into the living room, chatting and carrying their mugs of coffee. Professor Theopolous had his book tucked under his arm.

"That was your Mother on the phone Allie," Mrs. Widgit sat down next to me on the couch. I resisted the urge to scooch away from her. "It seems you two have been forgiven for being miscreants, and that Andie's parents have said she can spend the night here again."

Dad eased himself down next to Andie while Professor Theopolous sat in the chair at Aunt May's desk and resumed reading his book. Mrs. Widgit was blocking my view out the window, so I picked up a book from the coffee table and pretended to flip through it. *Decorating Your Alpaca for Any Occasion.*

"So I imagine we should start preparing for Vala's return," Mrs. Widgit said lightly.

Vala's return? Please. I snorted and continued to flip absently through the book.

If Mrs. Widgit noticed my interior monologue or exterior huffing she ignored it. "I imagine he will want to try again as soon as possible. There's no time like the present after all."

Andie watched me but didn't say anything. I flipped my pages a tad too fast now to fool anyone. Dad raised his eyebrows and blew the phrase, "Oh boy," quietly across his coffee mug before taking a sip.

"We still have plenty of time if you think about it," Professor Theopolous commented from Aunt May's desk. "Vala could even reopen the Gateway tomorrow if he wanted."

I flipped a page a little too violently and ripped it. Frustrated, I slammed the book shut. "And if he does, which one of you is going to take Pettikin through this time?"

Wow, that sounded nasty. Pettikin stirred from his dog fur bed, but I avoided his gaze.

Mrs. Widgit put her mug down on the coffee table. "It has to be you Allie, you know that."

"I don't know that," I was surprised at how angry I sounded. "I didn't do anything special at all. The alpacas led the way through the dimensions, any one of you could have followed them. Or let them take Pettikin home alone for all I care. They seem to know a lot more about this stuff than I do!"

"You agreed to take on this responsibility," Professor Theopolous' voice was stern.

"Theo," Dad growled a warning.

Andie jumped to my defense. "You can't make Allie go back again after what just happened. We're not used to this. It's not easy for us to *do* this stuff!"

I shot her a wan smile of thanks.

"And what about poor Pettikin?" Mrs. Widgit asked.

"Viola!" Dad's voice was sharper now as he set his mug down on the coffee table a little too roughly.

Pettikin cringed and burrowed deeper into Socks' fur.

I threw my hands up in the air, exasperated. "I love Pettikin! I want to help Pettikin! But I don't think I'm helping! I almost got us killed!" I was shouting now.

Mrs. Widgit, Professor Theopolous, Andie, and Dad all started shouting at once. I clenched my jaw and blinked back tears of frustration and anger.

"Everything OK here?" A softer, gentler voice.

Vala. He was standing over by the window, arms folded across his chest, smiling at us. A soft, golden light swirled around him.

Andie was on a roll. "No, Vala, it's not OK! These psychos are trying to tell Allie she has to go back through the Gateway again after those bat things almost killed her!"

"Now, we are not psychos." Professor Theopolous stood up.

Andie jumped up off the couch. "Oh yeah? I bet we could get Allie's mom down here to run a few tests or something."

"OK, I'm not sure this conversation is useful at this point." Mrs. Widgit stood up and placed herself physically between the two of them.

Vala caught my eyes.

"Want to go for a walk?"

A beat. Then, "Sure." I stood up.

The others fell silent and stared at us as we walked out of the room.

18

Vala held the front door open for me and brushed his hand across my back as we stepped out of the cottage. I wrapped my arms around my stomach in an attempt to conceal what I was sure must be visible butterflies. The air was getting chilly again, so hopefully, he just thought I was cold.

"Want to walk to my pond?"

"OK."

He walked slowly, which made it easier for me to keep up with him. He had changed into a black hoodie, white T-Shirt, jeans and tennis shoes, his appearance every inch a normal seventeen-year-old boy, except for the soft glow he gave off. He seemed relaxed and happy and not at all upset about what had just happened.

He really is handsome, I thought, and then remembered, horrified, that he could probably hear what I was thinking. *Oh jeez, oh no!* I turned my head away from him, trying to beam my thoughts in the opposite direction.

He chuckled and moved a little closer to me so his arm brushed mine. My heart beat a little too quickly for just the exertion of walking.

It took us about five minutes to reach the pond, and we still hadn't said anything. Vala paused.

"Rock or campsite?" he asked.

"Uh."

"Campsite." He started walking again.

I wondered if all people were as decision-impaired around him as I was.

I hesitated as we passed the big rock, then quickly dipped my right hand and foot in the water and put a palm print and foot print on it, feeling ridiculous. He stopped and waited for me without saying anything. I hurried to catch up with him, wiping my hand on my jeans, the cold water turning my knuckles red.

When we reached the campsite, Vala sat down cross-legged on the ground and gestured for me to sit down next to him. I hesitated and then lowered myself to the ground, leaving a safe distance between us.

"So," he said, "Tell me everything!"

Did he mean about what had happened in the dimensions? Didn't he already know?

"I'm not omniscient," he said. "I can know many things in the universe, but I can't know exactly what's going on inside here..."

He tapped my forehead with his forefinger.

"...unless you tell me."

"I was under the impression that you could read my mind."

"I can feel what you're feeling and know what you're thinking to a certain extent. For example, I know you're upset, but I don't know exactly what's upsetting you or why. I need you to tell me."

A million emotions swirled like a black cloud in my mind, but I couldn't explain what I was feeling.

"Did something happen in the dimensions that upset you?"

The black cloud in my mind solidified into a funnel cloud of bats in a void. I shivered. Hadn't he been there? Hadn't he seen?

He moved closer so his shoulder touched mine. "I need you to tell me." He peered down at me, concerned.

"I, well," my throat felt dry. "Those...*things*. In that last dimension. Actually I don't even know if it was a dimension. I don't know how we ended up there, it wasn't like the other dimensions it was just a dark void, and those...those bats..." I broke off.

"Sslorcs. Yeah. They take some ugly forms in some of the dimensions."

"And they just kept coming, and there was nothing I could do, until the light..." I swallowed. *Was that you?* I put an icy hand up to my neck where I had felt the creatures around my throat. I was trembling.

"But you're OK now. They're not here now." Vala took my hand from my neck and rubbed it between both of his. I felt the terror of the bats draining away, and a soothing feeling pouring into me.

"I guess that's true," I said, but my voice didn't sound convinced.

He stopped rubbing but kept my hand in his. "It's a strange mistake I notice most people on Earth make. You experienced that moment, and it was real for that moment. But moments are transient—they come and go. We can label them as good moments or bad moments, but it doesn't make them any more real. When something bad happens to you, you can carry it with you forever, or you can learn to let it go. You can realize it's just something that happened to you—it isn't who you are."

His earnest expression was almost too much for me to handle. I looked away. Was I as terrified of him as I was of the bats?

He gave my hand a gentle shake. My charm bracelet slipped out from under my sleeve, and he held one of the charms between his fingers.

"Where did you get this, Allie?"

"I found it on Aunt May's night stand. I thought it would be alright for me to wear it since she left everything she owned to me."

The stone flashed once. So it really could do that? I hadn't imagined that before?

"It's a summoning stone," Vala said. "It's ancient magic. The stones themselves have been around since the time of the Ancients. It's a very powerful talisman. It can help you in times of great need. It's a tricky kind of magic though because you can't control it. Even I can't control it. It will do what it wants, bring to you what it believes a situation warrants and not necessarily what you might want or think you need."

He turned the stone over in his fingers.

"So May had a summoning stone," he mused.

He closed his eyes. The stone glowed, a white light tinged with lavender, then faded.

"I tuned it to you instead of May," he said. "You can keep it."

He placed my hand back in my lap but remained with his shoulder touching mine. I fiddled with the stone on my bracelet.

"OK, what else? It's obviously not just the sslorcs that are upsetting you."

Why was I having such a hard time articulating my thoughts?

"I'm upset," I said, fighting to keep my voice steady, "because I failed. And I've never failed at anything before. And now, the one time it really mattered, I completely blew it. I failed Pettikin, I failed you…"

"But you didn't fail. What makes you think you did?"

Was he crazy? "Um—keys? Gateways? Tests? Getting Pettikin home? I certainly didn't *succeed* at any of that."

"Yet."

My mind went blank.

He shrugged. "For me, success and failure are just two sides of the same coin. Mostly what you call success or failure is just you placing some arbitrary judgment on any given experience." He leaned toward me. "If you can learn to just let experiences be, to just let them come and go without judging them as good or bad, right or wrong, then it will be easier for you to live, to do what you need to do, and allow others around you to live and do what they need to do. We all have some burden to carry, and we're all just doing the best we can with it. Don't judge yourself and others so harshly all the time."

I felt a bit ashamed, but the frustration I had been feeling was gone. I also felt a strange kind of gratitude toward him. He talked to me in a way that no one ever had before. Here he was, a Guardian of the Universe, and Professor Theopolous had basically told me I wasn't worthy of him, but Vala talked to me like I *was* worthy, like he was interested in what I had to say, like I mattered to him as a person.

Across the pond a frog chirped and disappeared into the water with a small splash, sending ripples in our direction.

"So, what else? Did anything *good* happen while you were in the dimensions?"

"Well...the *knarren* were pretty cute."

We both started laughing at that. He grinned at me, and I grinned back, a big, dorky grin, which seemed to make him happy.

"So what were the keys I gave you, do you know?"

I was about to say no, I didn't know, but then I thought about it.

"Willpower," I said finally. "In the red dimension the key was willpower. That's how I got us through."

"Good girl. And the blue dimension?"

I looked away from him. "Love."

"The most powerful force in the universe and always underestimated," he mused. "It's bigger than you and me. It transcends everything—time, space, even ephemeral happiness. And the gold dimension?"

I hesitated. "That one I'm not sure."

He tapped the center of my forehead. "So that's the one we have to get right this time."

I felt a warm glow behind my eyes and felt suffused with peace and happiness. He was completely golden. Radiant. I smiled at him.

He leaned toward me and put one hand under my chin. My heart was pounding.

"Don't you see? This is who you really are." He bent his face toward mine.

Wait, were Guardians allowed to do this?

He closed his eyes. "You're a beautiful person." He kissed me gently, and everything dissolved in light.

19

When we got back to the cottage, Andie was spread out on the floor next to the fireplace doing homework while Pettikin slept, curled up against Socrates. Professor Theopolous and Mrs. Widgit were reading on the couches. Mrs. Widget had donned a pair of rhinestone encrusted reading glasses with giant, teardrop shaped lenses.

"Where's Dad?"

"Allie!" Pettikin woke up, ran over, and hugged my leg.

"Your father went up to the house to get something, Allie. How was your walk?" Mrs. Widgit peered up at me and Vala from over her glasses, a knowing expression on her face. "Crisis averted?"

Vala walked over to the couches and folded his arms. "Yes, well, in terms of problems of the universe I have to deal with, Allie's crises are pretty easy for me." He winked at me, his voice full of humor.

Pettikin gazed up at me with wide, worried eyes. "Do we get another chance, Allie?"

"We do, Pettikin." I hesitated. "Tomorrow?" I asked Vala nervously.

He nodded, his eyes soft. "Tomorrow. You need some sleep tonight."

The front door opened, and my dad came in wearing an old suede barn jacket and wool cap. He had a book and several DVDs tucked under his arm.

"Ah, you're back! Everything OK then?" He unzipped his jacket.

Mrs. Widgit closed her book. "Everything," she announced, "is just fine. And Theo and I will be leaving now."

They pushed themselves up from the couch and made their way past my dad into the hallway. Mrs. Widget's tote bag was on the bench by the door. She placed her book in it, then slung the bag across her shoulders. Professor Theopolous opened the door for her.

"We'll see you tomorrow, girls! Have a pleasant evening!"

We were all quiet for a few moments. Vala watched out the window as Bob emerged from the alpacas' barn and joined the Professor and Mrs. Widgit as they walked off. I wondered where they all spent the night. Sunshine poked her head out of the barn, staring after Bob.

"I brought you some movies," Dad said finally. "And your Mother is going to call Coccia House right at five o'clock to order a couple of pizzas. I'll go pick them up."

"Seriously, if you don't call right at five you'll have to wait two hours for a pizza on a Saturday night," Andie said.

"So I'll be back tomorrow then," Vala said to me. Then to my father, "Make sure she eats something tonight."

"I will."

I opened my mouth to say something, but he was already gone.

Andie got up from the floor, took the DVDs from my dad, and flipped through them.

She grinned. "Bugs Bunny cartoons. Four DVDs worth."

I laughed. "That sounds like just about what I can handle tonight."

Andie walked to the small den behind the living room where the TV and DVD player were.

"C'mon, Pettikin. I'll show you one of our finer Earth creations."

Pettikin followed her.

"Here, I brought this for you." My dad handed me the book he was carrying, a light blue paperback with purple letters: *The Poems of Theodore Roethke.* The cover was creased and stained, the pages yellowed and curled up at the edges.

"Did you drop it in the toilet or something?" I joked as I flipped through it. A faded black bookmark with a red dragon marked the page with "The Waking"—the poem Aunt May left me at her funeral. I scanned it quickly.

I learn by going where I have to go.

"Thanks, Dad."

He patted me on the back. Then he zipped up his jacket, stuffed his hands in the pockets, and prepared to leave. When he reached the door, he hesitated.

"You never asked me about the bet I lost with Aunt May."

"I thought you said you didn't actually lose the bet."

He looked a little sad.

"Years and years ago, before you were even born, Aunt May told me that she would not be the last Gatekeeper on Earth, that in my lifetime there would be another. I guess I was young enough that I didn't even want to consider that possibility. In answer to my obstinacy, she bet me that not only would there be another

Gatekeeper in my lifetime, but that I would love that Gatekeeper even more than I loved her."

I felt my throat tighten. He raised one corner of his mouth in a half smile. "I lost."

I focused on the tattered book cover in my hands, not sure what to say.

Dad sighed. "Yep, I lost, and the wager, naturally, was good old-fashioned public humiliation. Gotta love Aunt May." He reached for the door. "I'll be back in a bit with the pizzas," he said and left.

I stared at the book for a few seconds more, set it down on the coffee table, and went to join Andie and Pettikin in the den. They were sitting about a foot away from the TV, Andie cross legged and leaning back on her hands, Pettikin in his V-stance. I grabbed a pillow from the old couch that was pressed up against the back wall of the room and joined them, lying face first with my elbows on the cushion and face propped in my hands like a little kid.

It was a wonderful few hours of normalcy. Dad returned a little later with Coccia House pizza, salad, and a pint of Chunky Monkey ice cream, then built us a fire in the fireplace before leaving for the night. We ate pizza and ice cream (Pettikin just ate ice cream) and watched Bugs Bunny cartoons until we wanted to strangle something every time we heard the theme music for a new episode. We turned the TV off and made our sleeping nest by the fire.

It wasn't very late, not even ten o'clock, but by the time I crawled into my corner of the nest, I felt like I was running on fumes. Images of Bugs, Daffy and Wile E. Coyote swirled in my mind, then flickered and became disfigured, morphed into bat creatures swirling in a void. I willed the images away, tried to replace them with happier images of Pettikin, Andie, and the alpacas, but no matter what I did, the creatures reappeared, whirling and buzzing until they were a funnel cloud in my mind. It was too hard to fight them, and the last thing I remember before I passed out was an overwhelming feeling of despair.

I opened my eyes to complete darkness. The air was dank and cold like I had descended into the creepy basement of human consciousness. I was suspended in mid-air, with nothing to refer to and nowhere to go. I wrapped myself into a ball, legs tucked to chest, arms around legs, trying to feel safe. I didn't know what to do. Then I heard faint music. Melancholy notes, struck one by one on the keys of some unseen piano, echoing through the void, each note louder than the first, until the melody surrounded me. A light appeared in the distance, so I unwrapped myself and willed myself to move toward it. I saw a figure standing there, and as I drew closer, I realized that it was Vala, still wearing his jeans and hoodie from our afternoon walk, his expression somber. He opened his arms, and I moved toward him. He wrapped his arms around me and pressed me to his chest. Relief washed over me.

That's the last thing I remembered until morning.

20

I awoke in a warm tangle of blankets, radiators hissing softly, a beam of sunshine on my face. The despair I felt the night before was gone, but gone the way the pain of a toothache is gone after you get a shot of Novocain. Your tooth is numb, but you know the pain is still there, below the surface, waiting to return when the shot wears off. I rubbed my eyes and rolled onto my side, hoping to drift back to sleep.

A loud pounding on the front door caused all three of us to gasp and sit up. Socrates trampled over us, galloping toward the door, barking wildly. Andie and I gaped at each other with wide eyes and extreme bed hair. Pettikin shrieked and dove under a pile of blankets, which at least muffled the noise.

I jumped up and almost immediately slipped on the mess of blankets on the floor. I caught myself with my right leg out and hands on the ground in an awkward lunge, then pushed myself up again and ran for the door.

"All right, all right, we're coming!"

I yanked the door open and was instantly struck on my forehead by Mrs. Widgit who was talking to Professor Theopolous.

"Ow!" I rubbed my head.

"Oh, sorry dear! I thought you were the door." Mrs. Widgit picked up her totebag and a basket that was sitting next to her on the porch and breezed into the house. "Rise and shine, everyone!"

"We are risen," Andie grumped as she padded out into the hallway, yawning and rubbing her arms. Pettikin's shrieking had died down, hopefully because he was no longer scared and not because he had suffocated under the blankets. Socrates twirled, snorted, and slobbered on everyone, reminding me of the Tasmanian devil from the cartoons the night before. He finally dashed out the front door, which I shut behind him.

Mrs. Widget's blue and purple patchwork dress, embroidered with small pink flowers, could easily have been converted from a quilt. She wore pair of thick, gray wool socks with her Birkenstocks. Professor Theopolous was in the same outfit he had been wearing the past two days, as if he had been propped up in a corner all night instead of sleeping.

"Where's Bob?" I asked.

"He's with the alpacas, dear," Mrs. Widgit called over her shoulder as she made her way into the kitchen. She set her basket down on the counter and began unpacking eggs, peppers, milk, and cheese.

"I'm under strict orders to feed you a good breakfast," she announced, rummaging through the kitchen cabinets for a frying pan.

"We have to start getting ready already?"

She freed a frying pan from underneath a stack of pots and lids and placed it on the stove.

"I should say so—it's almost eight o'clock."

She found a cutting board and long knife and started rinsing a bright red pepper in the sink.

"That's the middle of the night in Teenage Weekend Standard Time," Andie opined.

Professor Theopolous turned on Aunt May's stereo in the living room and the second movement of Beethoven's seventh symphony was crept into the kitchen. The portentous melody made me feel uneasy, and I could feel my emotional Novocain starting to wear off.

"Is that really appropriate, do you think?" I asked him, as he emerged from the living room and placed an armful of graph paper and books down on the kitchen table. I gestured to the air as if he could see the musical notes floating there.

"Oh, it's just what was on the radio." He took a seat and smoothed out a sheet of paper in front of him.

I wanted to tell him that the original set of maps he gave us hadn't been all that useful, but decided against it. Let him be all old-school about it if he wanted.

Mrs. Widgit was fighting her breakfast war on several fronts now, brewing, toasting, and frying as the music crescendoed. I retreated to the living room with Andie to clean up the bed sheets and get dressed. We found Pettikin wrapped like a mummy in a blanket and unraveled him, me holding him steady while Andie pulled the blanket.

I took a quick shower, then pulled on the same jeans I had worn the day before and a clean t-shirt. Instead of drying my hair, I pulled it, still wet, into two tight braids so it wouldn't be in my way all day.

I tried to fight the growing apprehension I was feeling, but by the time Andie and I sat down at the kitchen counter for breakfast, my stomach was twisting itself into knots. I ate about half of my eggs and then pushed my plate away.

Mrs. Widgit frowned.

"I ate most of it. I'm not going to starve, Mrs. Widgit."

She pressed her lips into a thin line but didn't say anything as she cleared my plate away.

Andie glanced at me in mid-chew, then looked down at her plate.

Pettikin sat next to me on the counter finishing a waffle. The cotton puff of his Santa hat flopped down next to his cheeks, which were still rosy from sleep, or possibly the exertion of screaming. Three drops of maple syrup stuck to his beard. I felt my chest tighten and my eyes well up with tears.

I jumped up before anyone could see and walked toward the front hallway, blinking furiously.

"Oh, Allie," Mrs. Widgit said lightly. "Since you're up, I wonder if you might do me a favor."

I took a deep breath and turned around.

She was pouring coffee into a small red thermos. "Would you be a dear and take this out to the barn for Bob? I don't think he has eaten yet, and I'm worried it might be a little chilly down there."

She winked at me as she handed me the thermos, then started wiping off the counters.

The thermos felt warm in between my hands. "Sure, I'll do that."

"Andie, do you want to help me make some cookies?"

Andie had been watching me and assessed my mood in about a second.

"Sure, Mrs. Widgit, I'll help."

She got up and carried her plate to the sink. Mrs. Widgit rinsed and wrung out her dish rag, hung it over the kitchen faucet, then dried her hands on her apron. She fished through a large pocket in her dress and pulled out the purple clamshell device. It was humming quietly.

"Not time yet," she murmured, returning the device to her pocket. She poured herself another cup of coffee and began unpacking baking ingredients from her basket.

Pettikin hopped down from the counter, scurried across the floor, and up to my shoulder. I felt my anxiety lessen and wondered if that was because I liked his company or if it was some strange gnome magic at work. I found my hoodie draped over a couch in the living room and shrugged into it, Pettikin placing his hands on my head and stepping over each sleeve as I tugged.

I opened the front door to a bright blue sky, red and gold leaves dappled with sunshine and frost sparkling on the grass like tiny, terrestrial stars. I hopped down from the front step, tucked the thermos under my arm, and zipped up my hoodie, breathing in the smell of rotting apples, fallen leaves, and woodsmoke from the main house. When I exhaled I could see my breath, but the sun cut through the chill of the air, warming my arms under the fabric of my sweatshirt.

I walked across the western yard of the cottage, toward two old apple trees whose branches form a fragrant canopy over the path to the barn every fall. Johnny Appleseed supposedly planted the trees in the early eighteen hundreds. I kicked a couple of small, green apples that had fallen into the path out of my way. Aunt May used to gather them every fall and make pies. I wondered if she had ever taken any of those pies to Pettikin in his world.

"Pettikin, sometimes I can't believe we've only known each other for two days. After everything we've been through, it feels like we've known each other forever."

"But we have known each other forever."

I frowned. "What do you mean?"

He was quiet for a few moments. "Time must be really weird here on your planet. I don't really understand it," he said finally.

"How could time be any different here than it is anywhere else? Isn't it one of those universal constants?"

"Did you think time was the same in the dimensions as it is here?"

We reached the fence, and I lifted the metal loop latch that secured the gate to the fence post next to it. I thought about the disconnect I felt the day before when we returned—that only a few minutes had passed when I thought we had spent hours or days in the other dimensions. But there had been no markers in the dimensions for the passage of time, no sunrises or sunsets, no sleeping, nothing for me to know how long we had actually been there.

"No," I said slowly, refastening the gate behind us. "It was weird. It was like there was no time while we were there, but when we got back here I felt like not enough time had passed. But even if it we did spend more than a day together, how can you say that we've known each other forever?"

Something about the tone of Pettikin's voice made me think that if I could see his expression it would be as incredulous as it was when he learned that I couldn't talk to alpacas. "On Arcorn we don't differentiate between *now* and any other time. So we know that anyone who is our friend *now* has always been our friend, and always will be our friend."

I didn't know what to say to that and felt tears welling up in my eyes again. Apparently I was going to be an emotional mess until this whole ordeal was over.

We walked across a rickety, makeshift bridge over a narrow drainage ditch that cuts across the pasture in front of the barn. The barn itself was as old as our house, a dark red, two-story structure, with wide, weathered boards and a steeply pitched gray metal roof. Two sets of double stable doors on either side of the main level were separated by a narrow door that led to a center tack room. Above them was a hay loft door with black hinges and a bright white X in its center.

The top half of the stable door on the right was open. I eased the lower door open just enough so I could squeeze myself through sideways without letting any alpacas out. Inside it was dark and cool and smelled like hay and grain and insect repellant. The alpacas were munching hay from a row of hay racks on the left hand wall. They startled when we entered, then hummed hellos as they came over to greet us. I buried my fingers in the soft hair on Suzy's neck, while Taos pressed a velvety nose to my cheek and exhaled in my ear.

Pettikin transferred himself from my shoulders to Sunshine's. The door to the tack room was just beyond the hay racks. I paused with my hand on the rusty latch. I thought I heard low voices and wondered if Bob was listening to the radio. I pushed the door open.

A single, dim bulb cast an orange glow on knotted, wooden beams and ropes of ancient cobwebs that were so pervasive, they seemed part of the architecture. The room was long but narrow. About halfway down on the left, beside the built-in wooden ladder to the hay loft, two bales of hay were stacked neatly against the wall. A third bale, with its twine cut, had fallen into flakes on the floor. A shovel, rake, and pitchfork hung on large hooks on the opposite wall, alongside two brooms and some empty buckets.

Bob was standing just past the hay loft ladder on the right, one of the alpacas' costumes draped over an old saw horse next to him. He was mending it with a needle and thread.

"Hey, Bob, I brought you some coffee—" I said and then gasped.

Leaning against the far wall, his arms folded across his chest, was Vala. He was wearing jeans, black boots, and a gray V-neck sweater with a white T-shirt underneath.

"There she is," he said, his lips twisting into a bemused smile.

"Oh hey, Allie," Bob said shyly, "we were just talking about you." He set his sewing down and stepped forward to take the thermos from my frozen, outstretched hand.

"Oh, really?" My voice was a little too loud. I folded then unfolded my arms, took a few steps to the side, and tried to lean casually against the wall to my right. Instead, I accidentally knocked over one of the brooms, which caught the lip of an empty bucket, flipping it on its side as it clattered to the ground.

"Whoa." I set the bucket upright and tried to lean the broom against the wall, but the one next to it started sliding over. I had to steady them both again twice before they stayed straight.

I wiped my hands on my jeans, folded my arms, and shifted my weight awkwardly. Bob and Vala grinned at each other. I wondered if Vala thought that beet red was my normal skin color.

Bob poured coffee into the lid of the thermos, which doubled as a cup. "Vala was just telling me how brave you are," he said, as he placed the thermos carefully on a low shelf in front of him.

"Brave?" I asked. That couldn't be right.

"You are very brave," Vala said. "Ask Bob. He's one of the bravest people I know."

Bob? Shy, mousy Bob? Somehow he was the last person I expected Vala to laud for his bravery. I suddenly felt whatever energy I had left washed out of me. I picked up the bucket I had knocked over just moments before, flipped it over, sat down on top of it, and put my face in my hands.

"I'm not brave Bob," I said. "I'm terrified. I've been terrified all morning and I don't know what to do."

Bob glanced over at Vala, who nodded at him once.

"You know, Allie," Bob said as he set his coffee down on the shelf next to the thermos, "I'm not like Mrs. Widgit and Professor Theopolous. I don't come from the higher worlds or even a forbidden world." He picked up his sewing and gave the needle a gentle tug. "I'm from a shadow world."

"A shadow world?" I was confused. "But... but you're *good!*"

Bob paused and regarded the wall in front of him. "Do you think so? There was a time when I wasn't sure." He returned his attention to his sewing, pushing and pulling the needle through the fabric of the costume.

I wasn't sure what I should say. Vala had closed his eyes.

"Where I come from, there are a lot of beings like the ones you encountered in the void and a lot of people who are far, far worse than Mr. Cutter. For someone like, well, like *us* Allie, living there is almost unbearable. There is so much fear and despair and an overwhelming feeling that you can never get out." He pressed his lips together into a thin line.

"How did you get out?"

"By some miracle—" He stopped sewing, shook his head, and laughed. "I found a book."

"A book?"

"A book that talked about the Guardians. Honestly, I'm not sure how it even got there. There weren't a lot of books on my world, but I found it, and read it. Everyone told me it was just a fantasy, that the Guardians weren't real, but I believed it with all my heart, and, every night, I begged the Guardians to save me, to get me off that world."

"I thought the Guardians don't go to the shadow worlds anymore."

"There are no Gateways to the higher worlds on the shadow worlds, but the Guardians will go anywhere in the universe if we're needed. Some of us are specifically designed for that purpose." Vala opened his eyes.

"For years I begged the Guardians to help me," Bob said, "but nothing ever changed. I wanted to give up hope so many times, but I guess, even in the darkest times, something in me always believed that the Guardians *must* be real. I had to believe that there was more to the universe than the darkness and misery I saw in front of me every day."

"So what happened?"

"Well, there aren't any Gateways to the higher worlds on the shadow worlds, but the Guardian Gateways, as you know, aren't bound by anything except the will of the Guardian. One night, Vala appeared to me in a dream and gave me the keys I needed to find his Gateway. But it was only after I passed a series of trials, which I imagine are similar to what you're going through now, that he finally pulled me through. The sslorcs fought me every step of the way and were furious when I finally made it out. Once I did, Vala brought me here to your Aunt May, and I've worked for the two of them ever since."

He stopped sewing again. "So I understand a little bit about what you're feeling right now."

"But *how* did you do it? I mean, obviously you are brave if you stood up to the sslorcs all on your own. Why weren't you afraid?"

"I *was* afraid. I think what Vala is trying to tell you is that being brave doesn't mean you're not afraid to do something. Being brave means you're terrified, but you do it anyway."

Vala was watching me with a serious expression. I was suddenly acutely aware of how I had been judging Bob in my mind—thinking he was weird and quiet and that there wasn't much more to him, when in truth he had been through more and survived more than I ever had. I was also starting to suspect that this entire conversation had been 'facilitated' by Mrs. Widgit.

"So Aunt May knew you were from a shadow world?"

"She did. She never said anything, but I must admit I had my suspicions over the years about how that book found its way to my dimension."

"May had some interesting ideas; there is no doubt about that," Vala said.

Bob sighed, knotted his thread, and clipped the needle free with a small pair of scissors that had been resting on the shelf next to him. He put them on the shelf and picked up his coffee cup.

"Well, I think that about does it. Shall I get the alpacas ready?"

"Yes. Better get started before it gets too late." Vala straightened himself up. "Allie, I'll help Bob down here for a few more minutes. You should take Pettikin up to the cottage. Your father is waiting for you."

When we got back to the cottage, Dad was in the kitchen, already wearing his suit for church. I had completely forgotten it was Sunday. I stopped just past the doorway as I entered the kitchen from the front hallway. Andie and Mrs. Widgit were finishing a batch of white chocolate macadamia nut cookies. My stomach growled, and I thought about the eggs I hadn't finished earlier.

"There you are, Al," Dad said when he saw me. "How are you feeling?"

"Fine," I lied.

"Well, assuming you're lying, I wanted to give you some good news, specifically that things should go a little smoother from our end today, since I can almost guarantee that Mr. Cutter won't be a problem this morning."

"How can you do that?"

Dad put an arm around my shoulders. "It's communion Sunday, my heathen daughter, and Mr. Cutter is a Deacon so he will be busy for quite some time after the service." He kissed the top of my head.

"Oh! That's pretty good actually."

"It is indeed, and I hope that you," Dad said pointedly to Andie as she walked past with a tray of cookies, "are paying attention to this triumphant moment of teaching through example, my young ally friend."

Andie slid the cookies off the baking sheet onto a wire rack on the counter to cool. "All I could come up with was letting the air out of his tires, so, yeah," she grinned at me. "You're kind of screwed in the future, Al."

"I doubt there would be any trouble from this end today anyway." Professor Theopolous finished his maps and was stacking his books on the kitchen table. "The damage was already done yesterday, and we can only guess what the repercussions of that sslorc getting through the Gateway will be."

Whatever momentary sense of relief I was feeling disappeared.

"Professor, my old friend," Dad walked over and clapped him on the back, "I'm starting to understand why Vala fired you."

A buzzing noise caused Dad, Andie, and I to all reflexively check our pockets for our cell phones, but it was Mrs. Widgit's pocket that was humming and vibrating and shooting out little puffs of steam. Pettikin sucked in his breath and tightened his grip on my head.

"It's time, it's time! Oh, good thing you've returned, Allie. We've barely had time to finish one batch of cookies—we'll have to make do with the leftovers from yesterday."

"As long as we have enough for the knarren…"

Mrs. Widgit wasn't paying attention to me. "Andie, quickly, help me get these bagged up. Where is Vala? And where is Bob? We need the alpacas. Bob!"

"Right, then," Dad said, as Professor Theopolous pushed himself up from the kitchen table. "I have to get to church, but I'll expect a full report when I get home." He stopped as he passed me on his way to the front hallway and put his hand on my arm. "Good luck, Al. You'll be fine." He gave my arm a gentle squeeze and left.

There was commotion everywhere, but I saw it in slow motion. Mrs. Widgit bustled around the kitchen. I heard her calling out to Professor Theopolous, and the vague, grumpy tones of his reply. Andie frantically bagged cookies while yelling something at Mrs. Widgit, but I couldn't hear what she said. I felt like I was under water. Movements were slow, sounds were muffled and indistinct. Mrs. Widgit and the Professor pushed their way past me, out of the kitchen, and out the front door. Pettikin said something to me, but I couldn't make out the words. He was like a weight on my shoulders, holding me under the water. Even my breathing seemed to be in slow motion. I felt the air leaving my lungs in one long exhale, and I was sure I was going to suffocate.

And then Vala was there, standing next to me, arms folded across his chest. He leaned into me, nudging my shoulder with his arm.

"Everything OK?"

The bubble burst, and everything returned to normal. I inhaled deeply. Someone had left the front door open, and we could hear Mrs. Widgit giving orders and the terse replies of the Professor and Bob. An alpaca hummed.

Andie pushed past us clutching two bags of cookies, tossing a harried "Hey" at Vala before hollering, "I'm coming Mrs. Widgit," and dashing outside.

Vala jerked his head toward the door.

"C'mon".

He spun on one leg, and walked outside. I followed behind him, Pettikin clutching my braids like reins.

Everyone was walking across the eastern lawn toward the Nexus Gateway. Suzy had her ears pinned back and tugged on the rope Bob was leading her with, as Professor Theopolous tried to stuff a map into her day pack. Sunshine shied away from Mrs. Widgit, who was trying to stuff more cookies into hers.

Andie fell into stride next to me, frazzled.

"It turns out facilitator is just another word for insane taskmaster," she said.

We stopped in front of the beech trees and watched Vala. He paced in front of the two trees, powerful and calm, pausing occasionally to stare fiercely at something in the sky unseen by the rest of us. I felt like a moth watching a flame, intensely attracted to him and frightened by him at the same time.

And we all know how that ends for the moth, I thought.

An electric current was building inside me. My skin buzzed; my hair stood on end. My throat felt dry, my stomach queasy.

"Don't worry. I asked some friends of mine to help look after you this time," Vala said.

"Friends of yours?"

"They were watching you before. They thought you were cute."

Cute. Not brave, not capable, not really a Gatekeeper. Cute. I guess at least they didn't *dis*like me.

"Are you ready?"

No, my brain replied. I didn't even bother to answer out loud.

He waved his left arm in a giant arc over his head. A shower of gold light and sparks shot up in the air, following the path of his arm, then trickled down and coalesced into a glowing web of light filaments between the two trees. His physical form dissolved into a vortex of swirling golden light which grew into a giant, ghost-like figure as tall as the trees.

Yeah, not really human, I reminded myself.

Guardian Vala turned toward me. My heart pounded and I was afraid I was going to be sick. Was this it? Wasn't I going to get any further instruction? Some tips on how to avoid the mistakes I made last time?

I didn't even notice that Bob was beside me, holding the alpacas. He grabbed my hand and closed my fingers around their leads. He held my fist in between both his hands, caught my eyes briefly, then dropped my hand and backed away slowly.

"Good luck, Al, you'll be fine," Andie's voice was strained, her gaze locked on the Gateway as she backed away with Bob.

"Pettikin."

Pettikin gripped my braids and made a small noise, like air leaking out of a balloon.

"Here we go again." I took a deep breath, and before I could change my mind, dove headlong through the Gateway.

21

Twelve pairs of glowing white eyes surrounded us. Twelve translucent, pastel, feline forms emerged from the moonless glow of a red, desert world. My less-than twenty-four hour absence had apparently brought the knarren to the brink of starvation. They pressed forward, yowling, pawing at my legs and butting their heads against me.

The alpacas pinned their ears back and pulled on their leads, humming with dismay. Pettikin climbed further up onto my head emitting breathy, pulsated whimpers that threatened to turn into full on shrieking.

"OK, OK, kitties! Give me a chance to get the cookies."

"Kitties?" Pettikin gurgled.

I was worried I was going to lose my balance between the knarren pushing and the alpacas pulling. I reached for Suzy's day pack and freed a bag of cookies, selfishly hoping they were the leftovers from yesterday and not the fresh ones. I gripped the bag in my teeth so I could re-zip Suzy's pack, and then unclipped the alpacas from their leads. They shied and fled toward an outcropping of rocks and cacti a safe distance away from us, honking their displeasure.

Two paws landed between my shoulder blades knocking me forward a half step. I wondered if I was about to become the subject of an Animal Planet two hour special, *"Eaten by the Knarren"*. I snatched the bag of cookies from my mouth, opened it and doled out cookies to each of the knarren as fast as I could. They trotted off one by one, flinging their cookies in the air, or batting them around on the ground like unfortunate prey before eating them.

I broke the last remaining cookie, handed half to Pettikin and crammed the other half into my mouth. Leftover chocolate chip. I crumpled up the empty bag and shoved it into my back pocket, not wanting to further sully the reputation of Earthlings by littering in a foreign dimension. I dusted my hands off on my jeans and tried to brush Pettikin's cookie crumbs out of my hair without dislodging him.

Lightning flashed around the jagged peaks of the distant mountain range, which I now knew was our goal. The air was cool and buzzing with electricity, and I felt oddly energized. The fear and anxiety I had been feeling was gone.

"Well that's strange."

"I know, I feel it too," Pettikin said. His whimpering had subsided, and he was sitting calmly on my shoulder again.

"That the fear is gone?"

"Yes, and it *is* strange. I never thought of emotion as being associated with a dimension before."

"What do you mean?"

"On Arcorn I don't usually worry. Only when something exceptional happens, like when your Aunt May was sick. But on your world I worry a lot."

"What are you saying? That the fear and worry come from Earth somehow? That we wouldn't feel that way if we were somewhere else?"

"I don't know. I always thought emotions were specific to us. What if sometimes they are, but not always?"

"Maybe we should ask Vala about it when we get back."

Pettikin didn't reply, and then I remembered that if all of this worked out, he wouldn't be coming back with me. I felt a jab from somewhere inside me.

"Nevermind. Maybe we should just get going," I said.

"OK."

The knarren were scattered across the red and gold sand beads, licking their paws and wiping their faces, some making a throaty, growling noise which I hoped was their version of purring. The alpacas hummed at us from their outcropping of rocks. I took what I thought was a normal step toward them but instead sprang forward several yards, almost losing my balance. I had forgotten about this part. I waved my arms until I got my bearings, then closed the rest of the distance in a single determined step.

Taos hummed.

"He says this is the last time he will show you through this dimension. After this you'll have to do it on your own."

Another stab from somewhere in my soul. Why was everyone talking about leaving me just when I was getting comfortable with all of this?

"Fine, let's just go."

The knarren stood up and turned toward me, forming ranks.

"You're coming with us, kitties?"

The knarren were silent, but the one in the front of the formation, a translucent orange cat with yellow stripes, circles and triangles on his back blinked his glowing white eyes.

Taos hummed and bounded away, Suzy and Sunshine following after him. I gripped Pettikin's legs to keep him steady against my shoulder and set off at an easy jog, flying across the slippery gel sand beads. I tried to pay attention to the surroundings so I would know which way to go if I ever had to do this on my own, but the dessert terrain seemed both too uniform in terms of components—sand, rocks, cacti—and too random in terms of their placement for me to distinguish any meaningful landmarks. Our overall direction was toward a low depression in the mountain range, which I supposed was the valley where we had encountered the warriors before.

We ran for a long while without talking, and I could feel the energy of the dimension building up in my body. Gradually the desert sand gave way to the rocky outcroppings that marked the foothills of the mountains, and I recognized the semi-circle of tall stones where we camped before. Once again Taos stopped and indicated that we should rest. I supposed that was something I should remember for the future—not to go past this point without resting.

The knarren emerged from the darkness, glowing white eyes appearing first, then translucent bodies. They arrayed themselves in a semicircle several yards behind us. Were they our protective guard, or just waiting for a tasty snack later?

I retrieved a bag of cookies from Taos' pack, my head buzzing and my hands shaking. White chocolate macadamia nut, still soft and chewy. I sighed as I chewed, and felt such a feeling of wellbeing that my eyes welled up with tears. I handed out cookies to the knarren, then grabbed a new bag, and Pettikin and I climbed up to the top of the large, flat rock we rested on the last time we were here. We sat and ate without saying anything, gazing at the stars and the looming mountain range in front of us.

I gasped.

"What is it?" Pettikin asked.

"The maze-that creepy maze we had to go through last time-where is it?" I scanned the horizon for the imposing landmark which should have been visible by now.

"You're right. It's not here," Pettikin said.

I went and got Professor Theopolous' map from Taos' pack. Pettikin and I unfolded it, smoothing it down over the rough surface of our rock, turning it around a few times, trying to orient it correctly. Like before, neither of us could make much sense of it.

"There's this group of concentric circles here which could be the mountains..." I said.

"Then this thick line in front of them could be the barrier we saw before, but it's definitely not here now," Pettikin replied.

Taos hummed.

"What does he say, Pettikin?"

"He said that the maze is one of the protective measures put there by the Guardians to keep anyone who enters this dimension from reaching the Gateway to the higher worlds. Since you have the key to this dimension now, the maze no longer appears for you. It's like the dimension trusts you."

From behind us, one of the knarren made a sound between a cat's meow and a lion's growl, causing Pettikin to stiffen momentarily, and then relax.

"That's the first time I could understand them. They agree with what I just said."

"So the dimension really does appear different for different people." I rubbed my hands up and down my arms, trying to dispel the prickly energy that was building up again. I dumped a few cookies from the bag onto Professor Theopolous' map. Might as well use it as a placemat.

Taos hummed again.

"He says that anyone who comes through this dimension without you will encounter that maze and become lost, never reaching the Gateway. Even if they should make it through the maze somehow, the knarren and warriors will be waiting for them, ensuring they will never get through."

I remembered the terrifying, arctic gaze of the warriors and shivered.

"Will we get through this time, Pettikin?"

Pettikin didn't reply.

I watched the night sky and let my mind go blank. From the corner of my eye, I thought I saw a figure, a warrior? I turned, but the figure slipped away behind a large boulder. Had it disappeared because I hadn't used my 'other sight'? I felt uneasy. The warriors had always seemed ethereal. This seemed like something had physically been there and slithered away, like a snake.

No one else was unsettled. Pettikin was quiet, and the alpacas stood with their eyes closed, chewing their cud and humming softly. The knarren were grooming themselves or sitting very still, like Egyptian statues.

I don't know how long we stayed like that before the alpacas stirred. I stretched and nudged Pettikin.

"Should we go?"

He crawled up to my shoulder. I hopped down, wadded up our placemat, and shoved it into Taos' pack. Taos led us away, at a somewhat slower pace, the knarren still following behind.

The path we followed eventually wound around the base of a large hill into the clearing in front of the red, diamond-shaped Gateway at the base of the mountain. Two warriors still stood on either side of it, solemn, dark, imposing. They didn't acknowledge us, but echoes of an icy, howling wind in my mind made my stomach drop. One by one the alpacas stepped through the Gateway, but my legs started to tremble. I half considered going the long route just to avoid the warriors. With the knarren behind us, maybe it wouldn't be so bad. Of course, at the moment the knarren were busy grooming themselves and purring, so maybe my plan to turn them from terrifying killers into chubby house cats was backfiring.

"What should we do, Pettikin?"

Pettikin tightened his hold on my braids.

I took a shaky step forward, heart pounding. The warriors didn't move. I clenched my fists and walked forward until I was standing directly in front of the Gateway. The warriors towered over me, stone features and crescent moon headbands glowing in the eerie light of this world. I was suddenly petrified.

One of the warriors stirred and I cringed, preparing for the worst. He lifted his sword, still in its sheath, and then—*smack*—whacked me from behind, pushing me, stumbling, through the Gateway.

An unsettling feeling of dematerializing and being sucked straight up, then spit out and turning solid once more. Three bored alpacas, eyes half-closed, chewed their cud in front of the white diamond Gateway.

"You did it Allie!" Pettikin said.

Taos hummed, not nearly impressed enough with me, I thought.

"So was that it?" I asked. "They're going to let me through from now on?"

Taos hummed again.

"He says they will. They recognize you as the Gatekeeper now."

This journey was a million times easier than the one yesterday. Maybe this whole gatekeeping thing wouldn't be so impossible after all.

Taos hummed and pressed his nose to my face, an alpaca kiss, then stepped off to the side. Suzy and Sunshine stepped through the next Gateway, Pettikin and I following behind.

Blue sky everywhere, shining with the warm light of a thousand invisible suns. Why had I ever left this place? I stretched and tried to let blue sky ooze into the nuclei of all of my cells. I closed my eyes and thought about taking a sixteen-hour nap.

No, wait. I opened my eyes again. I wasn't supposed to do this, right? There was something else I was supposed to do.

A foot-long gnome drifted past me, spinning slowly.

"Hi Allie!"

"Hi Pettikin! Wow, what are you doing here?"

Wait a minute—that was ridiculous. We had come here together, how in the world had I forgotten that?

"I think I just got here, but I think we should stay here forever!"

"No, no wait Pettikin, I remember. We can't just stay here in this blue sky—we've got to go down to the bouncy-cloud, music world." I should have asked someone if these dimensions had real names. Professor Theopolous would probably be offended. I wonder if he had written the names somewhere on the maps that we kept not using.

An annoyed, light brown alpaca head poked through the sky. Sunshine honked at me, her ears pinned back, a sour expression on her face.

"OK, OK, we're coming this time, I promise."

I pressed my hands and feet down, willing the sky to coalesce around me in a soft, spongy surface.

"Pettikin do you remember how…"

"Wheeeee!" Pettikin shot past me, careening through the sky in what I assumed was a downward trajectory.

I took off after him, knees slightly bent, slaloming through the sky until it became translucent and we could see the first hints of the world below. I felt the sky molecules becoming less dense around me until they dissolved, dropping us through the boundary between the worlds. We fell onto a cloud, bounced up and over onto rainbows, and finally down to the springy light blue ground. Suzy and Sunshine were waiting for us.

Music swelled around us. Pastel trees waved and rustled their leaves, vibrant stringed gourds hummed, and flowers like irises whistled like pan flutes. Blue and green turtles bouncing balls of light on their shells kept time, and four roly-poly, pastel colored elephants, not much taller than Pettikin marched past us trumpeting the melody through their trunks. Truly, if I had to pick a world to stay in forever, this would be it, I thought.

Suzy hummed, and I felt a sinking feeling, like my spirit had been zooming around overhead and was now descending to the ground.

"She's telling me that's part of the trap, isn't she?" I asked.

Pettikin had been bouncing up and down in time to the music, but stopped when Suzy hummed.

"Yes. The trap of this world is that it makes anyone who enters it so happy that they forget who they are and want to stay here forever instead. Unless they come with a Gatekeeper whose heart is strong enough to stay true in the face of the fleeting happiness, they will never find the Gateway into the higher realms. And even if they did, they couldn't get through the barrier around it."

"So, we can't ever stay here forever then," I said a little wistfully.

Suzy hummed a little more gently this time.

"She said as long as you are always true to your heart, then you will be OK."

I wasn't entirely sure what she meant by that, or how it answered my question, but also wasn't sure what to ask to clarify further.

"So should we just go directly to the Gateway?"

Sunshine hummed and lead us into the forest, bouncing in time to the music. More tiny elephants joined us, whistling and trumpeting as they marched along with us.

A small dissonance crept into the harmony and then quickly resolved. It was the first time I had heard something like that on this world. I didn't think much of it until I heard it again, and this time I turned around. I thought I saw a shadow slip behind a tree, and as it disappeared, the dissonance resolved again into the harmony of the world.

I felt uneasy and wondered if I should say something to Suzy or Sunshine, but neither of them seemed to have noticed, and the music soon washed away any anxiety I was feeling. I probably just imagined it.

The music began to fade, and we arrived at the lake. Sunshine walked a few steps onto the sparkling sand, then stopped and hummed.

"She said this is the last time she will help you through this dimension," Pettikin said.

I sighed and draped an arm over her neck. "Yes, yes, I get it. I'm on my own after this."

Suzy was already dragging a leaf from the nearby grove of pink and yellow trees, so I kissed Sunshine's cheek and went to find one for Pettikin and myself. Pettikin climbed aboard and installed himself up in the narrow bow like before. I pushed us off from the shore and seated myself cross-legged in the stern, Suzy already floating ahead of us toward the shimmering diamond in the distance. Some of the elephants had joined Sunshine on the beach, humming and swaying softly as they watched us drift away.

The music faded into the stillness of lapping water. I sighed and closed my eyes, feeling the warmth of the light of this dimension, soaking it up like I would the sun at home.

We drifted like that for a timeless time when I felt a strange twinge in my stomach. I opened my eyes, but everything was still warm and peaceful. Pettikin and Suzy were dozing. A ripple in the water a few inches away from the boat expanded and drifted in uneven concentric circles away from its point of origin. I peered over the side of the leaf into the water and thought I saw a dark shadow swimming away.

"Pettikin, are there fish here?"

Pettikin's eyes were closed, a peaceful smile on his face.

"Probably," he answered, without opening his eyes. "I can hear them singing the music of this dimension even from up here."

So the music hadn't stopped, only I could no longer hear it, the same way I couldn't understand the alpacas, I guess. Underneath the water, the shadow was gone, so I relaxed again. I closed my eyes and lost track of time.

Suzy hummed, startling me out of my reverie. We were approaching the Gateway, and this time, no protective crystal dome surrounded it. As with the maze in the red dimension, it seemed that a barrier once dissolved remained dissolved.

Suzy drifted through the Gateway ahead of us and disappeared.

"This is getting easier, don't you think, Pettikin?" I asked as our leaf approached the Gateway.

He didn't answer but turned around and smiled at me, his eyes shining, and then everything went white.

I felt like my soul was being tuned to a different frequency, stretched like a string so it would vibrate faster. I opened my eyes and was engulfed in the dazzling light and profound silence of the gold world. My body was in its lighter, almost transparent form. Suzy and Pettikin were shimmering apparitions in front of me, standing on the golden path that lead to the shining mesa in the distance. Curious ghosts floated by, but seemed less concerned about our presence than before, some ignoring us completely as they glided past, carrying their gourds of liquid light or bundles of golden flowers.

Suzy began floating down the path, Pettikin following behind her. For a moment, like before, I couldn't move, and it made me anxious. I closed my eyes and tried to relax. I reasoned with myself that, since nothing bad had happened in this dimension, I must be relatively safe here even if things seemed a little strange or scary. I felt my breathing slow, and after a few seconds, I opened my eyes and drifted, slowly and fitfully at first, but then more smoothly along the path behind Suzy and Pettikin.

Despite my shaky start, it did feel a little less strange to be in this world than it had before. I felt a happy, peaceful feeling spreading through me, similar to being in the blue dimension, but quieter and deeper somehow, more inward than outward.

Suzy and Pettikin stopped when they reached the diamond-shaped Gateway at the base of the mesa and waited for me. Ghost beings dissolved through and emerged from the shimmering web of light. One or two glanced at us as they passed, but most ignored us. Suzy waited until I joined them, and then we stepped, one by one, through the Gateway and zoomed up to the city on top of the mesa.

Colorful ghosts drifted in and out of the crystalline buildings as we drifted toward the central dome. We passed a small park where a bright red being sat elegantly on a platform, a group of ghosts gathered in a semi-circle in front of the dais gazing up at him.

"*They are playing music,*" Pettikin said.

"*Music?*" I hadn't heard anything since we arrived here. Like before, the silence of this dimension was deafening.

"*It's not played out loud here—it's composed and played telepathically. You can hear it the same way you can hear me if you concentrate.*"

I stopped and focused on the red ghost, trying to silence my mind, which I was starting to think might be the noisiest thing in this world.

He turned his head toward me and grew brighter, as if he were smiling at me. I felt a strange, new presence in my mind, like a small thread or ribbon of light unravelling. As I focused on it, I suddenly felt, rather than heard, a beautiful, ethereal music, like a celestial choir holding and sustaining heavenly chords which shifted and resolved periodically, but never rested. It was less overtly joyful than the music of the blue world—deeper and more transcendent and completely mesmerizing. I stood transfixed and let the composition engulf me until I felt a gentle pressure in my head.

"*Suzy?*" I surmised.

"*Yes. She says we need to go.*"

I smiled at the red being, trying to convey my thanks. He nodded at me once, almost imperceptibly, then returned his focus to the group in front of him.

The two guards were still standing on either side of the ornate double-door Gateway entrance to the central dome, and even though, like before, they made no move to stop us from entering, I felt anxious. I wondered how my heart could be pounding faster when I was in this translucent, silent body. Did I even have a physical heart at the moment? Maybe my soul remembered that feeling from my regular body and was projecting it for my benefit. I was really going to need someone to explain the physics of all of this to me when I got home. I stepped through the soft curtain of light filaments into the dimly lit hall on the other side.

Suzy and Pettikin were waiting for me just past the doorway. A universe turned slowly in the domed ceiling above us, and twelve golden beings, intense and powerful, watched us from their thrones.

And now I was scared. Up until now, everything seemed much easier this time. But this was the part where

I blew it before and blew it big time. The universe above us was already spinning, slowly at first, then faster and faster, zooming in on a planet and then on a Gateway. One by one a series of Gateways flashed by until only one remained, strands of light woven into dizzying patterns, filling the ceiling above us.

This time I knew it was the right Gateway. I also knew that I wasn't sure I could get us through it safely. This Gateway wanted me to dissolve completely to go through it in a way the others didn't. Whatever key Vala had given me for this dimension had utterly eluded me. I couldn't go through this Gateway and still be me. How could Vala want this? How could any of them want this?

Don't be afraid.

The voice in my head wasn't Pettikin's.

The Guardian on the throne closest to me beckoned to me with a thin, arm-like appendage.

I checked my immediate surroundings to make sure I wasn't going to run into anything, and then willed myself toward her.

She turned her head so I felt like she was looking into my eyes, even though she had no eyes. I felt waves of happiness and reassurance pouring into me. Part of me felt buoyed, like everything was going to be fine, but another part of me resisted that feeling—like a stubborn child in my mind who was determined to be terrified no matter what.

I wondered inanely what my mom would think if she knew how many "mes" were running around in my head.

The Guardian shifted her gaze lower, focusing on the area around my shoulders. I felt a sudden tightening in my throat and reached my hands for my neck. My mind flickered to the bat things, and I felt the grip of some invisible rope in my neck pulling tighter and tighter. Were they still in there? Had I been carrying them around all this time?

The Guardian's countenance shifted somehow so her gaze felt strong and fierce. The invisible cords binding my neck loosened somewhat and partially dissolved. I drew in a shaky breath and let my hands fall to my sides.

The Guardian turned her gaze away, and, feeling that I had just stepped out of the beam of a lighthouse, I exhaled.

"*I have no idea what just happened.*"

Suzy snorted a telepathic huff in my mind.

"*What should we do, Allie?*" Pettikin sounded as nervous as I was.

The Gateway pulsated above our heads.

I felt a pressure in my forehead from somewhere behind my eyes. Suzy gazed at me for a long moment and then flicked her ears.

"*I guess we just try again, Pettikin. What else can we do?*"

Pettikin floated over to me and grasped the leg of my phantom jeans. I swallowed and shifted my focus to the ceiling, willing myself to move toward the Gateway. We ascended, slowly at first, Pettikin being towed along after me. The higher we rose the lighter I felt, like the molecules of my being were being dispersed. I closed my eyes.

I was suddenly in a completely different world, as if I had gone through a Gateway or fallen asleep and entered a dream instead of just closing my eyes. I was standing in a vertical tunnel of light, and, to my surprise, Vala was standing above me in his familiar, human form. He held out his hand.

"*Come with me.*"

I reached my hand up and his fingers closed firmly around mine.

He gave my arm a strong tug and pulled me after him, flying upwards faster and faster until everything became a blur. Golden light rushed past me, and I felt like it was washing away everything in me, layer by layer—all of the fear I had felt, all of my thoughts, all of my hopes, all of me. At every point when I thought there could be no way to go any higher, nothing more to be washed away, Vala pulled me even further into a blazing, blinding silence. It was nothing, but it wasn't the cold, black nothing I feared, but a bright white light beyond anything I had ever known, something else, another side, another time, something I had forgotten long ago.

A strange feeling of release, and a flood of light more overwhelming than anything I had ever experienced rushed through me. My mind dissolved into a million gold and white sparks, drifting for one endless moment until they disappeared forever in the current of light.

22

I stood on top of a hill overlooking a green valley. Two suns, one about the size of ours and a smaller one to the right and slightly below it, shone in a vivid blue sky. Fluffs of clouds tinged with cotton candy pink drifted above us. Creatures about the size of chubby cows with long, lavender fur dotted the hillside, snorting as they chewed their grass. The air was clean and cool, and the only sounds were the occasional chirp of a bird or whir of an insect.

I felt different. Strong and calm, as if some ethereal connective tissue inside of me had been reinforced with diamond-like hardness. Allie 2.0.

Pettikin let out a squeal that reverberated painfully against my left eardrum and scrambled to the ground. He ran along the hillside, his arms outstretched, then stopped and spun in a slow circle, raising his arms into a gnome V for victory.

"Allie, you did it!"

"So is this Arcorn, Pettikin?"

"No, we're on Semba. But I know this world, and I know where the Gateway is that will take me home."

He ran over and wrapped his arms around my leg like a tiny tourniquet. He was happy in the blue dimension, but he seemed different here—more at home. I felt a small twinge of sadness that he wasn't able to feel this way on Earth. Earth must have been as pure as Semba once.

The steep hill on the other side of the valley leveled off into a broad road with a pine forest on one side. On the other side, a white stone castle with round turrets perched on top of another hill. A tall stone wall encircled the castle grounds.

"So, where is this Gateway of yours, Pettikin Periwinkle of Arcorn? If I recall, it is my duty to accompany you there."

Pettikin leapt up and grabbed my hand with both of his, then pulled his way up my arm to my shoulder. He grabbed my braid and gave it a gentle tug.

"I'll show you. Forward march, Allie Thomas of Earth!"

I set off at a trot down the steep slope of the hill, arms out for balance, my hoodie puffing up around me. Some of the purple cow creatures raised their heads startled, huffing or mooing their surprise.

"I assume *those* things are friendly?" I paused mid trot.

"Those are fluffermus," Pettikin said.

"You're kidding."

I held out my hand to the aptly named creature closest to me on the hill. Its head was rounded, and it had a wide pink muzzle more reminiscent of a hippopotamus than a cow. It stared at me with large blue eyes and flicked its ears. When I didn't move, it ducked its head, pawed the ground once, and lumbered toward us.

Up close, its lavender fur was caked with mud at the ends, and threads of mucous dripped from its nose. It stretched its head cautiously toward my outstretched hand and blew a blast of warm, moist air on my palm. I scratched the bridge of its nose, and when it didn't complain, I reached up to rub its head in between the ears. It closed its eyes and swished a long, thin tail with a lavender puff on the end.

"They're so cute. Does someone take care of them?"

"Yes, there are people on this world, but not very many. They are a little...different from the people on Earth."

I scratched under the fluffermu's chin and gave its neck a good clap before setting off again down the hill.

We reached the bottom and started our climb up the slope on the other side. The tall weeds and wildflowers reminded me of the milk thistle, Queen Anne's Lace, and buttercups we had at home. I wondered if everything in the universe was made from standard templates that were housed somewhere. Maybe in the gold dimension.

"Are we heading for the castle, Pettikin?"

"No. If you go toward the forest, there's a small bridge that joins to the stone wall of the castle grounds."

"An overpass?" I shielded my eyes with my hands.

"Yes, you can see it from here. The Gateway is on the other side of the bridge, in the castle wall."

"I see it. Just think Pettikin. All this fuss and worry, and now you'll be home in just a few more minutes."

We crossed the road. A few hundred yards from the edge of the forest, just as the ground began to level off, a dark figure emerged from the trees and walked toward us.

I froze.

"Is that...it can't be..." I said, and then my voice trailed off.

It was a man in a black business suit. His head bent toward the ground as he walked, and a black smoke or haze hung in the air around him. I felt a strange throbbing in my throat and a wave of nausea. He stopped a few feet away from us and raised his head. It was unmistakably Mr. Cutter.

"Allie Thomas. You're making this so easy for me."

Pettikin whined and tightened his grip on my braids.

"What...what are you doing here? You're supposed to be in church."

Mr. Cutter laughed, and the black haze around him darkened. His voice reverberated within it, so it sounded like different voices laughing with him and echoing through the air.

"That's priceless. Is that what your idiot father thinks? That he's protecting you?"

As much as I didn't like Mr. Cutter at home, I preferred him infinitely to whatever version of him was standing in front of me now. He seemed deranged, like he wasn't completely in control of his own mind.

"How did you get here? How did you get through the Gateway dimensions? There's no way—"

I took a step backwards, but the ground seemed to rise up and catch my foot too quickly, throwing me off balance.

"How? We came with you, *Gatekeeper*. Thanks for the ride."

Allie 2.0 experienced a major fault, and my brain was rapidly downloading and reinstalling Allie 1.0.

"No, that's not—" I felt a sudden jerk in my throat, an invisible rope or cord tightening, cutting off my air supply. I clutched my neck.

"Allie, what's wrong, what's happening?" Pettikin screamed.

I tried to answer but couldn't speak. Mr. Cutter dropped his gaze to the ground again, his eyes half closed, concentrating. The cloud or haze around him grew darker and began rotating around him in a counterclockwise motion.

I squeezed my eyes shut and strained with my whole being against whatever was in my neck. The strangling sensation gave way enough to let me breathe. I inhaled and let out a kind of low growl that finally dissolved it. I opened my eyes, panting a little.

My brain flashed through our last journey through the Gateway dimensions—the shadows I had seen in the red world, the dissonance in the blue world, the uncomfortable feeling in my neck in the gold world. Had I carried the sslorcs with me somehow, ever since that moment when they attacked me in the void? Had I really brought them here?

The cloud around Mr. Cutter was swirling and growing bigger. Small black flecks appeared in the smoke and morphed into bat-like creatures.

"Allie!" Pettikin was hysterical.

I scanned the area around us desperately. The bridge to Pettikin's Gateway was only about fifty yards ahead of us to the right. If nothing else, I had to get him home.

I clamped his legs down against my shoulder with one hand. "Hold on."

I sprinted past Mr. Cutter toward the bridge. He laughed a sickening, mocking laugh that echoed through the expanding cloud around him. I willed my feet to run faster.

By the time we got to the wooden beam bridge, my heart was racing, and I was completely out of breath. I stopped in front of it and bent over, sucking in huge gulps of air. On the other side of the bridge, a rusty metal gate in the stone wall led to the castle courtyard.

I checked behind us. Mr. Cutter hadn't moved, but new creatures had formed next to him, the dinosaur shaped creatures Andie had described, only less developmentally challenged.

I grabbed Pettikin and set him down on the bridge. I knelt in front of him holding his shoulders.

"Pettikin you have got to go—as fast as you can."

"I'm not leaving you Allie," Pettikin wailed in between sobs.

I gave his shoulders a small shake. "Pettikin, you *have* to...."

Something on my wrist caught my eye. My charm bracelet slipped out from under my sleeve, and the summoning stone was glowing. I flipped my hand over, catching the stone in my palm. It glowed brighter and started to pulsate.

"Pettikin, this is it, I'm sure of it. Vala said this stone is a powerful, protective talisman. I don't know how I know, but I'm certain it will protect me. I'll be fine, but you have to go now."

Pettikin hesitated, tears streaming down his face. The orb of light emanating from the summoning stone began to grow, first to the size of a baseball, then a grapefruit. A horrific roar behind us made me cringe.

"Pettikin! Go. You have to go. Go, and I'll come and visit you soon. I am the new Gatekeeper after all..." I broke off because I was crying, tears streaming down my cheeks, snot dripping from my nose, the whole works. I laughed at myself, a choky, sobby laugh, and wiped my nose with the sleeve of my hoodie.

Floppy Santa hat, snow white hair and beard, and big blue eyes awash with tears. I could barely see him through my own tears. He lunged forward and hugged my arm, pressing his face against me.

"I love you, Allie."

"I love you, too, Pettikin."

He released my arm, turned, and ran across the bridge. As he approached the Gateway, the metal suddenly came to life. An electric blue light that started in the center travelled through each metal bar until the whole Gateway was illuminated.

"Goodbye Allie!"

The blue lines of the Gateway became briefly transparent. On the other side, instead of the castle grounds, I saw a faint glimpse of a different world—blue sky, green grass, and Pettikin standing next to a light brown mushroom with white speckles. He was waving at me.

I choked back a sob. I raised my hand to wave back, but the picture had already faded, replaced by a rusty metal Gateway in an old stone wall.

Another roar from behind me. I stood up and placed myself squarely between the bridge and the approaching mess of sslorcs. I held the summoning charm out in front of me, praying it would be enough.

Mr. Cutter walked toward me slowly, an army of bat creatures swirling in a vortex around him. Three grotesque creatures, maybe eight feet tall, standing upright on powerful back legs, followed behind him. Their arms were tiny but their heads were large, with red beady eyes set deep in their foreheads. Gray, pus-like drool that smelled like rotting compost oozed out of their gaping mouths, which seemed to be perpetually unhinged.

I raised the growing sphere of light from the summoning charm higher, hoping it might intimidate them.

"It's too late Mr. Cutter! Pettikin is already home!"

My arm was shaking.

"Pettikin?" Mr. Cutter cocked his head to one side and laughed. "Wow, you really are dense aren't you? And you're supposed to be the smart kid."

I scowled at him and set my jaw.

"We don't care about the gnome. The only thing we care about, besides having access to all of these wonderful resources in all these wonderful worlds—" he waved his hand in an arc encompassing the pristine landscape, "—is killing you."

"But... but why? Why would you want to..."

Mr. Cutter's eyes narrowed. There seemed to be nothing left of the Mr. Cutter I knew. This was the Contractor, and whomever or whatever he had made a contract with was talking through him.

"Eliminating a Gatekeeper here, in the higher worlds, is the ultimate triumph. It was never possible while that old hag was still alive. She was much too powerful. But you're nothing. It will be easy to overpower you, and once you are gone, not only will this world be ours, but the secret Gateways and Earth as well. It won't be a shadow world, it will be a shadow realm."

I felt sick. It was everything Professor Theopolous had feared. If Aunt May were still alive, none of this would have happened. If Vala had simply left the Gateways closed, all these worlds would have been protected. This was what they had planned all along.

The summoning stone blazed in my hand, my last and only hope. But the orb of light around it had stopped growing. Why had I been so certain it would protect me? Vala himself had said the charms were unpredictable. It certainly hadn't saved Aunt May's life when she was in trouble.

Mr. Cutter, or rather the Contractor, also observed the stone, and must have come to a similar conclusion. He raised his hand up over his head in a fist with only his index finger extended.

"Die, Gatekeeper."

He swung his arm down and pointed directly toward me. An army of screeching bats left the funnel cloud around him and flew at me.

My mind went completely blank, cold, emotionless, and my body moved on its own. I crouched down and raised my right arm over my head, palm facing out, using the summoning charm like a shield.

A blinding white light poured forth from the charm, arching up and over me like a dome. It *was* acting like a shield. The bats beat down on it, some igniting when they hit the light and burning into cinders, others bouncing off it and fleeing away, shrieking. I could feel the blows reverberating through my joints and braced my right arm with my other hand, gritting my teeth.

The light poured forth for several seconds until there were no more bats, at which point it started to sputter. The remaining light emanating from the charm swirled into a violet colored vortex which spun in the air for several seconds before it dissolved completely. An object clattered to the ground in front of me.

It was a small knife, no larger than a kitchen cutting knife, carved from a crystalline substance like a lavender quartz. It glowed softly.

I looked up at the hulking, stinky sslorcs drooling behind Mr. Cutter, then down at the tiny knife.

Really?

Mr. Cutter raised his arm again, then swung it down to point at me. The three sslorcs behind him roared and lumbered forward.

I lunged for the knife. As soon as my hand closed around it, I felt a percussive blow, like someone played a bass note with the subwoofer turned all the way up, and everything around me shifted into photonegative, the way it had when Vala changed the color of the cottage. I could still see the forms of the sslorcs and Mr. Cutter, but now they were white streaks against a black sky. A series of glowing purple lines tethered each sslorc to Mr. Cutter's hand, and, more sickeningly, a thinner purple line, more like a thread or hair but definitely there, extended from Mr. Cutter's hand to my throat.

The first sslorc was almost on top of me in all of its creepy, photonegative glory. It roared and droplets of foul smelling pus rained down on me. I brandished the small knife in front of me, praying it might suddenly transform into a sword or perhaps a chainsaw, but it didn't appear to have any magic powers other than making me see funny, and it didn't deter his progress.

A terrifying noise rang out from behind me, like the roar of a thousand angry lions echoing off the walls of the universe. Something flew over my head, and I cowered. Twelve knarren arrayed themselves in a semi-circle in front of me, beams of photo-reversed dark light streaming from their eyes, halting the sslorcs, driving them back as they screeched and flailed their arms.

I whirled around. The Gateway which had glowed blue for Pettikin glowed red, and the towering figure of a warrior stood in front of it. In photonegative he was even more terrifying than usual, ghost white hair pulled into a sleek ponytail, his eyes gaping silver holes, his headband a black swath with a shining crescent moon on it.

He leapt up in the air, clearing the small valley easily without using the bridge, and landed a few feet in front of me. He locked his gaze on Mr. Cutter and drew his sword.

"Contractor."

I had never heard the warriors speak, and the sound was almost more terrifying than the sslorcs. It was airy but loud, as if the word were being carried into this world on a howling, icy wind from some ancient depth of the universe, each syllable drawn out for almost a full second.

The expression on Mr. Cutter's face would have been comical if I hadn't been so scared myself. He turned to run, but the warrior overtook him easily. Mr. Cutter put his arms up to cover his head and screamed in a hilariously feminine falsetto. The warrior grabbed him roughly by the neck and yanked him about three feet off the ground. As Mr. Cutter kicked the air and clawed at the giant fingers around his throat, the warrior's hollow silver eyes locked on mine.

"Gatekeeper."

I felt like ice was being injected directly into my veins, crystalizing throughout my body, and I shrank away from him.

"Break the Contract."

What?

I straightened myself up slowly and tightened my grip on the purple knife.

I felt another percussive blow. The photonegative effect around me intensified, bringing the glowing purple lines between Mr. Cutter, the sslorcs and myself into greater focus.

The knife glowed and pulsated, alternating between violet and white light. I raised it up toward my neck. My hand was shaking. I took a deep breath and slashed through the purple thread that stretched from my neck to Mr. Cutter's hand.

There was a blinding flash of white light and another percussive beat. I felt like blood was rushing to my head and a feeling of relief washed over me, like I could breathe freely again. Had that thread really been there ever since my first experience with the bats in the void? Had the warriors been able to see it? Did they know? Did Vala?

The warrior was still brandishing Mr. Cutter in front of him.

"Break the Contract."

Hadn't I already broken it? The lines binding Mr. Cutter to the sslorcs were still there. If the line I just cut represented the hold the sslorcs had on me, I guess those lines represented the original contract Mr. Cutter made with them. Pulses of energy flowed from Mr. Cutter down the lines to the sslorcs. I wondered if that was what was keeping them alive. Were they feeding off of his energy? Was I supposed to save him too, after everything he had done?

Although, if I hadn't been fully aware of the line binding me to him, could it be that he wasn't fully aware of what he had done, the effect that those purple lines were having on him? Part of me didn't want to believe it. Hadn't I been an unwilling participant and hadn't he always been greedy, seeking money and power? Still...I gripped the knife and strode across the field to where the warrior held him.

"No, no." I must have had a scary expression on my face because Mr. Cutter sounded panicked. "Please don't kill me, Allie, please. I give up. I promise I'll let you go. You can have the Gateways, I won't bother you again on Earth—"

"Shut up, idiot. I'm not going to kill you. I'm saving you."

I strode past him to the first purple line.

Slash. A flash of light more powerful than before, and, this time, the ground shook with the reverberation of the noise. Mr. Cutter cried out, and the first sslorc shrieked and began withering in the light from the knarren's eyes. It backed away and tried to flee, but one of the knarren took off after it.

I waited until the ground stopped shaking so I could regain my balance, took a deep breath and then *slash, slash* I cut the remaining two bonds in quick succession. The lightning flashes and reverberations that followed were too powerful. I lost my balance and staggered, the purple knife falling to the ground.

The photonegative effect disappeared and the world came into focus. Without the power of the bonds, the sslorcs were dissolving in the light from the knarren's eyes. They tried to flee but the knarren chased after them.

Mr. Cutter had lost consciousness and was hanging limp from the warrior's hand. The warrior tossed him roughly to the ground.

"Take him back."

I ran over to Mr. Cutter and crouched down next to him. He was unconscious but breathing. The knarren roared in the distance. I wondered if I should do something else since it was my fault the sslorcs were in this world. Had any kind of permanent damage been done?

The warrior answered my unspoken thoughts.

"We handle them. You take him back."

His eyes held no emotion when he talked to me. He obviously wasn't protecting me out of some kind of compassion or kinship, so I assumed he was here because Vala had asked him to be. Which meant he and Vala were friends.

What type of being would you have to be to be friends with this guy?

The warrior turned and walked away. I shivered and turned my attention to Mr. Cutter. No black haze surrounded him anymore. He looked like the Mr. Cutter I knew from home, his face pale and clammy.

I poked his arm.

"Hey, Mr. Cutter. Are you OK?"

He didn't respond. Crap. He weighed almost twice as much as I did. I would never be able to carry him. I grabbed his shoulders and shook them, hoping, too late, that he didn't have a serious head injury. So much for CPR training.

He groaned and put one hand up to his face.

"Hey. Yay. You're awake. Can you stand up? We need to get out of here."

He opened his eyes, saw my face, groaned, and closed them again.

"Hey. Dude. C'mon. We have to get out of here before they change their minds and come back for you too."

His eyes flew open and, he sat up, turning his head toward the carnage in the distance. The knarren had already dissolved the larger sslorcs and were now dissolving a few stray bats that the warrior flushed out from the edges of the forest with his sword. A gray, putrid haze hung in the air around them, slowly expanding and drifting in the afternoon breeze.

Mr. Cutter pushed himself up, staggered, clamped a large, unwelcome hand on the top of my head to catch his balance, then, over my annoyed protests, shoved himself the rest of the way up.

He seemed to not be able to use his left arm, the one that had been bound to the sslorcs. It hung limp against his side, and he reached over and clasped it near the elbow with his right.

"Get me out of here. How do we get out of here?"

He was giving me orders now? I stood up and marched toward the bridge, not even bothering to check if he was following. I stopped at the edge of the bridge, staring at the metal Gateway in front of me.

"Why are you stopping? Is this how we get home?"

I suddenly realized that I had no idea how to get home. I could hear Vala's voice in my head, telling me that the last part of the Gatekeeper's test was to see if I could find my way home. How was I supposed to do that? Could I go through this Gateway, or did I have to go find the one that we used to enter this world initially? Did I have to go back through each of the Gateway worlds we had gone through on the way here in reverse order? The thought of dragging a conscious, human Mr. Cutter through the gold world wasn't appealing.

"What's wrong? What are you waiting for?"

"Give me a second," I snapped. I wished I were still traveling with Pettikin instead of him.

The thought of Pettikin brought a flood of memories. Little, screaming Santa on the kitchen table flinging cake, sitting on my shoulders, riding Socrates, peeking out from behind Vala's head, bouncing down a rainbow slide. My brain zoomed in on a particular memory, an image of when we first met, of him telling me with wide, blue eyes how he had accidentally come to Earth.

"When I thought about being with her, I found myself here."

I stared at the Gateway. I thought about Andie, Mrs.Widgit, Professor Theopolous, and Dad, all waiting for me at home.

Vala. Would he be there waiting too?

A blue green light formed in the middle of the Gateway, traversing all the metal rods until the whole thing glowed turquoise.

I reached back, grabbed Mr. Cutter's sleeve, and pulled him in front of me. I gave him a small shove from behind.

"Come on, we're going home."

23

I felt like I was sinking, becoming heavier, more solid, more real. I saw a fuzzy glow in front of me, like static on a television, and stepped through it into the dim, gray light of an October afternoon in Ohio. Mr. Cutter stood beside me.

We were in the yard on the eastern side of the cottage in front of the Gateway. Mrs. Widgit and Andie were talking a few feet away from us. Andie had her arms folded across her chest, perhaps because Mrs. Widgit's arms were animated enough for both of them. Professor Theopolous and Bob stood a regulation-safe distance away from Mrs.Widgit's arms, and Dad paced in front of the two of them, rubbing his head. Everything felt a little too heavy, looked a little too real.

Mr. Cutter took a step forward and collapsed on the ground.

Everyone froze, and then Mrs. Widgit, the Professor, and Bob rushed forward to help him in a flurry of motion, while Andie and Dad accosted me, a jumble of hugs and questions.

"Oh my God, you're back, are you alright?"

"Is everything OK? What happened? Are you hurt?"

"What's Mr. Cutter doing here?"

"Is Pettikin home?"

I opened my mouth to answer, but my brain couldn't quite formulate words fast enough.

I felt a presence behind me, like the sun radiating against my back. I turned.

Vala, in his human form, leaned against one of the old beech trees. His arms were folded, and he looked tired but happy.

"Welcome back, Gatekeeper."

He closed his eyes, and I felt a feeling of warmth and light descend around me.

"Gatekeeper! Allie you did it!" Andie grabbed my arm.

Vala pushed himself up from the beech tree and walked over to Mr. Cutter. He knelt down and put the palm of his hand against his forehead.

"Is he OK?" Mrs. Widgit sounded skeptical.

"He's OK. He's just unconscious," Vala said.

"Was he with you this whole time?" Andie asked me.

"Yeah. I mean I guess so? Apparently. I dunno." My brain-word output unit was still malfunctioning. Vala grinned up at me, and I felt a strange tingling in my head like he was repairing or rearranging my synapses.

"I mean, I'm not sure I understand all the technicalities about what just happened, but he definitely wasn't in church. Speaking of which, why are you here, Dad? Didn't anyone go to church this morning?"

Everyone but Vala looked at me as if I were insane.

"It's four o-clock, Al. You've been gone for *hours*. Even the alpacas came back already. We thought you were dead," Andie said.

So last time I felt like I had been gone for days, and it had only been minutes. This time I felt like the trip had been much faster, but I was gone for hours.

"Time must be really weird here on this planet—I don't really understand it at all," I said, echoing Pettikin's words from this morning. What was he doing now? Was he happy to be home on Arcorn?

Did he miss me?

My eyes welled with tears.

Andie gave my arm a gentle tug. "Are you OK, Al? What happened? Is Pettikin OK?"

I laughed and wiped at the tears that spilled down my cheeks. My hands were shaking.

"Pettikin's great. He's home." I took a deep breath and recounted the entire story as best as I could—the almost uneventful trip through the dimensions, the beauty of Semba and the fluffermus, the horror of encountering Mr. Cutter and the sslorcs, the bittersweet goodbye with Pettikin, and the final ordeal with Mr. Cutter.

When I finished, Vala stood up and held my gaze for a long moment, his bright green eyes pouring light and warmth into whatever gaping hole Pettikin had left in my heart.

"So you didn't just save Pettikin, you broke the contract!" Mrs. Widgit sounded amazed.

"I thought the contract couldn't be broken," Andie said.

"Couldn't be broken on Earth," Vala corrected. "Not without killing Mr. Cutter. That's ultimately why May sacrificed herself. The sslorcs attacked her before she had time to formulate a plan to both break the contract and save Mr. Cutter's life. Rather than kill Mr. Cutter to defend herself, she allowed herself to be killed, knowing I would close the Gateways. But unbeknownst to the sslorcs, the summoning stone brought Pettikin here at that moment."

"The stone summoned Pettikin?" I asked, surprised. "I thought he came here accidentally."

"It probably seemed accidental to him, but even with the sincerity of his feelings, I don't think he could have stepped through a Gateway to a forbidden world so easily. From the moment Mr. Cutter made the contract with the sslorcs, there were two possibilities—the possibility that Earth would become a shadow world, or part of a shadow realm, or the possibility that the contract could be broken in the higher worlds, the sslorcs eliminated, and the Gateways reopened. The summoning charm saw the possibilities and brought Pettikin here to ensure the second possibility. The sslorcs were fooled into thinking everything was going according to their own plans because they underestimated Allie and Pettikin. They never saw them as a threat."

"Breaking the contract wasn't even part of the test," Mrs. Widgit said.

"Extra credit," Vala said and grinned. "What do you say to that, Theo?"

Professor Theopolous made a noise that sounded like a backhoe hauling gravel through his throat. "I will admit that Allie performed admirably, although I don't think we should assume that this proves out your teaching methods, Vala. It seems that this entire affair involved a great deal of risk."

"So much so that I'm almost wishing I hadn't been filled in on the details." Dad said. He had been twisting his cap in his hands while I spoke, his face a bit peaked.

"What happens to him now?" I pointed at Mr. Cutter, who was still lying on the ground.

"He won't remember anything when he wakes up," Vala said.

"Nothing at all?"

"Not a thing, not even his original contract with the sslorcs."

"But how do we know he won't make another contract with them?"

"He can't. At least for a while. He doesn't have enough personal power anymore."

"So what should we do with him?" Mrs. Widgit asked.

"Andie," Vala's lips twisted into a mischievous smile.

"Uh, yeah?"

"Would you like to do the honors?"

"The honors, you mean you want me to… to…"

"You got it."

Andie gave me a funny look and took a few steps toward Mr. Cutter.

"You know I have no idea what I'm doing or what happens to him when I do this," she said to Vala.

"Don't worry, I do. He'll wake up at home with no memory of what happened. Actually, Dan, perhaps you could assist in that."

"I'll stop by to check on him later with a plausible cover story. It's amazing what can happen to Deacons at church after everyone's left," Dad said.

Andie shook her head. "This is all so wrong." She bent over Mr. Cutter's inert form.

"Please go away!"

And he was gone.

Dad made a funny noise that sounded like "Gyah" and stepped backwards.

"First time you've seen her do that?" Vala asked.

"I had no idea…"

"Not your average ally," Vala said.

"No, not average at all," Dad said slowly, staring at the spot on the ground where Mr. Cutter had been.

"Well!" Mrs. Widget said briskly. "That's one person down."

One person down? Were we planning to do this to everyone? And then I remembered.

"Oh my God. I totally forgot you guys still need me to take you home."

The thought of going through the dimensions
again today made we want to cry.

"Oh heavens no, Allie, I should have told you
right away. Vala has asked us to stay and do a job for him
here on Earth. It will probably take us several months, so
you won't have to take us through until then. That should
give you enough time to rest and recharge."

"And practice," Professor Theopolous added.

"Pfft. I'll get you through, Professor, with only
maybe a fifty percent chance of us getting lost in a void,
killed by sslorcs, eaten by knarren…"

I doubt my bravado really hid the relief I felt, but
everyone laughed politely anyway.

"And on that note we should be going," Mrs.
Widgit said. "Bob. Theo. Shall we go tidy up the cottage a
bit and be on our way?"

They left, and Vala walked off in the other
direction, his gaze skyward, his gait uneven and
meandering. He stopped in front of the Gateway and
seemed to be waiting.

"Hey, Mr. Thomas, weren't you going to, uh,
show me that thing in the cottage?" Andie asked.

"Thing? Oh right, the thing! That I wanted to
show you. In the cottage. Come, other daughter." Dad
draped an arm over her shoulders, winked at me, and
steered her toward the cottage with the others.

Vala's arms were folded, his attention on the
Gateway. Was he leaving? Did he want me to join him, or
did he want to be alone?

As soon as I thought it, he turned to me and
smiled. I took a few halting steps toward him and then
stopped, unsure.

"You can hug me if you want to," he said gently.

If I wanted to. I walked over to him. He smiled
and opened his arms. My heart pounded so hard, it was
probably audible as I put my arms hesitantly around his

neck. He pulled me to his chest and wrapped his arms tightly around me. I squeezed his neck and closed my eyes.

After a moment, he released me and smiled down at me.

"So," he said.

I didn't know what to say.

"Do you still want to be my Gatekeeper?"

"Yes," I answered immediately.

"Because you do have a choice, you know. You can stay in my world of magic and gatekeeping, or you could just visit for a little while…"

"I want to stay."

He nodded slowly. "OK."

He closed his eyes, and soft gold light descended around him, then swirled outwards and enveloped me. It was warm and silent.

He opened his eyes.

"What was the last key I gave you, do you know?"

I hadn't even thought about it. The key to the Gold dimension—why had I been able to get through this time?

"I don't know—you were there, Vala, that's all I remember, you pulled me up this time."

"Up how?" he asked curiously.

Had that been him or not? Was I hallucinating? Didn't he remember?

"I was doing a few different things at once—multitasking, you know how it is," he grinned. "Help me remember what I was doing there."

"Well, before in that dimension, I felt like I was dissolving the higher I went, and I got scared because I didn't want to disappear. But this time, you kept pulling me upwards, and after a while, I realized that the stuff that was dissolving…maybe it wasn't really me after all. It's like there was something else behind it all along…that I could just let everything go, and it would be OK…" I wasn't explaining this well.

"So that's a type of wisdom then," Vala said. "To see that there is more to you than you realize, Allie Thomas. Well, it's a start anyway. Good girl."

"Vala?"

"Hm?"

"You could see...before, you could see that those sslorcs or Mr. Cutter or the contractor...whoever, you could see that they had some kind of hold on me, that line to my neck."

"Yes."

"Why didn't you tell me? Because, I mean, I didn't even realize, I didn't know..."

"I didn't want to worry you, and there wasn't a lot you could have done about it anyway. Worrying would only have made it worse—made the bond even stronger. Being with your friends and family made it weaker, easier to break. It's better that it never had a chance to get a hold of your heart."

I put a hand up to my neck. "But it's gone now, right? You would tell me if it was still there?"

"It's gone now. There's a small scar, but that will fade with time." He traced one finger delicately across my neck, giving me goosebumps, then brushed it down my cheek before letting his hand drop to his side. His expression turned serious.

"So then, Allie, I have to go for a little while."

"OK."

I wanted to ask a million questions, about what I should do, what would happen next, and when I would see him again, but OK is all that came out.

He put both hands under my face and kissed the top of my head.

"See you soon."

He turned and waved one arm over his head. The Gateway sprang to life, a million glowing filaments of light between the beech trees. He stepped through without looking back and was gone, the light fading after him, until the Gateway was dark. I thought I could see just the faintest shimmer between the two trees, woven threads of time and space waiting to be reactivated.

A chilly wind rustled the trees and kicked up the dry leaves on the ground around me. I shivered, rubbed my arms, and walked back to the cottage.

Mrs. Widgit, Professor Theopolous, and Bob were all ready to leave by the time I got there. Mrs. Widgit promised to return soon and hugged both Andie and me. Then they left, wandering west, past the barn, to wherever they spent their evenings.

"Well, girls," Dad said, "I'll head up to the house and see what we can do by way of feeding the two of you. Maybe you should lock the cottage when you're done, Al?"

"Sure."

He left, and Andie and I stood alone in the foyer. The only sound was the steady ticking of the cuckoo clock.

"It doesn't seem right to be here without Pettikin," Andie said.

"I know. I wonder if we'll ever see him again."

More silence.

"We have to go to school tomorrow," we both said at the same time, and then laughed.

"Ugh. C'mon let's go do something normal before then," Andie said.

We made a quick pass through the living room to pack up our stuff. I shoved *Introductory Gatekeeping* and *The Guardians* into my backpack. Andie took her *Book of Useful Phrases* ("There might be something else good in here," she said) and a book called *Famous Allies*.

We looked around the room one last time.

"At least we won't be bored," Andie said.

I flicked off the light. We locked the cottage door and walked back to the house together.

ACKNOWLEDGMENTS

I gave up on writing this book so many times that it most certainly would not exist were it not for the dogged encouragement, counsel, and support of the following people and institutions, in roughly chronological order:

Thank you to my family and the town of Wooster, OH for giving me a great education and a childhood where I could wander in the woods and dream of bigger things.

Thank you to the Gotham Writer's Workshop and my instructors Thomas O'Malley, Masha Hamilton, and Carolyn MacCullough for teaching me useful basics for fiction writing, such as: "These vivid characters should probably exist in some sort of setting."

Thank you to Chris Baty, muse-incarnate and founder of National Novel Writing Month, for making me laugh and for providing a forum in which a few rough, meandering chapters could be transformed into a rollicking-bad first draft of a novel. Thank you also to NaNoWriMo first-elf Grant Faulkner for continuing to support my quest to finish my book year after year.

Thank you to my former manager and long-time friend Gregg Evans, who probably deserves something closer to a co-author credit for: encouragement on early chapters, use of first-born dog, generating names for other-worldly creatures and places, back-filling gaping plot holes, and copyediting services. I can't stress enough the importance of finding a reinsurance actuary to read the early drafts of your middle-grade fantasy novel.

Thank you to my friend Ethel Greene, who in no way bears a purely coincidental resemblance to Mrs. Widgit, for supporting, encouraging, enthusing, and raging over early chapters in the way only she could.

Thank you to my old bestie Amy Schuesselin Henricksen for bravely offering up her eldest child, Ms. Madeline Henricksen, as my first age-appropriate beta reader. ("We're sharing the brain three ways now, Ab.") It is due to Madeline's efforts that the word 'shinnied' now appears in this manuscript only once.

Thank you to my older brother Justin Smith and nephew Adam Smith for reassuring me that the book "actually wasn't too bad!"

Thank you to my step-niece Alyssa Pratt-Miranda for finding me an army of beta-readers. And a huge thank you to young beta readers Cole Bhella, Aidan Dehays, Sarah McGarrity, Zoe Parkinson, and Oona Woodbury for their comments and feedback. You guys gave me the courage to see this project through.

Thank you also to my many adult beta readers, including Rory Airhart, Tony Akkanen, Marsha Bell, Barbara Fox, Kate Fox, Jennifer Fry, Ellie Hastings, Alexia Marcous, Wolfgang Müschenborn, Michelle Roycroft, Tori Santos, Jill Sweeney, and my soul sister from Gotham Joan Turlington, who owes the world a book about Professor Roland. My apologies to anyone I inadvertently omitted.

Thank you to Dean Robbins (www.deanrobbins.net) for providing an early edit. Any flaws in the final manuscript are my own and no reflection on his talents.

Thank you to my dear friend and editor Karin Hanni (rambleom.blogspot.com) who understands the comma in a way I never will. And special thanks to Karin's kids, Tara and Dylan Wall, who were not only beta readers, but made my entire life when they sent me a photo album of Pettikin sharing their summer vacation adventures in Bellingham, WA.

Thank you to the amazing and delightful Sophie Mitchell (sophiemitchellillustrations.com) for bringing Pettikin to life with her magical illustrations and cover artwork. Thank you to Kellie Bonnici (kebowebdesign.com) for the beautiful website design.

Thank you to ONE OK ROCK for the inspiring music and for finally showing me, after all these years, how to think positively.

Finally, thank you to "My Guardians" for their endless love, patience, wisdom, encouragement, humor, support and inspiration.

ABOUT THE AUTHOR

Abby Smith is a database consultant and tech entrepreneur who has spent many meetings doodling and wishing an interdimensional portal would open up and take her home. In addition to writing, she enjoys hiking, traveling, and music. She lives in Connecticut with a revolving cast of pets and welcomes your correspondence at pettikin@gmail.com.

www.pettikin.com
www.facebook.com/pettikin
twitter: @pettikin
Instagram: @pettikinbook